A BODY ON THE BEACH

A gripping Welsh crime mystery full of twists

P.F. FORD

The West Wales Murder Mysteries Book 1

JOFFE BOOKS

Revised Edition 2022
Joffe Books, London
www.joffebooks.com

First published in Great Britain in 2020

This paperback edition was first published
in Great Britain in 2022

Cover art by Dee Dee Book Covers

ISBN: 978-1-80405-637-0

To my amazing wife, Mary. Sometimes we need someone else to believe in us before we believe in ourselves. None of this would have happened without her unfailing belief, encouragement and support.

CHAPTER 1

Monday 14 October 2019
King's Head public house, Llangwelli, West Wales

It was 10.30 p.m., and Kimberley Lawrence was angry and drunk. Not the steaming, no idea what you're doing, sort of drunk, but enough to make her throw her usual caution to the wind. She had no qualms about flirting with the handsome young guy at the bar and certainly wouldn't say no if he wanted what she was hoping he wanted. Usually, she would be a little more discreet and wait until her friends had all gone home. Tonight, though, she didn't give a damn.

She'd had yet another blazing row with her useless husband earlier and, frankly, she rather hoped he found out what she was about to do. Perhaps it would finally make him sit up and take notice if it got back to him that she had been openly flirting with some young stallion in their local pub. She knew the young guy was up for it; he'd been watching her for quite some time now, and she'd made sure she had done enough to encourage him.

Experience told her he was there for the taking. She probably had a dozen years on him but she knew she was in great shape, and it was a fact that lots of these young guys

1

liked an older married woman because in all probability there would be no commitment involved. It would be a simple case of 'wham, bam, thank you ma'am', and that suited Kimberley perfectly.

She looked at her three friends gathered around the table. They were talking kids' stuff as usual. Kimberley had no children and always found these conversations annoying. She forced a smile as she pushed her chair back and reached for her bag.

'Right then, who wants another drink?'

Her three friends declined. They'd had enough and were thinking about going home.

'Just me, then,' said Kimberley, rising from her chair and heading for the bar.

'She's starting early tonight,' said Pippa Roberts, nodding towards the bar. 'She normally waits until we've gone before she starts flirting.'

'She told me she and Greg had a huge row before she came out. That's why she's drinking like a fish,' confided Ruth Evans. 'The problem is it tends to loosen her knicker elastic.'

'She doesn't need a drink for that,' said Pippa. 'She probably isn't wearing any!'

'It'll be the young guy with the dark hair,' said Abbey Moore. 'She's been making eyes at him for at least half an hour.'

'She thinks we're that stupid we don't know,' said Pippa.

'Do you think Greg knows?' asked Abbey.

'Of course, he knows,' said Pippa. 'The whole village knows.'

'But why does he put up with it?' asked Abbey.

'I asked my husband that question. He says Greg knows but doesn't want to believe it. He's clinging on to some crazy idea that she's suddenly going to change and they'll ride off into the sunset together and live happily ever after.'

'That's a bit pathetic, don't you think?' asked Abbey.

They looked across to the bar where Kimberley only had eyes for the young man.

'Come on,' said Ruth, pushing her chair back. 'If she's going to screw him I'd rather not know. I like Kim, but I hate it when she plays the tart.'

Obediently, the other two gathered their things and followed her from the bar. The three friends had to pass Kimberley as they left, but she only had eyes for her new friend and ignored them even though they said goodbye and offered her a lift home as they passed.

CHAPTER 2

Tuesday 15 October 2019
Office of Slater & Norman, Private Investigators, Tinton, Hampshire,
England

The tall man stepped from his car and looked around. There
were only half a dozen businesses on the site, so it was quite
easy to spot the premises he was seeking. 'Slater & Norman',
he read on a small placard attached to the wall. Then, as he
approached, he could see the legend, 'Private Investigators'
was etched on the glass of the door. The man shook his head
as he read the sign, then knocked and waited.

After a minute no one had answered, and he considered knocking a second time. Then he thought better of it,
grabbed the door handle, twisted and pushed. As the door
slowly opened the left-hand side of the room came into view.
Two comfortable chairs stood either side of a small table. A
carrier bag full of shopping filled one of the chairs. Without
stepping into the room, he pushed the door open a little
further and peered around it at the other side of the room.

A desk was doing its best to survive under two enormous piles of newspapers. Beyond, the object of the man's
search was leaning back in an office chair, feet up on the desk

before him. He had his hands behind his head, and his eyes closed. Large headphones covered his ears, and anyone could see he was enjoying his listening.

The visitor entered the room and coughed loudly, but the reclining listener was oblivious. He walked across the room and coughed again, but again there was no response, so he walked around the desk, tapped the reclining man on the shoulder and called out.

'Hey, Norm!'

Deep in the embrace of Led Zeppelin's first album, the man called Norm nearly had a seizure as he jerked back into the present, inadvertently creating a slow-motion avalanche of newspapers that began to spill across the desk and onto the floor.

'Holy crap!' he yelled, snatching off the headphones. 'You could have given me a heart attack. Don't you knock?'

'I did knock, several times, but you didn't answer.'

Norman realised this might not be the best way to greet a potential client but then was suddenly distracted by the impending avalanche. Hurriedly he reached forward to try to stop it, but his clumsy effort only helped sweep the rest of the papers across the desk towards his visitor.

'Shit,' he hissed as he jumped from his chair, but he was too late to stop the last newspaper disappearing over the edge of his desk.

'Dammit!'

He hurried around the desk and sank to his knees at his visitor's feet trying to gather up the newspapers tidily, finally conceding defeat and scrabbling them into a heap which he then carried behind his desk and dumped on the floor.

'I'll sort them out later,' he muttered, turning back to his visitor.

'I'm sorry about that,' he said, extending a hand. 'My name's Norman Norman.'

He hadn't noticed the man's face before, but now as he looked his visitor in the eye, his mouth dropped open.

'Jeez! Nathan Bain? Where the hell did you come from?'

The man called Bain looked distastefully at Norman's hand, now grubby with newspaper ink, then reluctantly extended an arm, shook hands, and grinned.

'How are you, Norm?' he said. 'Still working in a mess, I see.'

'I'm great,' said Norman. 'You're not looking too bad yourself.'

'I heard you had a new woman in your life.'

Norman grimaced.

'Yeah, well, "had" is the word,' he said, sadly. 'I'm afraid it didn't work out.'

'Oh, I'm sorry.'

'Shit happens, right?' said Norman. 'It was a complicated situation for everyone, and in the end it just, well, you know, right? Anyway, what brings Inspector Bain to this neck of the woods?'

'It's Superintendent Bain, now, Norm. I thought it best if I came in person.'

Norman could see this was supposed to mean something significant, but for the life of him, he couldn't think what it was.

'Er, right. Well, you don't have to worry. I can assure you of my discretion at all times. Your secret will be safe with me.'

Bain looked stung.

'Secret? What secret?'

'Hey, look, don't get alarmed,' said Norman. 'What I mean is, whatever you want me to investigate will stay between you and me.'

'Investigate? For me?'

'That's what you're here for, isn't it?'

'You're serious, aren't you?' asked Bain.

Norman scratched his head through his unruly curls.

'Well, why else would you be here? I mean, this is a detective agency.'

Bain looked slowly round the untidy office.

'Really?' he said.

'I'll admit it's a bit of a mess right now, but I've been so busy I haven't had time to tidy up.'

'You don't look busy, and frankly, if I were a potential client, I would take one look around here and head straight back out again.'

'It's my day off,' said Norman, hastily. 'I took a day off so I could clean up. I was psyching myself up with some inspirational tunes before I start.'

Bain grinned.

'You always had a way with words. An answer for everything and a deflection from any situation.'

'What d'you mean?'

'You honestly have no idea why I'm here, have you?'

Norman stared at Bain's face as if for inspiration, but nothing came to mind.

'Okay, I give up,' he said. 'You'll have to give me a clue.'

'You were sent a letter about rejoining the police and resuming your duties as a detective sergeant. I sent it out personally.'

A light switched on in Norman's head.

'Jeez, that was weeks ago.'

'It was a month ago.'

'Yeah, that's what I said, it was weeks ago. I seem to recall the letter said you would be following up. I heard nothing, so I assumed that meant you must've changed your mind.'

'You know how it is. These things take time. We only have one vacancy, and we had a lot of applicants.'

Norman frowned.

'Seriously?'

'These jobs are in demand, you know.'

Norman snorted.

'Yeah, right. If there are so many others to choose from, why are you here?'

'I just want to make sure you understand the opportunity.'

Norman studied Bain for a moment, and then his face broke into a grin.

'Ha! I get it,' he said. 'What you mean is you're here in person because no one else wanted to know, and I'm your last resort.'

'What I mean is I didn't consider anyone else. You are the person I want for this job.'

Norman was both flattered and surprised.

'Really? I find that hard to believe. I mean, why me?'

'Can we sit down?' asked Bain. 'I've got a dodgy knee. It aches if I stand for too long.'

Norman pointed to the two chairs across the room.

'Sure, why not. I've got nothing else to do right now.'

'I thought you said you were busy.'

'Yeah, I did,' agreed Norman, thinking fast. 'I also said I had taken the day off. Ergo, I am not busy today.'

He led the way to the two chairs, removed the shopping, and indicated the other chair. Bain sat down opposite Norman, clicked open his briefcase and picked out a folder which he kept on his lap.

'D'you seriously think you can persuade me to join you?' asked Norman.

'Wouldn't it be better than kicking your heels here?'

'We do all right,' said Norman.

'That's not what I understand.'

'Well maybe you're not as well informed as you think,' said Norman.

Bain put his hands together and steepled his fingers.

'Let's see if I'm right,' he said. 'Your last job involved finding out what happened to a young girl who died in a road accident.'

'Correct! And if the police had done their job properly, that would have been cleared up at the time.'

Bain nodded his head.

'You're probably right about that, but my point is if that was your last job, it was months ago. What have you done since then?'

Norman shifted in his chair and folded his arms.

'I keep busy.'

Bain smiled ruefully.

'Your body language is letting you down.'

Norman hastily uncrossed his arms.

'Look, I have a business, and I have a business partner.'

'Ah yes, the former Detective Sergeant Slater.'

'His last position was Detective Inspector,' argued Norman.

'Yeah, for a few weeks,' agreed Bain. 'Where is he now?'

'He's on vacation.'

'With another former DI, I understand.'

Norman bristled.

'Stella Robbins had to retire through stress,' he said. 'It wasn't her fault some nut job decided to ambush her in her car.'

'You don't need to defend her reputation,' said Bain. 'I wasn't implying anything. I've seen her record, and I can assure you I have the highest regard for her abilities. What happened was a tragedy for her and her career.'

'Anyway,' said Norman. 'What's the problem with them going away together. They're both adults, and they're both single.'

'It's not who Slater's with that's the issue,' said Bain. 'The point is he's gone and left it all down to you, again. It's not the first time, is it?'

Norman couldn't keep the surprise from his face.

'What?' asked Bain.

'You seem to be damned well informed. Have you been spying on us?'

'Norm, when we worked together in the Met, I had the highest regard for you. I would never have let them crap on you the way they did if I had still been around. I kept an eye out for you after that. I was the guy who recommended you to Bob Murray.'

'You got me the job in Tinton?'

'Your record got you the job. I just suggested you would be a good fit.'

'So, you have been spying on me.'

'I've been looking out for you. It's not the same thing. Anyway, I had to check you out before I approached you. Wouldn't you do the same?'

'Well, yeah, I suppose,' said Norman. 'But it won't make any difference. I'm not going to let my partner down.'

Bain looked hard at Norman.

'I admire your loyalty, but don't you think it might be a little misplaced?'

'What do you mean, misplaced?'

'Well, now let me see. How many times have you and Slater started this business? What is it now, twice? Three times?'

'I'm not sure I'm following,' said Norman.

'Well, correct me if I'm wrong, but the first time, didn't you start a business, and then he left when he was head-hunted to become DI? He didn't worry about his loyalty to you and your business then, did he?'

'It was a good opportunity for him.'

'Which he subsequently wasted. He has a habit of losing his rag and throwing all his toys out of the pram, doesn't he?'

'He was affected by his father's death much more than he realised. In hindsight, he probably should have taken a much longer break before he came back to work.'

'My point is, he did it before, didn't he? How long do you think it will be before he does it again?'

Norman was beginning to feel uncomfortable.

'He'll be fine. He just needed a break. Now he's got someone he cares about he'll be a lot better.'

'So, you agree he has a problem.'

'I didn't say that.'

'Not in so many words,' agreed Bain. 'And what about Slater and Stella? D'you think they're serious? I understand Slater has a habit of discarding women at the drop of a hat.'

'It's not like that. Dave has, or at least, had, a problem with commitment. But this thing with Stella is different.'

'D'you think there's going to be a wedding in Thailand? I hear it's a beautiful place to get married.'

'Nah, he would have told me,' said Norman.

'Are you sure? He's unpredictable, so it has to be a possibility, don't you think?'

Norman felt slightly nauseated. He and Slater were supposed to be best mates. Surely, he would want Norm to be at his wedding? Wouldn't he? Who else would be his best man?

'You say he has changed, and maybe you're right, and Stella is for keeps,' said Bain. 'That'll be another test for his loyalty towards you.'

'I don't want to hear any more of this,' said Norman. 'You're just trying to drive a wedge between my best friend and me. I think you should leave.'

Bain took the folder from his lap and held it out to Norman, but he didn't reach for it, so Bain placed it carefully on the small table between the chairs.

'You said Slater leaving to become a DI was a good opportunity. What I'm offering is a better opportunity. I have some great young officers, but I need someone with experience to get the best out of them. And I promise you it's a beautiful place. It'll be a new start for you.'

'Who says I need a new start?'

'At least read through the folder and see what I'm offering.'

'You're wasting your time. I'm not turning my back on my best friend.'

Bain sighed.

'The problem, Norm, is that Slater only has one best friend, and that's himself. You're wasting all that experience and ability here. You need to start looking out for yourself, Norm.'

'When I had a heart attack, he saved my life.'

'I heard the heart attack happened because you were fighting with him.'

'It wasn't like that. I was trying to stop him from doing something stupid in the heat of the moment.'

As Bain's face broke into a grin, Norman realised what he was saying.

'Which illustrates my point, entirely, don't you agree? said Bain.

'You can say what you like,' said Norman. 'I'm not deserting my partner.'

Bain sighed.

'I'm sorry you feel that way,' he said. 'But perhaps, when you've had a chance to think about it, you'll reconsider.'

'No chance,' said Norman.

Bain took a card from his pocket and placed it on the table next to the folder. Then he stood up and headed for the door.

'Read the folder, Norm,' he said. 'I'll be waiting for your call.'

'Yeah, you do that,' said Norman.

Norman watched as Bain pulled the door closed behind him, then he turned his attention to the folder.

'New start? Who the hell does he think he is telling me I need a new start?' he muttered.

As he thought about his life right now, and the things Bain had pointed out, an uncomfortable truth began to dawn on him. Tinton had been a new start when he had arrived, but now, with no business, no partner, and no one in his life, he had to admit it wasn't working out the way he had hoped, was it? Maybe a new start wasn't such a bad idea after all.

He placed the folder on his lap, flipped it open and began to read.

CHAPTER 3

Wednesday 16 October 2019

Detective Inspector Sarah Southall was feeling distinctly uncomfortable. After a few days enforced leave she had been relieved to receive the call yesterday telling her she had to meet her boss this morning, but now her relief had given way to worry.

Why wasn't the meeting in his office? And why at 9.00 a.m.?

She stopped in front of a large plate glass window and quickly checked her reflection. She decided she didn't look too shabby considering she had endured yet another sleepless night. It was a shame about the hair, but in this wind, what could anyone expect?

She took the half a dozen paces to the small coffee shop, pushed her way through the door and scanned the interior. It didn't take long to spot Detective Superintendent Ian Melloway in the almost deserted shop. He had chosen a corner table as far away from everyone as possible, and he smiled and waved as soon as he saw her. She felt a pang of irritation as she noticed the two cups of coffee on the table before him. She was quite fussy about her coffee.

Politely he stood as she approached, and didn't sit down again until she was seated opposite him.

'How are you feeling, Sarah?'

'How should I be feeling, sir?'

A hint of irritation flashed in his eyes.

'I was hoping we would be rather more relaxed here than in my office,' he said.

'How do you expect me to be relaxed when I've spent the last twenty-four hours wondering why you wanted to meet me?'

'It's quite normal for an officer returning from,' he hesitated for a moment, 'for an officer in your situation to meet their immediate superior before returning to normal duties.'

'I had a week's leave,' she said.

Melloway leaned forward.

'No, I advised you to take a week,' he said. 'It's not the same thing, and you know it.'

Sarah sat back and rolled her eyes.

'It wasn't my fault. Robson disobeyed my orders.'

Melloway sighed.

'We've been over this at least a dozen times,' he said. 'As the officer in charge of the operation, you should have arranged for a firearms team to be there.'

'The intelligence we had didn't mention guns.'

'But the people involved were known to have used guns before, and although there was no hard evidence to say they had guns on this occasion, it would have been prudent to—'

'Prudent? Jesus, boss, we had half an hour to react. If we had waited for a firearms team, we would have been too late, and they would have got away long before we got there.'

'Yes, perhaps you're right, but at least Robson wouldn't have ended up in the hospital.'

Sarah looked at her boss. His face told her he was sympathetic to her cause, but she could also see he wasn't going to change his stance.

'So, that's the decision, is it?' she asked. 'Robson gets a pat on the back, and I get a kick up the arse? Okay, fair enough. I'll take my medicine and try and do better next time. Now, can I get back to work?'

Melloway shifted as if uncomfortable in his chair.

'Ah, yes, back to work. About that.'

'I'm ready,' she said. 'I'm annoyed the operation went wrong, but I'm not traumatised, and my confidence isn't affected.'

'I understand that, Sarah, but I'm afraid it's not quite that simple.'

'It is exactly that simple. I know it, and you know it; Robson got shot because he was a dickhead, not because of me.'

'If it was down to me—'

'What do you mean, "if it was down to me"? You're the boss, aren't you?'

'I have a boss, too, you know.'

Sarah felt her insides run cold.

'What are you saying? Have you called me here because you're going to fire me?'

'Of course not, you're far too good for that.'

'So, what are you saying?'

'This was your first case as DI.'

'Are you going to reduce my rank? You can't do that! I'll go to the union.'

'We're not going to reduce your rank.'

'What, then?'

'For God's sake, Sarah. If you stop interrupting, and just listen for a minute, I'll tell you.'

'Sorry,' said Sarah sheepishly. 'It's just that—'

Melloway raised a palm in her direction.

'Stop!'

'But, I—'

'DI Southall. I order you to stop speaking and listen to me!'

There was an awkward silence.

Red-faced, Sarah looked around the room. A face behind the counter was looking inquisitively in their direction but, fortunately, no one was close enough to hear. She breathed a sigh of relief and turned back to Melloway, who was speaking again.

'I asked you to meet me here because I wanted to afford you some privacy from your colleagues. I'm beginning to think that was a mistake. At the very least, you could afford me the respect I deserve as your senior officer.'

She bowed her head momentarily, then looked him in the eye.

'I'm sorry, sir. That was very unprofessional of me. Of course, I respect your position, and I respect you.'

'Are you going to let me speak?'

'Yes, sir.'

'Without interruption?'

'Yes, sir.'

Melloway studied her face. He admired Sarah's determination, and he had been firmly behind her promotion to DI. However, not everyone at headquarters had agreed with him, and now her first case as a newly promoted DI had gone pear-shaped, he had been put under a lot of pressure. He had fought tooth and nail to save her job but, in the end, the best he could do was a compromise. Now all he had to do was sell it to her.

He sighed and leaned back in his chair.

'It's budget time, and HQ has just passed down the latest round of cuts. As a result, I can no longer afford three DIs. I have to lose one. They wanted me to do that by firing the newest one.'

Sarah's eyes widened, and she leaned forward to speak, but he raised his hand again, to remind her of her promise.

'Don't worry,' he said, with a reassuring smile. 'I'm not going to do that.'

'I wouldn't go quietly, you know, sir.'

'I wouldn't expect you to,' he said. 'But if you got into that sort of fight, you would be on gardening leave for months, maybe even for years, and that would destroy your career whether you won or lost. Is that what you want?'

Sarah knew it was a valid point. That sort of inactivity would drive her mad.

'I've never quite managed to fit the bill with HQ, have I?' she asked. 'This is an excuse to push me out, isn't it?'

'To be fair, the Chief Constable didn't ask to have his budget cut,' explained Melloway. 'I'm not the only one having to make difficult decisions.'

Sarah knew she couldn't argue with that.

'You've been through a lot over the last three years, and both the Chief Constable and I think you've shown remarkable fortitude, and to have gone on to achieve the rank of Detective Inspector in the face of such adversity is nothing short of miraculous.'

'This is sounding awfully like a goodbye speech,' she said suspiciously.

'Despite what you've achieved, you can't deny you're a changed person.'

Sarah bristled.

'I think anyone would be in the circumstances, don't you? This is a situation I can't win, isn't it? Before I was too easy-going, now I'm too feisty.'

'Aggressive was the word used to describe you,' said Melloway, quietly. 'I think they would have accepted feisty.'

'So, what are you saying?'

'The Chief Constable thinks a change would do you good.'

'So, he has ordered you to fire me, is that it?'

Melloway sighed.

'Sarah, no one is going to fire you. On the contrary, we're trying to help you.'

'Help me, how?'

'There's an alternative solution to firing you, and you should know it was the Chief Constable who suggested it,' added Melloway.

'What is this alternative solution?'

'The Chief Constable thinks you still have a lot to offer, and he feels that shouldn't be allowed to go to waste, so we've found you another position.'

He sat back with a self-satisfied smile on his face.

'Another position? But how? Where?'

'It's with another force.'

'Sorry?'

'It means a transfer to a different area, but you would retain your rank. You would still be DI.'

'Where is this place?'

'It's in Wales.'

Sarah sat bolt upright.

'Wales? That's bloody miles away. It's another country!'

'It's still part of the United Kingdom.'

'So is Scotland, but that's not exactly half an hour down the road, either, is it?'

'They're crying out for a good DI, and I've heard it's a nice place.'

Sarah looked bewildered.

'Don't you think I've had enough shit piled on my plate these last few years?' she asked.

'Yes, of course,' said Melloway, 'and I've done all I can to support you through that. But you can't blame the police for problems in your personal life. I honestly think a change of scenery and a new start could be just what you need.'

Sarah stared at him, open-mouthed.

'Look,' he said, 'I know it's come as a bit of a shock—'

'A bit of a shock?' she said. 'You've just turned my world upside down.'

'Now don't do anything hasty, and don't write it off,' urged Melloway. 'At least think about it.'

'Do I have a choice?'

Melloway looked distinctly uncomfortable. Rather than look at Sarah, he looked at his watch.

'I don't, do I?' she asked.

'I have to go now,' said Melloway. 'I want you to take a couple more days off. At least promise me you'll think about it.'

'How long have I got?'

'I need you to decide by close of play on Friday.'

'You want me to decide on my future in just two days?'

'I'm sorry, Sarah, but it has to be signed off as soon as possible.'

'This has already been signed and sealed, and now it's been delivered, hasn't it?' she asked.

Melloway didn't say anything as he gathered his things and walked from the shop.

Despite her anger, Sarah had only recently been thinking about getting away and making a new start. Four years ago, over twelve long months, her world had unravelled catastrophically. Now, wherever she went in this town, there were painful reminders of what used to be. But where would she go, what would she do?

As the day wore on, she began to believe that perhaps having the decision made for her was the best thing that could have happened.

By the end of the day, she couldn't wait to leave.

CHAPTER 4

Friday 18 October 2019
Office of Slater & Norman, Private Investigators, Tinton, Hampshire,
England

Hi Norm,
    Having a great time. We're off to Australia for three
weeks on Sunday, then back here for a bit longer.
    We've been staying at the bar my dad used to own. We've
even been working behind the bar to help out, and guess what?
I think I might have found my calling!
    Don't know when we'll be back.
Dave

Norman read the email three times, cursed loudly, sat back in his chair and stared at his laptop.

'Is that it?' he asked, out loud. 'You've been away for over a month, and all I get is a piddling short email? What about, "How are you, Norm? How is business?" Don't I at least deserve that much?'

He jumped to his feet and paced around the room, the words of Superintendent Nathan Bain echoing loudly through his mind. He aimed a mistimed kick at the wastepaper bin as he passed, barely moving it.

'Well, that's it,' he said finally. 'I'm not doing this anymore.'

He turned back and aimed another kick at the bin, this time knocking it over, scattering the contents across the floor.

'I've had enough of being taken for granted. I'm fed up sitting around here, bored out of my mind, waiting for something to happen. Now I'm going to do something I want to do, just for me, and sod you, Dave Slater.'

He opened the drawer of his desk and fumbled around. Finally, he lifted the card out of the drawer and placed it on the desk in front of him.

He stared at the card for what seemed like an age, then reached for the phone.

'Okay,' he muttered as he keyed in the number on the card. 'So, you were right, and I was wrong.'

He continued muttering until he heard a voice in his ear.

'Nathan Bain.'

'Nathan, it's Norm.'

'Norm! It's good to hear from you.'

'I've been thinking about this offer of yours.'

'Are you going to take it?'

'I dunno. I admit the idea tempts me, but it would mean a fresh start, and I'm not getting any younger, you know? How about I come down for a couple of weeks and see if it works out?'

'Okay. How about a month's trial period?'

'What about accommodation?'

'I have a friend who owns a couple of small chalets. They're holiday lets, down near the harbour, but the season's ended now, so they're empty. As I said, they're not very big, but I already spoke to him about it, and he says you can use one of them until you sort something out.'

'I don't exactly have a lot of stuff to bring with me, so I don't need big,' said Norman. 'It sounds perfect.'

'When can you start?'

'I don't want to hang around. It won't take long to get things sorted here, and then I'm free. I can move in on Sunday if that's okay?'

'Let me know when you're on the way, and I'll make sure I'm there to help you get settled in.'

'It's not going to be a big job. As I said, I don't have much to bring. If it's okay with you, I'd like to get to know the area before I start. It's the eighteenth now, so how about I start work on Monday week? That gives me a week to find my way around and tidy up any loose ends I've forgotten up here.'

'That sounds good to me, Norm. If you call into my office towards the end of next week, I'll introduce you to everyone and get you ready to go.'

CHAPTER 5

Tuesday 22 October 2019
Harbour Road, Llangwelli, West Wales

The young fox padded silently along the middle of the deserted road, accompanied only by the dawn chorus, and the gentle shushing of waves upon the beach to his right. But now he stopped to listen as a new sound began to insinuate itself upon his acute sense of hearing. The unfamiliar noise was soft at first, coming from behind him, still distant but steadily getting nearer. Curious, he turned to look back down the road which stretched away for a hundred yards before it curved behind the trees to the right.

At first, there was nothing to see, but then, as the unfamiliar noise steadily grew louder, a young woman appeared, trotting round the bend in the road, heading his way. As if he couldn't quite believe his eyes, the fascinated fox sat down to watch the approaching jogger closing the distance between them. She was within fifty yards before his instincts told him getting close to a human was a risk he shouldn't entertain. In a flash, he took off across the road and vanished into the trees.

Back down the road thirty-year-old Detective Constable Catren Morgan, the jogger, watched the fox disappear into the trees. For a moment, she had thought he was going to let her get close, but she knew that had been wishful thinking. Still, it had been something different to see and had broken the monotony of her morning run.

She felt vaguely guilty that she should feel bored. It was, after all, a beautiful, peaceful place to run, what with the trees to her left and the sea air coming in on a gentle breeze from her right. But she also thought whoever had said 'you can't have too much of a good thing' had been talking bollocks. The fact was, even this beautiful place could do with livening up now and then.

There was still the best part of a mile to go before she reached the harbour and took the road back towards town, and now the foxy distraction had fled the scene she returned to her thoughts. At the forefront was the new boss who had arrived yesterday. Detective Inspector Sarah Southall had been a last-minute substitute for the man they had been expecting. Consequently, all the research they had done was useless.

They had known nothing whatsoever about Southall, but it soon became apparent she also knew very little about them or their situation. Catren thought this made sense in a weird sort of way for surely no one in their right mind would choose to join them. So, DI Southall was either mad or had messed up and been condemned to the career black hole that was Llangwelli Station, just like everyone else in the team.

To be fair, the new DI had certainly done her best to appear positive about her new job when she had met them for the first time yesterday, and she seemed determined they would become a first-class detective team and solve every crime that came their way. This announcement had been news to everyone else in the room. They had become used to handing anything but the most mundane and straightfor-ward crimes on to Region.

The way the smug arseholes in Region explained it, the only reason any of them were still employed as police officers was because someone had to man Llangwelli Station. It was a public relations exercise to reassure the tourists.

DI Southall appeared blissfully unaware of this, and no one had had the heart to break the news to her on her first day when she seemed so keen. Catren had later been volunteered by the rest of the team to break the news to her today. Quite how she would broach the subject, she had no idea.

On her right, as she ran, she was now approaching the final stretch of beach before the harbour. Ahead, on her left, a small church nestled halfway up a hill, overlooking the harbour. Legend had it the church was built to look out for the small fishing fleet which used to operate there. A packed graveyard bore testament to the number of men who had perished to feed their community.

The tide was out, so the gently sloping beach ran a long way out to the distant waters of the bay and, unsurprisingly at this time on a fresh October morning, was deserted. She could just make out a handful of gulls investigating an object on the beach, but from this distance, couldn't quite make out what it was and thought it was probably a discarded fishing net, or perhaps one of the dead seals that were occasionally dumped on the beach by the incoming tide.

More and more gulls were joining the crowd, and as she squinted at the object from under the brim of her baseball cap, one of them began to tug at something, until it gave way and, with a triumphant screech, the bird took to the sky. As it flew off the other gulls immediately took its place and began arguing over the prize.

As she got closer, the object began to take shape, and involuntarily she slowed down, finally coming to a stop. Then she started to sprint as fast as she could. She rushed through the gap in the barrier, and down the steps onto the beach. As she neared the bundle on the beach, she began waving her arms and screaming at the greedy gulls.

'Go away, you bastards!'

As she reached the gulls, she kicked out at one or two who were in no hurry to leave.

'Go on, bugger off, all of you!'

The startled gulls had scattered, but they weren't going far, not when there was a meal so close.

Horrified, Catren stared down at the bundle.

'Oh my God,' she muttered.

She had seen a dead body before. Two in fact, but they had both died of natural causes. And of course, she had been shown some gruesome scenes of crime photographs during her training, but now she knew nothing would be adequate preparation for something like this. It was a good thing she ran before breakfast because, if she had eaten, she surely would have been unable to keep from throwing up.

She took a couple of deep breaths and tried to recall the correct procedure? Come on, Catren, think. What are you supposed to do in a situation like this? There wasn't much point in checking for a pulse; she didn't need to be a doctor to know this had ceased to be a living being several days ago.

She tore at the velcro strapping her mobile phone to her arm, found the number she wanted and pressed dial. As she waited, she wondered what the response from the new boss would be this early in the morning.

'Good morning, Catren,' said an unexpectedly bright voice.

Catren was surprised her new boss had remembered her name, then realised it had probably come up on the phone's screen.

'Morning, ma'am. I'm sorry to wake you, only you did say we should call if—'

'Don't worry, I'm already up, showered, dressed and fed. What can I do for you?'

'I was out running, down by the beach. There's a body. I think it's a woman.'

'A body? Are you sure she's dead? It's not just—'

'I'm sure this one's been dead for days, ma'am. I've just stopped a gang of seagulls pulling lumps off her for their breakfast. I can't leave, or the bloody things will be all over her.'

'Where are you?'

'About a hundred yards past the harbour heading north.'

'I'll be there in ten minutes. In the meantime, get some uniforms out there to secure the scene. You know the drill, right?'

'Yes, ma'am.'

The phone went dead. Catren glared at the seagulls who seemed to have no intention of giving up anytime soon.

'If you bastards think you're getting near her again, you can forget it,' she told them. 'I'm not moving. I can make my phone calls from here.'

CHAPTER 6

It took Sarah Southall precisely twelve minutes to reach the scene, which she thought was quite impressive considering she was so new to the area. She was pleased to see two patrol cars and three uniformed officers had already arrived.

Morgan was waiting by the roadside as Southall pulled up and joined her. They watched one of the uniforms doing his best to drive the seagulls away.

'He's not trampling all over the crime scene, is he?'

'He's doing his best not to, ma'am. But the gulls are very persistent.'

'Have you called the duty doctor?'

'It hardly seems necessary, but yes, I have.'

'It's the correct procedure, so yes, it is necessary. What isn't required is for you to address me as if I were the queen. It's okay for you to call me "boss". I told you this yesterday.'

'Sorry, I was a bit . . .'

Southall put a reassuring hand on Morgan's arm.

'Is this your first body?'

'I've seen a couple of natural causes before, but this is something of a first.'

'Bad, is it?'

'It's a woman. She's got a rope around her neck, and she's bound with what looks like fishing line.'

'Let's take a look.'

'You'll need a strong stomach.'

'Fortunately, I have one. Come on, show me.'

They headed towards the body.

'The good news is you probably won't see this sort of thing very often,' Southall assured the younger woman. 'The bad news is I can't guarantee you'll never see another one.'

'Should I call Region or will you?' asked Morgan.

'There's no rush.'

'Yes, but we usu—'

'We can notify them later when we send a preliminary report.'

Morgan stopped walking.

'A preliminary report? You mean we're going to investigate?'

'Isn't that what we're here for?'

Sarah had carried on walking and Catren had to scamper after her.

'We usually just secure the scene and then pass the case on to Region.'

'Why would we do that?'

Morgan thought this was as good an opportunity as any.

'I asked that question when I was first here. It's because everyone at Llangwelli Station had proven they were so useless they couldn't find their arses without a search party.'

'Who told you that?'

'One of the guys from Region.'

Southall smiled.

'And what do you think? Are you useless?'

'I think I made a mistake, and I accept I needed to learn a lesson. But I also think that, if what I did wasn't bad enough to get me fired, I should be given a chance to redeem myself.'

'So do I, and that's exactly why I'm here.'

'It is?'

'Weren't you listening yesterday when I said my job was to help Superintendent Bain build a crack team?'

'Well, yes, but . . .'

They were standing a few yards from the body now.

'I think that's close enough until SOCOs have had a chance to look the scene over,' said Southall. 'What can you tell me about this body? Did it drift in on the tide?'

'I'm no expert, boss, but I would think so.'

'We're not too high up the beach?'

'The sand's still damp.'

Southall nodded.

'I tend to agree with you.'

She studied her young colleague's face.

'D'you fancy being bagman on this one?'

'What, me?'

'Why not? You found the body.'

'But I'm not sure I'm ready. I'm only a detective constable. Isn't that a job for a sergeant?'

'Yes, but I don't have one, do I?'

'But, I've never been given that sort of responsibility before.'

'Well, it's high time you were.'

'What if DS Marston comes back tomorrow?'

'That's a good point, so how about if you fill his shoes until he comes back?' suggested Southall.

She was suddenly aware of the clunk of a car door closing back by the road and turned to see who it was. A tall, bearded man, wearing a suit, was talking to the uniformed officer who pointed towards them. The man looked in their direction and then began walking their way.

'Who's that?' asked Southall. 'He's not Marston, is he?'

'No, boss. That's DS Hickstead. He's from Region.'

'What's he doing here?'

Morgan shifted uncomfortably, grateful Southall was still looking the other way.

'Dunno, boss. Perhaps he's the "on-call" officer, and he was just passing.'

They watched as the newcomer made his way over to join them. There was a distinct swagger about the man as if he owned the place. Southall sighed.

'Oh great,' she muttered wearily. 'A walking ego. That's all we need.'

'Morning, girls.' The man smiled condescendingly. 'The cavalry's arrived now so you can get off and do your makeup.'

'And you are?' asked Southall.

'DS Hickstead, from Region.'

'Can I ask what you're doing here?'

'I'm taking over.' He looked around. 'And I have to say I'm quite impressed.'

'I'm sorry? Impressed?'

'Yeah,' said Hickstead. 'It looks like you've done everything right so far, but now you can leave it to me. I'll take it from here.'

'How did you know we were here?'

Hickstead raised an eyebrow and leaned towards her.

'I don't have to explain myself to you.'

At six foot two, he towered above Southall, but she had experienced this sort of behaviour countless times before. If Hickstead thought he could intimidate her, he was sadly mistaken.

'I wouldn't be so sure about that,' she warned. 'But, go on, humour me.'

'If you must know, I'm the on-call officer, and I just happened to be passing.'

Southall turned to stare at Morgan, who seemed to have found something interesting down by her feet.

'Now there's a coincidence,' she said, turning back to Hickstead. 'Do you live around here?'

'No.'

'So, why would you happen to be passing this godfor-saken place at this time of the morning?'

'At Region, we like to keep an ear to the ground.'

'Do you mean you drive around all day hoping to stumble across a crime scene? Or did someone tell you to come here?'

Hickstead struggled to think of a quick answer.

'Let's just say I like to keep my finger on the pulse.'

'Is that right? Well, we don't need your finger on this particular pulse.'

'Look, I understand you must be new here, but we always take these cases. That's just how it works.'

'You mean, you always *took* these cases. That's not going to happen any more. And, trust me, if I find you have a mole in my camp they will soon be seeking a transfer somewhere else.'

'Your camp?'

'Yes, my camp.'

Hickstead clenched his fists, and his face began to redden.

'Look, luv, I don't know who you are, but—'

Southall smiled.

'Oh, didn't I say? Or perhaps you didn't have the courtesy to ask when you barged in. My name's Southall, that's Detective Inspector Southall, and I suggest you show some respect for my rank and back off, right now!'

Hickstead took a hasty step back. He licked his lips and cast a sideways look at Morgan, but she studiously avoided making eye contact with him. His mouth opened and closed a couple of times, but he didn't seem to be able to speak.

'My team found the body, and it's in my area,' continued Southall. 'From where I'm standing, that makes it my case. That's how it's supposed to work, isn't it?'

Impassively she watched as Hickstead ground his teeth, still unable to form any words. Then finally, he managed to speak.

'Now listen. I don't think you understand.'

'Trust me, Sergeant, I understand perfectly.'

Hickstead ground his teeth even harder.

'What was your name again?' she asked. 'Dickhead, was it?'

'Hickstead,' he growled.

'Ah, yes, Hickstead. Sorry, my mistake. Right then, DS Hickstead, as I'm the senior officer here, you will listen to me, and you will not argue. There is only one person here having a problem with comprehending the situation, and it's not me. But I always try to be helpful, so, let me make it simple for you to understand.

'This,' she indicated the area with a sweep of her arm, 'is my crime scene, and my team will carry out the investigation. The only thing that will change that situation is a direct order from my commanding officer. Is that clear enough for you?'

'My guvnor's not going to like this.'

'I'll try not to lose too much sleep over that.'

'I'll speak to you later, Catren,' hissed Hickstead, as he turned away and headed back to his car.

'Oh, by the way, Hickstead,' called Southall.

The angry man turned to face her.

'If you ever dare to try and intimidate me, or call me "luv" again, I promise you I'll do my very best to make sure you're back in uniform. Is that clear?'

Hickstead glowered as he thought about a response, but she had already turned her back on him. Instead, he directed a glare at Morgan, then turned and stomped away.

Morgan watched until Hickstead was halfway back to his car before she turned to find Southall studying her face.

'What's that all about?'

'Boss?'

'Is there something going on between you two?'

Morgan stared down at her feet.

'No, boss.'

Southall turned and stared out to sea.

'Let me give you some advice, Morgan. If you're going to lie to me, you need to be a hell of a lot more convincing than that. Should I assume you were the one who told him about this case?'

Morgan looked up at Southall but said nothing.

'I'm not going to ask if you're sleeping with him. What you do in your own time is your own business,' said Southall. 'But it will become my business if I think your relationship is affecting your work. Or affecting the security of my team.'

Back at the roadside, a white van had pulled up, and the sound of car doors slamming drew their attention.

'That must be the pathologist and the SOCOs,' said Morgan.

Southall looked at her watch.

'I'm sure our friend from Region is going to be making waves, so I think it's only fair I brief Superintendent Bain, before the shit hits the fan, don't you?'

Morgan nodded.

'What shall I do?' she asked.

'I want you to make sure this whole area is cordoned off and get some screens around that body. I don't want the public gawping at the poor soul. Then I'd like you to stay here until SOCOs have finished and let me know when they remove the body. If anyone from Region appears, call me straight away, okay?'

'Am I still bagman on this case?'

'I'm going to have to think about that,' said Southall. 'It's not been an auspicious start, has it?'

'I'm sorry, it's just that—'

'I don't want your excuses. What matters is what you choose to do next.'

'Boss?'

'You should understand, I value trust very highly. You heard what I told Hickstead about his mole. I must admit I found you much sooner than I expected, but now you need to decide which side you're on.'

'I'm not sure I understand. Do you mean you want me out?'

'If you want to work with me, I can help you rebuild and develop your career. All DS Dickhead is going to do is continue using you to develop his career. You need to decide what you want and then make a choice, but if you choose him, then yes, I will expect you to request a transfer.'

Morgan stared after her new boss as she started back towards the road. After about ten yards, she turned and called out.

'Don't take too long making up your mind. I only want people in my team who want to be there.'

'Yes, boss,' said Morgan, unhappily.

CHAPTER 7

Superintendent Nathan Bain was six foot three and very lean for such a tall man. He had a habit of standing with his hands in his pockets when deep in thought and now, as he stared out of the window of his office, a long nose, and developing stoop made him look not unlike a heron awaiting its prey.

During a long career as a detective, Bain had managed to solve more than his fair share of significant cases, but he had also made a habit of speaking his mind and ruffling feathers. This had made him many enemies in high places which, in turn, had resulted in more than one sideways promotion in attempts to keep him out of harm's way.

Despite this, he had attained the rank of Detective Superintendent and, much as the powers-that-be wanted to keep Bain quiet, there was no denying his record and no one had wanted to deprive this once brilliant detective of his hard-earned pension. So now, in the twilight of his career, he had been put back into uniform (still as Superintendent) and sent to command the backwater that was Llangwelli Station where it was felt he could do no further harm while he saw out his last two years of service.

In an attempt to humour him and keep him happy, they had even indulged his seemingly crazy dream to retrain all the reject officers under his command. Of course, if he succeeded, HQ could claim the credit. If he failed, well, at least it would keep him out of their hair. They had even interviewed, and recruited, a 'suitable' Detective Inspector to assist Bain in his task.

Resigned to the arrival of what he knew was going to be a spy in his camp Bain couldn't believe his luck when, just a week before he was due to take his position, the chosen man had turned out to be on the payroll of not one, but two, drug dealers.

For a couple of days, it looked as though fate was conspiring to allow Bain free rein to run his station his way, but then suddenly a last-minute substitute had been found in the form of DI Sarah Southall. Bain naturally assumed she was also hand-picked to spy on him although, in truth, he knew almost nothing about her except she was a recently appointed DI, and hence inexperienced in the role. He felt entitled to think this was a further attempt to make life difficult for him.

He leaned forward to get a better look at the woman climbing from her car. He sighed as he watched the small, suited figure walk across the car park until she disappeared from view as she entered the building. He regretted not making an effort to learn something about her, but then what difference would it make? If Region had appointed her, she must be a spy. He was stuck with her, like it or not.

He turned from the window, sat down at his desk, and regarded the mountain of paperwork with another sigh, and not for the first time, wondered why they had felt the need to stick him out here in Llangwelli. Didn't they realise he didn't have the energy to fight any more and was just seeing out his time?

His thoughts were interrupted by a knock on the door. 'Come in.'

The door opened, and the woman he had been watching stepped inside. Confidently she closed the door and walked across to his desk, hand held out in front of her.

'Superintendent Bain? I'm DI Southall.'

Bain climbed stiffly to his feet and shook her hand.

'I'm sorry we haven't had a chance to speak before,' confessed Bain. 'I should have been here yesterday when you arrived.'

'That's okay, sir. It was all a bit of a rush. I didn't even know I was coming until Friday.'

'Yes, that's when I found out,' admitted Bain. 'I'm afraid I'm rather in the dark. I wasn't even aware they had interviewed a second candidate, and I haven't even seen your application.'

'I understand I wasn't your first choice.'

'Let's be clear about something right from the start,' said Bain. 'DI Harding was never my choice. He was foisted upon me by Region. I had no say in the matter, any more than I've had any say in your appointment. At the very least I should have been present at your interview.'

'Interview? There was no interview, sir.'

'There wasn't? Then how . . .'

'Can I speak frankly?'

'Of course.'

'A month ago, I was a newly appointed DI waiting for a chance to prove I could lead an investigation. When the chance finally came, I was unfortunate enough to have a maverick under my command who ignored orders and got himself wounded. I was put on gardening leave until last Wednesday when I discovered I could either take this position or lose my rank.'

Bain's right eyebrow had raised as Southall told her story.

'So, you haven't been selected by Region?'

'I've not even spoken to anyone from Region. Superintendent Melloway, my old boss, told me an unexpected opening had come up, but I had to take it there and then.'

Bain struggled to conceal a grin.

'Unexpected opening? Yes, you could say that. It turns out Region's darling, DI Harding, had become badly tainted by two drug dealers.'

'Ah, that's a bit embarrassing.'

'Superintendent Melloway, did you say? I don't think I know him.'

'I can give you his number if you'd like to speak to him.'

Much to Bain's irritation, the phone on his desk began to buzz like an angry wasp.

'Oh, bugger,' he muttered.

'That's okay, sir. You should answer it. It might be important.'

She watched as Bain reluctantly reached for the phone and raised it to his ear. He listened for a moment, grunted once or twice, said, 'Tell him I'll call back in five minutes,' then placed the phone back in its cradle. A smile tugged at the corners of his mouth. This time he didn't try to conceal it.

'That was DCI Davies, from Region,' he said. 'Apparently, my new DI has upset one of his detective sergeants. Care to explain?'

'Yes, sir. DC Morgan called me early this morning after she found a body on the beach. DS Hickstead arrived on the scene not long after me, announced he was from Region and tried to take over. I merely pointed out that it was our crime scene, and there was no need for Region to get involved.'

'Hickstead, you say? Yes, that sounds like the sort of thing he would do. Arrogant bugger likes to think he's a modern-day Sherlock Holmes. I bet having a woman tell him what to do put his nose out of joint!'

'He was very persistent. I had to pull rank in the end. I hope I'm not going to cause a lot of trouble for you.'

Bain was laughing now.

'Trouble? Oh, don't worry about that. Trouble used to be my middle name.'

'Used to be?'

'I've always been a pain in the arse to my bosses. I speak my mind when they would rather I did as I was told. I'm nearing the end of my time now; hence I've been parked in this backwater. They expect me to sit here and twiddle my thumbs for the final two years of my career. I'd more or less accepted my fate.'

'Are you telling me this is a dead-end?' asked Sarah.

'Well, now, here's where I think I owe you an apology,' said Bain.

'Apology?'

'To be honest, I was getting tired of the fight. I know for a fact DI Harding was supposed to make sure we handed everything over to Region. I assumed you were sent here to do the same. I can see my assumption was quite wrong.'

Southall smiled.

'I'm not very good at tugging my forelock,' she said. 'I know my place, but I'll always argue for what I think is right. Besides, Superintendent Melloway told me this job offered me a chance to help you train a team of young detectives. I don't see how we can do that if we pass all the good cases over to Region.'

Bain leaned back in his chair, a broad smile on his face.

'That is an excellent point, Sarah,' he said. 'But I should warn you Region won't be happy with this.'

'You're my boss, sir. I'm only concerned about you being happy with it.'

'I don't think you need to worry about that,' said Bain. 'I'm sure I would quickly have become bored just sitting here biding my time. Now I can show them there's life in the old dog yet. This is going to be much more fun.'

'So, you'll back me?'

'One hundred per cent,' said Bain. 'I believe we're going to get on rather well. And if you need anything at all, you just let me know.'

'There is one thing. DS Marston? He's off sick. Do we know when he's likely to be back?'

'Between you and me, he doesn't know it yet, but he asked for a transfer, and his request has been approved.'

'But he's my only sergeant. Who's going to take his place?'

'It's already in hand. I've managed to recruit a guy I worked with at the Met twenty years ago. He's a good man who's never been afraid to share his knowledge with younger officers.'

'When is he going to arrive?'

'He'll be here any day now. I'll let you know as soon as I know.'

Southall wasn't entirely convinced, but she had only just met Bain, and he seemed okay. She would just have to trust the new guy was on the way and manage without him for a few days.

'Anyway, if that's all,' said Bain. 'I have to call DCI Davies back and tell him the good news.'

'Yes, of course. I need to get things organised downstairs anyway.'

Southall got to her feet and headed for the door.

'We'll talk later,' said Bain. 'As I said, Region will make this hard for us, so keep me up to date with the case, and let me know whenever they try to obstruct you.'

'Yes, sir, of course.'

CHAPTER 8

Catren Morgan surveyed the crime scene with a degree of satisfaction. Screens now hid the victim from the road, and a tent had been erected to keep the weather off. A team of SOCOs were busy scouring the area for clues, and the forensic pathologist had finally arrived to carry out a preliminary examination of the body.

She had never had this sort of responsibility before, and she just hoped she hadn't forgotten anything. Her career had been drifting since she had been at Llangwelli, and after she had been so easily caught out by DI Southall this morning, she felt she had reached a crossroads.

But, then, perhaps a kick up the backside was just what she had needed. Despite being so busy, she had played the scene over in her head at least a dozen times. She still couldn't quite believe her new boss had given her a second chance! Well, you know what? She was going to seize the opportunity and make the most of it.

What had her fling with Hickstead brought her anyway? She knew in her heart that he was a total arse, and Southall was right when she said he was only using her to further his career. Well, not anymore!

Her thoughts were interrupted by a voice on the radio.

'This is Thomas. I've got some old bloke here says he's the new DS.'

She turned towards the road where all the vehicles were parked. DC Jimmy 'Dylan' Thomas was the duty officer booking authorised people in and out of the scene. She could make out a figure standing next to him.

'What new DS?'

'Well, yeah, exactly. It's news to me, too. I've told him we're not expecting a new DS, but he won't go away.'

'What does he want?'

'He says he wants to speak to the officer in charge. That's you, isn't it?'

Morgan had been too busy to give it much thought, but now Thomas had mentioned it . . .

'Yes, I suppose it is,' she agreed. 'Tell him I'm on my way.'

As she walked across the sand, the figure next to Thomas began to take shape. From here he certainly didn't look like any detective sergeant she had ever met. She spoke into the radio.

'Tell you what, Dylan, if he's a time-waster I'll let you arrest him; my treat.'

'I can think of a better treat than that.'

'In your dreams, Thomas, in your dreams.'

The man standing next to Thomas was a good deal shorter. She knew Thomas was about six foot tall, so she guessed the man was maybe five foot eight-ish. He was wearing a pair of training shoes, a dark blue hoodie and a pair of knee-length shorts that revealed two spindly, pasty white legs. It certainly wasn't standard uniform, but it was the unruly mass of curls that seemed to be trying to escape from his head that drew her eye.

'I'm DC Morgan,' she said as she reached the man.

The man raised his eyebrows.

'You're in charge?' he asked.

'I'm the senior officer on site. How can I help you, sir?'

The man held out his hand.

'I'm the new DS. Officially I don't start until next Monday, but I was here anyway, and I saw there was a crime scene. I thought maybe you could use some help.'

Morgan looked suspiciously at the extended hand, but she didn't shake it.

'As far as I'm aware we don't have a new DS starting next Monday, or any other Monday. We already have a DS. Can I see your warrant card?'

The man appeared to be ready for the question.

'Ah, yeah, I'm afraid that's a bit of a problem. You see I haven't been issued with one yet.'

Morgan crossed her arms and regarded him with a mixture of irritation and curiosity.

'You're not a police officer, are you?'

'Well, actually, it's quite a story. You see I was, then I had to retire, and now I've been recruited back under the Rejoiner scheme, so I am again if you see what I mean. As I said, I haven't checked in with Superintendent Bain yet. That's why I don't have my warrant card.'

Morgan exchanged a look with Thomas, who raised his eyebrows, and shrugged his shoulders. Then she turned back to the man.

'I have to warn you, impersonating a police officer is a serious offence, and so is wasting police time. As you can see, we have a lot going on here at the moment, and you're getting in the way. I'm going to ask you to leave quietly, or if you'd prefer, I can get DC Thomas here to arrest you. Which is it going to be?'

It looked as though the man was going to argue, but then a wry smile crept across his face. He nodded his head appreciatively, raised his hands and took a step back.

'Okay,' he said. 'I see your point. You're right. Why should you believe me when I don't even have a warrant card?'

'Can I ask why you're here?'

'I just moved in at the weekend. I was taking a look around the area to get a feel for the place. Then I saw there was a crime scene and, as I said, I thought you might need some help. I didn't think about not having a card with me.'

'Can I ask your name?'

'Sure, it's Norman Norman.'

CHAPTER 9

Southall's phone was ringing as she reached her office.

'It's Morgan, boss.'

'How are you getting on?'

'Okay, I think. SOCOs are everywhere, and the patholo-gist says he'll be moving the body soon. He says he'll do the post-mortem this afternoon at three.'

'That's good. Anything else I should know?'

'It's probably nothing, but some guy was trying to get onto the crime scene. He said he was a new DS, and wanted to help, but he had no warrant card. I sent him away but sug-gested if he wanted to help, he should come in this afternoon and make a statement.'

'Did he give a name?'

'Norman Norman. It sounds pretty unlikely to me. I reckon he's some sort of fantasist. You know the sort; wanted to be a police officer but didn't make the grade. Once I warned him about impersonating a police officer and wast-ing police time, he was quick enough to back off. Apart from that, it's been pretty straightforward.'

'Good. Well done. Once the body has been moved, and as long as SOCOs are happy, you can come back here.'

'Is it okay if I go home and have a shower first? I'm still in my running gear!'

'Of course. I'll see you later.'

Southall felt as though she had hardly put the phone down before Bain walked into her office and closed the door behind him.

'We have a problem,' he said. 'Region have been checking you out.'

'That was quick,' she said, 'but that shouldn't be a problem. My record is clean enough.'

'That's not the issue. They're saying you're not qualified as a Senior Investigating Officer. Is this true?'

In the rush to get here and then the sudden finding of a body, Sarah had forgotten entirely about this. In her old job, she would have started things rolling and then called her boss. Damn! Surely, she hadn't messed up on her very first case.

'I'm sorry, sir. I'm afraid it is. I've completed the training course, but I haven't completed the Professional Development stage. I didn't intend to mislead you. It's just that everything's happened so fast—'

Bain held up a hand.

'Hush now,' he said. 'I'm not looking for an apology. These things happen when appointments are rushed, and interviews are skipped, but it's not your fault. I've spoken to Ian Melloway, and he speaks very highly of you. He didn't go into detail, but he assures me you've had a rough time and deserve my support.'

'Thank you, sir. I appreciate that, but does this mean we've got to hand the case on to Region?'

'Nonsense. If we mavericks don't stick together, the suits will win, and anyway, how are you ever going to finish your professional development if we give it to them?'

'But how can we manage the case without a qualified SIO?'

Bain beamed at her.

'As I have just pointed out to Region, we do have a qualified SIO. I might wear a uniform these days, but I still have the necessary experience and qualifications.'

Southall felt her stomach lurch.

'So, you're taking the case away from me?'

'Not at all. You are going to run the case as part of your ongoing development, and I am going to supervise.'

'How exactly is that going to work?'

'Don't worry, I'm not going to be breathing down your neck all the time; I'm sure that would drive you mad! Even so, we have to be aware of your lack of experience. I have a couple of suggestions as to how we can make this work so I can keep an eye on things but not get in your way.

'The first suggestion is that you brief me at the end of every day. The second is that you don't hesitate to ask if you need advice. Can you do that?'

'Yes, sir, I think so.'

'Good. And don't forget Region will be watching, and hoping we screw things up. They may even try to interfere and trip us up but, if we work as a team and stick together, there's no reason why we can't prove we're up to the job.'

Bain reached for the door handle.

'One more thing,' said Southall. 'You mentioned a new DS. What's his name?'

'Norman Norman.'

Southall began to laugh.

'I know. It sounds unlikely, doesn't it?' said Bain. 'Apparently, it's a family name. Even his father is called Norman.'

'It's not that. He turned up at the crime scene earlier, offering to help. But Morgan threatened to arrest him unless he backed off.'

'She did what?'

'She told him to clear off and stop wasting their time.'

'Why?'

'He wanted access to the crime scene, but she had no idea who he was, and he had no warrant card. To be fair, I would have done the same.'

Bain's face creased into a smile, and he laughed.

'Ha! That'll teach old Norm,' he said. 'It's his fault. He's a short notice arrival like you. He told me he was moving in this weekend but that he wouldn't be starting for another week. He said he wanted to get a feel for the place before he started.'

'Do you know where we can find him?' asked Southall. 'An experienced sergeant would be a godsend.'

'Leave it to me,' said Bain. 'I'll get hold of him and get him here right away.'

CHAPTER 10

The inquiry room at Llangwelli Station wasn't exactly the biggest, but then they were only a small team, so the four desks crammed into the space left just enough room for someone to stand at the front and command attention.

Catren Morgan sat before one of the desks, writing a report on what had happened this morning. Her desk could never be referred to as tidy, but she liked it that way, and she felt it was more critical she knew where everything was.

By contrast, the next desk was so neat and tidy it almost looked unused. This was the domain of DC Judy Lane who liked everything to be 'just so'. Just looking at what she saw as the untidy mess on the other desks was enough to drive her to distraction. Right now, Lane was staring at her computer screen as she trawled through the photographs from missing person reports, hoping to find a match for their victim.

The third desk was the most haphazard of the three. It belonged to DC Thomas who was supposed to be contacting the Coastguard to find out about tides, winds, and currents but was currently staring into space trying to figure out why he still hadn't got inside Catren Morgan's knickers. She'd even said he wasn't her type! How could that be possible?

He was forever paying her compliments (like down on the beach earlier when he told her she had a nice arse) yet somehow his charm wasn't making an impact. Then he realised there could only be one answer. She must be a lesbian. Yes, that's the only thing that could explain it!

It was just at this definitive moment in Thomas's thinking that the door burst open and Superintendent Bain came into the room followed by DI Southall, and another man dressed in a shabby suit. The man had thick, curly hair which didn't appear to have any particular style.

All heads turned, as one, to view the arrivals.

'Shit!' hissed Morgan, turning to look at Thomas. 'It's the old bloke from the beach. What's he doing here.'

'He did say he'd come in and make a statement,' said Thomas.

The 'old bloke' had heard Morgan, and now he looked in her direction, smiled, and raised a hand in greeting.

'Listen up, everyone,' said Bain. 'This is DS Norman Norman who's come to add his years of experience to the team and help with your training. He's arrived a week earlier than planned, but given the circumstances, I think that's a good thing. I do owe you an apology for not warning you he was on the way, but I hope you'll overlook that and make him welcome.'

Morgan missed the rest of Bain's introduction as she became lost in thought, wondering what the new man was going to think of her behaviour earlier. She had already stepped out of line with DI Southall, and she figured she was hardly likely to be flavour of the month with the new DS either.

Norman smiled happily at everyone as Bain made his short announcement. After he had gone, Norman made a point of going from desk to desk, shaking hands and saying hello. He left Morgan until last.

'Hi,' he said when he got to her desk. 'It's Catren, isn't it?'

'God, this is embarrassing,' she said, sheepishly.

He extended his hand.

'If you're talking about what happened earlier, it shouldn't be,' he said, shaking her hand. 'I think you handled the situation very professionally.'

She couldn't hide her surprise.

'You do?'

'Sure. It was entirely my fault. I rushed over to help, but I didn't think it through. You don't know me from Adam, and I had no ID.'

'But I threatened to have you arrested.'

'Yeah, well, maybe that was a bit over the top, but I would have been disappointed if you'd let me wander around your crime scene in those circumstances.'

'Really? Are you saying it was a test?'

'No, not at all. I'm afraid I'm a bit rusty. I've just spent three years not needing to carry a warrant card, and I didn't think about it until you asked. If anything, I should be the one apologising.'

'So, you're not annoyed? I was worried I might have put you off before we even got started.'

'No way. I thought you did great.'

Southall had walked over to join them.

'I understand you two have met.'

'Yes,' said Morgan. 'It's a bit embarrassing.'

'DS Norman says you did the right thing.'

'Yes, he's just told me that, but I still feel a bit awkward.'

'You haven't got time for that now,' said Southall. 'You're coming with us.'

'Where to?'

'Post-mortem at 3 p.m., didn't you say?'

'Yes, but I thought now you've got DS Norman here you wouldn't need me to be bagman anymore.'

Southall pursed her lips.

'Yes, that's true, but I'd still like you to come. DC Lane is going through missing persons, and Thomas is contacting the Coastguard. There's not much more we can do at this stage so you might as well join us. You can bring DS Norman up to speed while we drive.'

CHAPTER 11

The pathologist wiped his hands and sighed.

'Okay, so the first thing you need to know is that this body has been in the water for some time and, because of that, it's difficult for me to be as accurate as I'd like to be.'

'I hope you're going to give us something,' said Norman. 'I'd hate to think I watched you slice and dice for nothing.'

'I thought you looked uncomfortable.'

'It's nothing personal. It's just that I detest this part of the job. Given a choice, I'd sooner be notifying someone their loved one had just died than watch you working, and no one likes doing that.'

'Can you at least tell us how the long the body has been in the water?' asked Southall.

'The coldness of the water would slow down decomposition.'

'How about an educated guess?' suggested Norman. 'Right now, we could do with anything, just to give us a start.'

The pathologist scratched his head and mumbled quietly to himself.

'Okay. I would guess at least a week, but it could be as much as ten days. But remember that's just a guess at this stage. I won't be able to offer anything more accurate for at least a couple of days.'

He looked at the three police officers, but no one said anything.

'When I first arrived at the beach, DC Morgan suggested the body had come in on the tide, and that it looked as though the victim had been strangled with a piece of rope.'

'Was I right?' asked Morgan.

'Yes, and no. Everything suggests the body did come in on the tide, but I don't believe the rope was used to strangle her. For one thing, there are no rope marks on her neck consistent with her being strangled. There's a bit of chafing, but that appears to be post-mortem. There's also evidence of blunt force trauma to the back of her head.'

'Is that what killed her?' asked Morgan.

'It certainly would have rendered her unconscious.'

'Could a fall have caused it?' asked Norman.

'It's always a possibility, but the fact she was trussed up with fishing line makes it unlikely, don't you agree?'

'So, you think she was killed by someone bashing her head in?' asked Morgan.

The pathologist pulled a face.

'If only that were the case. But sadly, there is water in her lungs.'

There was a sharp intake of breath from Norman's direction.

'What?' asked Morgan.

'It means she was still breathing when she went into the water,' said Southall, grimly.

'I'm afraid so,' said the pathologist. 'I can't say for certain yet, but it looks as though she was probably unconscious when she went into the water.'

'Somehow, that's not much comfort,' said Norman.

'Even if she had been awake, trussed up like that, she would have been unable to do anything to save herself.'

'Jesus,' said Norman. 'So, it's possible whoever did this intended her to know she was drowning? He could even have trussed her up, waited until she came round, and then pushed her in?'

'That doesn't bear thinking about,' said Morgan.

'I would hope that's not what happened,' said the pathologist, grimly, 'but it is a possibility and, at the moment, I can't rule it out.'

'Holy shit,' muttered Norman.

'Any evidence of sexual assault?' asked Southall.

'After a week in the water, it's hard to say for sure. She wasn't wearing any underwear but, while that suggests the possibility, in itself it doesn't prove anything.'

'And I guess any DNA evidence would be useless,' suggested Norman.

'We'll test, of course, but I wouldn't hold out much hope. Some of her nails are broken which suggests she put up a fight, and they're long, so someone might well have some nasty scratches.'

'Anything under the nails?'

'I've recovered some material that could be human flesh, but it could also be something collected from being in the water.'

'Is there anything to help us identify who she is?'

'No obvious birthmarks, operation scars, broken bones, but dental records should be able to help us with that. However, I can tell you she was well-nourished, and despite being in the water for all that time, it's obvious she took care of herself. She had good muscle tone, which suggests she kept herself fit, and the clothes she was wearing bear some pretty expensive designer labels.'

'So, she's unlikely to have been homeless, right?'

The pathologist nodded. He had laid out the clothes she had been wearing on a nearby table, and now he pointed to a blue jacket.

'I don't know if it will be any help, but there's a tear here, and a piece of the fabric appears to be missing.'

'Could that have happened when she was attacked?' asked Norman.

'Quite possibly, but it could just as easily have happened while she was drifting in the sea.'

'Oh well, at least it's something we can look out for,' said Southall, as she studied the rest of the clothes. 'We have a blue jacket, white T-shirt and white skirt. But no shoes.'

'No, but that's hardly surprising. They could easily have been lost out at sea.'

There was a gloomy silence before the pathologist spoke again.

'I think she was married, too. Although there was no jewellery found on her, there's evidence to suggest she wore a wedding ring.'

'D'you think it might have been taken as a trophy?' asked Southall.

'There's no sign to suggest it was torn off, but it's possible.'

'Or, maybe she's no longer married,' suggested Morgan. 'Or perhaps she takes it off when she goes out without her husband.'

They all stared at her.

'Some married women do,' she added hastily. 'To advertise that they're open to suggestion, you know?'

'So, we have a woman who is, or perhaps was, married, with a good job, who was murdered, and then dumped at sea,' said Norman. 'Is that right?'

The pathologist shrugged.

'Your guess is as good as mine at this stage. All I can say for sure is that, at the very least, she would have been knocked out by the blow to the head, and then she drowned when she was put into the sea. Where exactly this happened, I have no idea. We'll analyse the water for diatoms and so on, and that might help us identify the site, but that will take some time.'

Norman sighed.

'D'you mean to tell me I've had to stand here struggling to keep hold of my lunch, and we're not much further forward than we were this morning?'

'I'll know more in a day or two when the results start coming in.'

CHAPTER 12

The information from the pathologist regarding the victim's identity had proved to be no use whatsoever, and despite what she claimed had been a thorough search through the missing persons records DC Lane had found no one who was even close to a match.

Thomas had eventually turned his attention to the Coastguard, but he'd left it so late the information wouldn't be with them until tomorrow morning.

'Right, everyone, it's six thirty,' said Southall. 'Let's call it a day and start again in the morning. I'm speaking to the Coastguard first thing. I hope they can give us something to go on, so let's have you all here for a briefing at oh-eight-hundred.'

Norman waited until the others had gone and then walked over to the map on the wall and studied it.

'Aren't you going home?' asked Southall.

'A holiday chalet might be great on a warm sunny day, but at this time of year it isn't my idea of a cosy home,' said Norman. 'So no, I'm not in any great hurry and I thought I'd take the opportunity to try and make some sense of what we do know.'

'That won't take very long. We know our victim is probably middle class, married, with a good job, and probably living in a nice area. But she doesn't seem to have been reported missing; we have no ID and no clues as to what happened and where. We have nothing unless you know something I don't.'

'What do you think about her being married?' asked Norman.

'You mean, why hasn't her husband reported her missing? What if he's away, or what if she's supposed to be away?'

'Yeah, that's possible, but wouldn't they have kept in touch? The pathologist says she's been in the water for at least a week, possibly longer.'

'Some married couples would love an excuse not to have to speak to each other for a few days,' said Southall. 'Or maybe she's divorced but still wears the ring.'

'Or, maybe the husband hasn't reported her missing because he killed her,' suggested Norman.

'It isn't always the husband.'

'But it often is.'

'That doesn't help much if we don't know who she is, although the dental records should help us with that. Maybe tomorrow.'

'Yeah, let's hope,' said Norman. 'D'you know anything about tides and currents? I mean, we're on the coast. When I look at this map, there seems to be one heck of a lot of places a body could wash in from, on the tide. I've always worked inland, so all this stuff isn't something I've ever needed to worry about before.'

'That makes two of us, then. Let's hope someone from the Coastguard can explain it to us.'

'What about the team?' asked Norman. 'I'm told they're young and inexperienced and need an old hand like me to help with their training.'

'Yes, that's what I was told, but I also learned this morning that they're all here because they can't be trusted with real police work.'

'Says who?'

'Apparently, that's what Region think of them. I checked with the boss earlier, and he says that's not necessarily true.

He says he believes everyone can improve with the correct training.'

'Is there anyone I need to keep an eye on?'

'I've only been here a day longer than you so I can't tell you too much. Catren Morgan has been having an affair with a DS Hickstead from Region.'

'Is that a problem?'

'Region is a problem. They think they should have this case.'

'But it's right on our doorstep.'

'Yes, but Region have always taken anything bigger than shoplifting. They think it's their right. I've told them it isn't any more and it hasn't gone down too well. You'll need to keep an eye out for them. Bain says they'll try to interfere.'

'So, is this affair of Morgan's going to be a problem?'

'I think Hickstead was using her to find out what was going on here, but I explained to her this morning that it stops right now, or she's out.'

'Can she be trusted?'

'I'm pretty sure she got the message, but I think we should keep an eye on her just in case.'

'I was quite impressed with what I've seen of her so far.'

'There's no doubt she shows promise. I just hope she chooses us and not him.'

'What about Lane? I notice she keeps her desk neat and tidy. People like that tend to be very thorough.'

'That sounds about right from what I've seen of her so far.'

'And Thomas?'

'Ah. Not sure about him. I'm not convinced he's mature enough to do this job, but I'll give him the benefit of the doubt for now.'

'You don't sound too sure about any of them.'

'A week ago, I didn't even know I was coming here, then I suddenly found myself with the choice of facing demotion, or coming here. I've worked too bloody hard to reach DI for me to step down over a budget cut, so here I am.'

Norman studied her face for a moment.

'Right,' he said. 'So, they still treat people like shit in the name of budget cuts. I have to say I'm not surprised.'

'You, too?'

'Oh, I never had any ambitions to be anything more than a sergeant, so it's not quite the same. I just became a convenient scapegoat when they needed one.'

'Yet you still came back?'

Norman smiled.

'I guess it's in my blood. Anyway, I needed a change of scenery, and I've heard it's nice here.'

'Sounds like we have a lot in common,' said Southall, with a grim smile.

CHAPTER 13

As Southall walked into the inquiry room and headed to the front, she was pleased to see every member of the team was at their desk.

'Right, listen up everyone. I've just spoken to the Coastguard, but unfortunately, we're no further forward as a result. They say the currents are variable along this part of the coast. Because of this, our body could have come from just about anywhere. Furthermore, if it's been in the sea for a week, it's probably been ten miles or more along the coast in each direction.'

She looked from face to face. DC Thomas clearly had something on his mind.

'Thomas? You look concerned. Is there a problem?'

'Can I ask a question?' said the young detective.

'Of course.'

'How come we're investigating this case? Shouldn't we have passed it on to Region? That's what usually happens.'

'I know that's what happened in the past,' said Southall. 'But that was before I arrived. It's not going to happen anymore.'

'But we don't have the experience to handle it,' said Thomas.

'Is that a collective "we", or are you speaking for yourself?'

Thomas looked at Catren Morgan, and Judy Lane, then back at Southall.

'I think I can speak for us three. We've never done anything like this.'

'And how will you gain the experience you lack if we hand all our big cases over to Region? Superintendent Bain, DS Norman and I have more than enough experience to handle a case like this. We're here to steer the ship and help you learn.'

'DS Hickstead told me I wasn't fit to be a detective, and that's why I'm here,' said Thomas.

'Ah, yes. I had the pleasure of meeting DS Hickstead yesterday. I suggest you ignore anything he says. The people at Region might think they're superior to everyone else, but the fact is it doesn't matter what they think. You work here, with me, at Llangwelli Station. Superintendent Bain is our senior officer, and you need to worry about what he thinks, and what I think, not what some jumped-up sergeant from Region thinks.'

Norman had been reading something on his computer. Now he rose from his desk and walked across to the printer which was clattering into life.

'Sorry to interrupt, boss,' he said. 'But I've just had an email from the pathologist. You need to hear this.'

'Has he identified the body?' she asked.

'That would be good, but I'm afraid it's not that. If anything, what he's found only confuses the issue.'

Southall groaned.

'Come on, then. Let's hear it.'

Norman gathered a couple of sheets of paper from the printer.

'He says there's a full report on the way, but this is additional to what he told us yesterday: although the victim's lungs were full of water, it was freshwater and not seawater.

However, the rope around her neck was soaked in seawater, and not freshwater.'

'Does he draw any conclusion from this?'

'He says his best guess is that she drowned somewhere inland, possibly in a river, and then the body washed out to sea where the rope snagged around her neck. Then the body was brought back in on the tide.'

'So, we can stop looking out to sea for a murder scene,' said Southall. 'And we can rule out strangulation with the rope.'

'He says bruises to her thighs and other evidence, suggest she was also sexually assaulted. But there were no usable DNA samples.'

Thomas was wide-eyed.

'Does this mean there's a sex maniac on the loose?' he asked.

'Let's not get ahead of ourselves,' said Southall, calmly. 'What we have is one body found on our beach. We don't even know for sure if it originated in our area so, at this stage, I don't see any reason to assume it's anything more than an isolated incident.'

She had pinned a map of the coastline up on the wall, and now she pointed to it.

'Okay guys, gather round the map.'

She waited until they were in a small huddle before the map.

'Now it's your turn. You have been here longer than Norman and me, so you know the area better. We've got precious little to go on so far, so let's see if we can "what if" our way ahead of the game.'

Their faces suggested this was a new concept for the young team.

'To put it another way, let's make a few assumptions based on what we know,' she suggested.

'Aren't we supposed to assume nothing, and check everything?' asked Morgan.

'That's correct, Catren. We can't build a case on assumptions, but we can use them as a starting point if we have nothing else. So, we won't speculate on the details of how or why she died, but let's assume the victim was murdered on our patch somewhere. That seems reasonable, doesn't it?'

Everyone was nodding, so she continued.

'The pathologist has suggested sexual assault, so let's assume the victim was abducted and taken somewhere quiet and out of the way. Then, let's assume the body was dumped somewhere and subsequently washed down into the sea. Once in the sea, it drifted up and down for a period before coming ashore where Catren found her.'

She was pleased to see she had everyone's attention, but then frowned as the phone in her office began to ring.

'Damn,' she said.

'Go ahead,' said Norman. 'I can handle this.'

Southall nodded and headed for her office.

'Okay,' said Norman. 'We also have to consider the possibility she could have been attacked in one place and then dumped in another. So, first, let's focus on where a body might have been put into the water.'

'Can I make a suggestion?' asked Morgan.

Norman smiled.

'Let's get something clear before we go any further,' he said. 'I have been here just a couple of days, and the boss only a day or two more. We might have years of investigative experience and knowledge we can share with you, but neither of us knows our way around this area. That means we're reliant on you guys to share your knowledge with us, okay?'

He looked at the three faces.

'Also, you will learn a lot quicker if you're willing to contribute. That includes suggesting ideas and asking questions. If there's anything you don't understand you should always ask. The way I see it, the dimwit isn't the person who asks the question, it's the person who's frightened to risk looking a dimwit.

'One more thing. I don't mind if you call me Norm, or Sarge, except when we're out in public, then it's DS Norman. Now, Catren, you had something to say.'

'I think we should focus on the river. I know there are plenty of streams that run down from the hills and out to sea, but most of them are quite narrow and twisty, which would make it easy for a body to get stuck. Also, the river is much more accessible. There are dozens of places you can park right next to it.'

'Now we're cooking,' said Norman.

He placed a finger on the mouth of the river and began to trace its course back inland.

'So how many likely sites are there?' he asked.

'Dozens,' said Judy Lane. 'In the summer lots of these places would be filled with potential witnesses in the form of tourists, but at this time of year . . .'

'Good point,' said Norman. 'I might never have thought of that. We didn't have many tourists where I lived before, so it wasn't a consideration.'

He thought for a moment. 'So, it's just the locals here now, right?'

'More or less,' agreed Lane.

'So, let's assume our killer is a local, which means who-ever we're looking for would probably know the best places to dump a body,' said Norman.

As he turned to face the three youngsters, he could see Southall standing in the doorway to her office. As she caught his eye, she beckoned him over.

'Okay,' he said. 'I think the boss wants me, so I want you three to come up with at least six good places to dump a body in the river. I'll be back in a minute.'

He walked across to join a frowning Southall.

'Have you got an ID for the body?' he asked.

'I'm not sure,' she said. 'It's a bit of a weird one. I've just been speaking to a woman called Avril Fisher. She's the secretary to someone called Kimberley Lawrence. Now, she says she hasn't seen Kimberley since Monday fourteenth, and that such an absence is totally out of character.'

'It fits the timeframe,' said Norman. 'Has she been reported missing?'

'That's where it gets weird. Avril told me that Kimberley's husband, Greg, came to her office on the morning of Tuesday fifteenth looking for her, but she hadn't come into work. Then, later that day, he called to say Kim wouldn't be coming to work as she was sick, but that he would keep Avril informed about how she was.'

Norman was confused.

'So, she's not missing?'

Southall raised a hand.

'Hang on; there's more. Avril hadn't heard by Friday, so she called Greg to see how Kimberley was. Greg told her he didn't know where Kimberley was and that he had been to the police and reported her missing. Avril was calling us to see why we hadn't been to interview her about her missing boss.'

'You got a description, right?'

'Without trying to make it too obvious, yes.'

'And does Kimberley fit the description?'

Southall nodded.

'Oh yes, she's a perfect fit.'

'So why didn't Judy Lane find her among the missing person reports?'

'That's what I want to know. Bring her over and let's ask the question.'

Norman walked back to the group working at the map.

'Judy? Can we borrow you for a minute?' he asked.

'Sure,' she said.

She followed him across to Southall's office.

'Judy, are you sure you went through all the misper files?' asked Southall.

'Yes, boss. I went back over a year. There was nothing even close.'

'How would you feel if I told you a woman who fits the description was reported missing just last Friday.'

'I'd feel obliged to argue with you,' said Lane, vehemently. 'I might not be perfect, but I know my way around those databases, and I swear there is no such report listed. I'll show you if you like.'

Lane's tone struck Norman. Could she be right? She seemed so confident.

'That's a good idea, Judy,' he said. 'Why don't you and I take another look?'

He glanced at Southall, who nodded her agreement.

Lane was correct in her assertion she knew her way around the database. Within seconds she had the list in front of her.

'Okay,' she said, pointing at her screen. 'So, this is in date order. Can you see a report posted last Friday?'

'What if you search by name?' asked Norman. 'Try Kimberley Lawrence.'

Lane sighed as she typed the name, added +12 months, and pressed the search button.

'See? Nothing, just like I said.'

'You're right,' said Norman. 'There's nothing listed. But someone just called the boss and told her—'

'I can search it as many ways as you like,' said Lane, truculently, 'but it still won't be there.'

'Okay, you're right, it's not there,' agreed Norman. 'I'm sorry we doubted you. But let me give you some advice. In this job, you'll often be asked to check your work. It's been that way for years, and it ain't gonna change just because you don't like it. It's how we make sure we don't make mistakes.'

'But I was right,' argued Lane.

'Yes, you were,' agreed Norman. 'But when the boss asks you to check something to make sure you haven't made a mistake, arguing with her isn't the way to do it.'

'I didn't argue with her.'

'But you were ready to, and I'm sure you would have if I hadn't got you over here. I'm telling you, you seriously need to do something about that attitude of yours.'

'What do you mean?'

'All that huffing and puffing when I asked you try a different search, for a start. You behaved like a spoilt kid, as if perhaps you think you're perfect and couldn't possibly make a mistake.'

Lane said nothing, so Norman continued with his lecture.

'Well, I have news for you, DC Lane. No matter how good you think you are, there will be times when you're wrong, and it's better to find out during an investigation, rather than when a defence lawyer tears your case apart in court.'

Lane still said nothing.

'And another thing,' added Norman. 'When you do mess up, have the good grace to hold your hand up and admit it. A little humility oils the wheels of forgiveness much better than any tantrum ever did.'

Lane stared at her desk. Norman couldn't decide if she was angry, or about to burst into tears.

'Do me a favour,' he said. 'Without sighing, do the name search again, but this time without a timeframe.'

She looked up at Norman and frowned.

'You're joking, right?'

He smiled down at her.

'It'll take just a few seconds,' he said. 'Go on, humour me.'

She did as he asked and stared at the screen.

'There you go,' he said.

'Jesus!' she said. 'How did you know that?'

'Who, me? I didn't know anything except we had nothing to lose by searching further back.'

Lane was reading the notes onscreen.

'This report was made five years ago, but she hasn't been missing all this time. She was found four days later.'

'Is there a photograph?' asked Norman.

'Yes, there is. Should I print some out?'

'Now you're thinking,' encouraged Norman.

'How many?'

'We need enough for everyone to have a copy and a few spares. Twenty should be plenty for now.'

Lane sent the information over to the printer.

'Good,' said Norman. 'Just remember to rein it in a bit, and you'll be fine. You're a bright young woman, and you have a chance to learn so much here; it would be a shame if you missed the opportunity because you didn't know how to behave. Now, let's go and tell the boss you were right.'

'Judy was right,' Norman explained to Southall. 'There's not a single misper reported that day, and a search for Kimberley Lawrence during this month gets no results.'

'That's strange,' said Southall.

'But she was reported missing five years ago,' said Norman.

'You're not suggesting she's been—'

'No, no,' said Norman. 'She was found four days later.'

'Is that significant?' asked Lane.

Norman shrugged.

'It could indicate a pattern of behaviour, but she's not been reported missing since, so maybe it was just a one-off. Who knows?'

'Either way, it doesn't help us much,' said Southall. 'Avril Fisher was adamant Greg Lawrence said he had been to the police last Friday.'

'Maybe your caller got it wrong,' suggested Lane.

'Or perhaps Mr Lawrence changed his mind about reporting her missing,' said Norman. 'Maybe he knew where she was all along.'

'Let's not encourage our young team to jump to conclusions,' said Southall.

'I'm just saying,' said Norman, with a wry smile. 'Anyway, what d'you want to do now?'

'I think you and I should go and see her husband.'

'What shall I do?' asked Lane.

'Are you all right doing financial searches?' asked Southall.

'Yes, sure.'

'Okay. I'd like you to take a look at the Lawrences' finances.'

'No problem.'

They watched as Lane walked back across to her desk.

'Is she okay?' asked Southall.

'I just gave her a lecture on humility,' he said.

'What?'

'I pointed out her attitude needs to improve and that she had better get used to having her findings called into question now and then if she wants to make a career out of this.'

'A little criticism never hurt anyone,' said Southall. 'Let's hope she takes it on board.'

'I think it came as a bit of a shock, but she'll get over it,' said Norman. 'Oh, and she's printed out some photos of Kimberley from the old report.'

'Smart girl.'

'Yeah, I reckon so.'

CHAPTER 14

The Lawrences lived on a small development of twelve detached houses.

'What does a house like this cost around here?' asked Norman as he turned off the main road.

'I haven't had a chance to look around yet,' said Southall. 'But I can tell you they're a lot cheaper than in England.'

'Houses like these would go for around half a million where I come from,' said Norman.

'Yes,' agreed Southall, looking at the houses either side of them. 'I think we can safely assume the Lawrence's aren't exactly struggling to survive.'

Norman swung the car onto the drive of number twelve and parked behind a battered, tired-looking, pick-up truck. He looked at the house.

'The curtains are closed,' he said.

'Perhaps he's not home.'

'Or, he's still in bed.'

'But it's eleven o'clock!'

'Maybe he works nights,' suggested Norman.

'How many builders do you know who work nights?'

'I can't argue with that,' he said, as he opened his car door.

Norman peered into the back of the pick-up as they approached the front door.

'Anything interesting?' asked Southall.

'Normal builders' tools, but it looks as if they haven't been used in a while. And this truck has a puncture. It looks like it hasn't moved in weeks.'

'Perhaps business is a bit slow.'

'Or non-existent,' said Norman, as he rang the doorbell.

They waited and waited, but there was no answer. Norman rang again, then bent down and looked through the letterbox.

'Someone must be here,' he said. 'I can hear a radio somewhere in there.'

He stood up and banged on the door, then stepped back and looked up at the windows. Curtains slowly parted in one of the upstairs windows, just enough for a face to show. Then a window opened, and a man's head appeared.

'Who are you? What do you want?' he asked.

Norman produced his warrant card, even though he knew it couldn't be read at this distance.

'Mr Lawrence? My name is Detective Sergeant Norman, and this is Detective Inspector Southall. We're from Llangwelli Station.'

'Is it about my wife? Have you found her?'

'We'd rather not speak like this, sir. Can you come down and let us in?'

Lawrence muttered a curse.

'I'm not dressed. Give me a couple of minutes.'

The head disappeared, and the window banged shut.

'He thinks we've been looking for his wife,' said Southall. Norman grimaced.

'Yeah, it sounds like it, doesn't it? Jeez, I hope this isn't going to be one of those situations where she might still be alive if only we'd been looking for her.'

'Maybe that's not what he meant,' said Southall.

'But you know it is, right?'

She sighed.

'Yes, I know. We'd better play this carefully and see how it pans out.'

There was the muffled sound of the door being unlocked, and then it swung open, and they got their first proper look at Greg Lawrence. They knew he had just got out of bed, and it looked as if he wasn't sleeping well.

Norman showed his card again, and Lawrence glanced at it.

'This is about Kim, isn't it?' he asked. 'You've found her, right?'

He looked at their car, obviously expecting her to emerge, then he looked enquiringly at them.

'Where is she, then? Didn't you bring her home?'

'Mr Lawrence, can we come in?' asked Southall.

Without waiting for an answer, they ushered him inside and closed the door behind them.

'What's going on? Kim's not in any trouble, is she?' asked Lawrence.

'Is there somewhere we can sit down?' asked Norman.

'Well, yeah, you can come through here.' He led them into an untidy living room.

'Why do we need to sit down? I don't understand . . .'

Now Lawrence's face fell, as he suddenly began to realise what they were saying. He slowly lowered himself into one of the armchairs. Southall and Norman sat opposite him.

Southall took a photograph from her pocket and showed it to him.

'This is Kimberley, isn't it?'

'Yeah, that's right. Look, what's going on?'

'I'm afraid we've found a body, Mr Lawrence,' began Southall. 'We think it's Kimberley.'

'What? No. No. It can't be. She'll be off with some bloke. She's done it before. She'll be back when she gets fed up with him. They never last more than three or four days. She always comes back to me.'

'When did you last see your wife, Mr Lawrence?'

Lawrence looked at Norman as though he'd spoken gibberish, and then he seemed to focus.

'Sorry? See her? Er, well, it must have been Monday.'

'This Monday just gone?'

'No, the Monday before that.'

'So that would be nine days ago, right?' asked Norman.

'Yeah, that's right.'

Norman looked at Southall, who nodded. Yes, it sounded about right.

'I'm afraid we have to ask if you'll come with us, Mr Lawrence,' said Southall. 'We need to confirm if the body we have found is Kimberley.'

He turned a stricken gaze at them.

'Do I have to?'

'I'm afraid someone has to, and no one knows her better than you.'

'Yes, of course. I suppose you're right.'

He summoned up all the resolve he could muster.

'Right. Okay. I'll do it.'

'Is there someone we can call for you?'

'No, thanks. Maybe after, but I should do this on my own. I owe Kim that. She wouldn't want anyone else to see her like that. She's very proud of her appearance.' He looked at them, guiltily, then corrected himself. 'I mean, she was very proud of her appearance.'

He studied the floor for a few moments, then looked up.

'Right, come on, then. Let's get it over with before I lose my bottle.'

* * *

The sky seemed to have been growing darker all morning and rain was now falling steadily. It seemed somehow appropriate to the mood in the car, and the otherwise deadly quiet journey to the morgue was punctuated by the monotonous weenk, wonk, weenk, wonk of the windscreen wipers.

Norman stared at the storm outside as he drove. He knew this was just the lull before the real storm for Greg Lawrence. First, he was going to have to deal with seeing his wife on a slab, and then he was going to have to answer some pretty searching questions. There was no easy way through this for him.

CHAPTER 15

The relatives' room at the morgue was suitably peaceful and comfortable. Southall and Norman had taken Greg Lawrence there after he had confirmed the body was Kimberley. Now they sat in silence as Lawrence slowly composed himself.

'I'm sorry for your loss, Greg,' said Southall.

'How did she die?' he asked.

'This is an ongoing investigation,' said Southall. 'I can't go into details.'

'But she was murdered, right?'

'I'm afraid so.'

He lapsed into silence again. Southall gave him a minute or two, then continued.

'I understand what a shock it must be for you, Greg, but we have to ask some questions.'

'What? Oh, yeah, of course.'

'You said you last saw her on Monday fourteenth.'

'That's right.'

'What time was that? Before she left for work? When she got home?'

'She came home from work at around quarter to six, had a cup of tea, showered and got changed, then left again at about half seven.'

'Can you tell us what she was wearing? We have the clothes we found her in, but there were no shoes.'

'I'm sorry, but I don't know,' said Lawrence. 'We had this argument, you see. Then she had a shower, got dressed and went out. She didn't come and say goodbye, or anything, so I didn't notice what she was wearing.'

'Can you tell us where she was going?'

'Girls' night out. There's four of them. They meet up once a month to have a meal and a few drinks.'

'Where do they meet?'

'The Kings Head.'

'That's a pub, isn't it?' asked Norman.

Lawrence looked at him as if he were stupid.

'I'm new to the area,' explained Norman. 'Still finding my way around. But I'm sure I've seen that pub. Isn't it in the centre of town?'

'That's the one,' said Lawrence.

'How did Kim get to the pub?'

'One of the other girls picked her up. They take it in turns, so only one of them has to watch what they have to drink.'

'Can you give us the names and addresses of the girls?'

'Not off the top of my head, but I've got them at home.'

'That's okay; we can do that later,' said Southall. 'So, she went out with the girls, but didn't come home?'

'Yeah, that's right.'

'You said earlier that Kim had done this before, but that she always came home after a few days.'

'Yeah, she's done it three or four times before.'

'So why report her missing this time?'

'Because she had been gone longer than usual.'

'I see,' said Southall. 'And you don't mind when she went missing like that?'

'Of course, I mind, but what can I do? I can't lock her up, can I?'

'It must make you pretty angry.'

'Not really. You can get used to just about anything when you love someone.'

'Where were you the night she disappeared, Greg?'

'I was with a friend. He's converted his garage into a games room. We were playing snooker.'

'What, all night?'

'I got there at about eight and came home at eleven-ish.'

'Does this friend have a name?'

'Nick Rose.'

'And where does he live?'

'It's a Welsh street name,' said Lawrence. 'Would it be easier if I wrote it down for you?'

Norman handed Lawrence his pen and found a clean page in his notebook.

'I spoke to Kimberley's secretary, Avril,' said Southall as Lawrence scribbled the address. 'She says you turned up at Kim's office on the morning of Tuesday fifteenth, looking for her.'

Lawrence glanced up from his writing, looking distinctly uncomfortable.

'Yeah, that's right. Avril phoned home to say Kim hadn't arrived for work. Her car wasn't in the garage so I was worried she might have had an accident or broken down, so I got Nick to drive me along the route she uses to get to work. We drove to her office, but we didn't find her on the way, so I called in to see if she had arrived yet.'

'What did you do then?'

'Went back home.'

'Couldn't you just have called her?' asked Norman. 'I assume she has a mobile phone.'

'It was switched off.'

'Did you leave a message?'

'Well, yeah, of course, I did.'

'So, you were worried enough to drive out to her office looking for her, but when you couldn't find her, you didn't you think you should report her missing?'

'I told you, she'd done this before. I assumed she'd gone off with some bloke.'

'Which bloke?' asked Norman.

'Take your pick,' said Lawrence, bitterly.

'I'm sorry, I don't follow,' said Norman.

Lawrence's eyes blazed.

'Whichever bloke took her fancy at the time. All right?'

'Oh, right, I see,' said Norman.

'Let me get this straight,' said Southall. 'You didn't report Kimberley missing because you thought she was with another man and that she would be back in a few days. Is that right?'

'Yes.'

'But Avril says you told her Kimberley was off sick.'

'I told her that because I was embarrassed to admit the truth.'

'But, if she had done it before, wouldn't Avril be aware of the situation?'

'She always used to do it when she had a week off work. This was the first time she had done it and missed work. She never missed work.'

'You were worried that she was missing work?'

'Yes.'

'But you still didn't report her missing,' insisted Norman.

'I did what Avril said. I reported her missing on the Friday.'

'Last Friday?'

'Of course last Friday.'

'Are you sure?'

'Yes, I'm bloody sure!'

'The thing is, we have no record of you reporting her missing. We have a report from five years ago, but nothing more recent.'

'Five years ago?'

'Yes. She turned up four days later. Is that right?'

'Oh, yeah. That was the first time she ran off with another guy.'

'But you haven't reported her missing on other occasions when this has happened?'

'Not after the first time.'

'Why not?'

'Because that first time she came back looking like she'd been on holiday. She couldn't understand what all the fuss was about. She made me look an idiot, and the detectives organising the search weren't too impressed.'

'And you're sure you reported it this time? Only like I say we don't have a report on file.'

'Well, you must have lost it then,' Lawrence's voice was getting louder.

'Where did you make the report, Greg?' asked Southall.

'Your place. Llangwelli Station.'

'Who did you speak to?'

'I went in and spoke to the guy on the desk, and he called one of your detectives out.'

'Can you remember the detective's name?'

'I can do better than that. I've got a card here in my wallet.'

He pulled a wallet from his inside pocket, fished a card from it and handed it to Southall.

'DS Marston,' she read from the card. 'He's off sick at the moment.'

'Have you spoken to DS Marston since?' asked Norman.

'He said someone would be in touch.'

'And you didn't chase him up?' asked Norman. 'I think I would have been calling him all the time to find out what was going on.'

'Maybe your wife doesn't make a habit of doing this sort of thing.'

For a moment Norman was thrown by the reply, but before he could think, Lawrence was speaking again.

'So, what are you saying?' he asked. 'Did this guy lose my report? If Kim died because you lot didn't bother to take me seriously, I'll make sure you're in some seriously deep shit.'

'Mr Lawrence, lost report or not, I'm afraid Kim was dead long before last Friday,' said Southall.

'You're just saying that to cover your arses. You're going to say it's all my fault for not reporting her missing earlier, aren't you?'

'I don't think that would have made much difference.'

'What's that supposed to mean?'

'We don't know for sure, but it looks as though Kimberley may well have died the night she disappeared.'

Lawrence stared, wide-eyed, as her words sank in. He seemed to deflate before their eyes.

'I think I've had enough now,' he said quietly. 'I'd like to go home.'

'Before you go, could I ask you for Kim's mobile phone number? We haven't found the phone, and it might help if we can get hold of her call records.'

Lawrence found the number on his phone and handed it to Norman who copied it into his notebook.

Southall nodded to Norman.

'I'll get someone to take you home,' he said. 'We can arrange for a family liaison officer to stay with you for a few days—'

'I'd rather not.'

'Would you like us to call someone for you?'

'It's okay. I can do that for myself.'

Catren Morgan had been waiting to drive Greg Lawrence home, and now Norman called her in.

'DC Morgan will drive you home, Mr Lawrence. If you could give her those addresses, I'd be grateful.'

Lawrence nodded.

'Sure, no problem.

'And, if you think of anything you need, just let her know. We'll come and speak to you in a day or two to keep you updated with the investigation.'

* * *

'What did you make of that?' asked Norman as they watched Morgan drive Greg Lawrence away. 'Would he really have no clue what she was wearing?'

'If they had a big argument, maybe she did walk out without saying goodbye,' said Southall. 'It's quite possible. He seemed genuinely upset.'

'Oh, yeah, the tears were real enough. I meant the other bit when he was blaming us for not doing our job, then suddenly seemed to run out of steam.'

'It could be delayed shock, but it happened when I told him we thought she died the night she went missing. So, I think it's more likely he's feeling guilty that he didn't do anything until she'd been missing for several days. I mean, who would do that?'

'Someone whose wife made a habit of running off for a few days?' suggested Norman. 'Or maybe someone who knew where she was?'

Southall studied his face for a moment.

'Let's not jump to conclusions,' she said. 'We're supposed to be the experienced heads. Consider all possibilities, remember?'

'I'm not excluding anyone; I'm just saying he is one of those possibilities.'

'Everyone is a possibility until we eliminate them from our inquiry.'

Norman nodded his agreement.

'Of course. So where shall we start? Lawrence's alibi, or DS Marston?'

'We can deal with Marston later. Let's start with the alibi. What was the man's name?'

'Nick Rose.'

CHAPTER 16

Nick Rose lived alone in an enormous, modern, four-bed-roomed house at the far end of a small estate of similar homes. Unlike the others, this particular house had a huge garden, and it was also the only one to have a Maserati Levante parked on the drive.

'Nice car,' said Norman, as they pulled up alongside it.

'Someone has some money,' said Southall. 'The most basic model costs north of sixty grand, and that one looks top of the range.'

'I guess it's okay if you like that sort of thing,' said Norman, as he parked their car. 'But a car is just a car. As long as it gets you from A to B, does it matter how much it costs?'

'That's a very philosophical approach, Norm, but it doesn't take into account the need for status symbols.'

'Yeah, well, that's because I don't feel the need to exert some sort of self-imposed superiority on everyone else.'

'You can't pass judgement yet; we haven't even set eyes on the man!'

'I'm not judging, I'm just saying a single guy who owns a big house like this, and a big car like that, is trying to prove something.'

'Come on, then,' said Southall, opening her door. 'Let's see if you're right.'

* * *

Norman couldn't explain why, but he took an instant dislike to Nick Rose. Maybe it was the condescending smile, or the superior attitude, or the way he looked at Southall. Or perhaps it was all three. And then there was the patronising way he responded when she introduced herself.

'A detective inspector of the female variety. That is unusual. You have done well for yourself.'

'Actually, it's becoming quite common these days,' said Southall.

'Not in this area,' said Rose. 'I know most of the detectives around here, and I've never heard of you. Are you new to the area?'

'As it happens, yes, I am.'

'Ah! That explains it, then. I expect I'll share a drink with you some time.'

'I don't drink,' said Southall.

'Oh, shame. I was hoping we might meet up at the Christmas ball.'

'Christmas ball?'

'That's right. The guys at Region organise a ball every year. It's just a glorified piss-up really, but it gets everyone together in the right spirit, if you'll excuse the pun.'

'We're not from Region,' said Southall. 'We're from Llangwelli Station.'

'Isn't that where they send all the numpties? Where they can't do any harm?'

Rose thought this was hilarious, but when Norman and Southall exchanged a look, he stopped laughing.

'Not funny?' he asked. 'Okay, right. My bad. So, anyway, what can I do for you?'

'We're investigating the murder of Kimberley Lawrence.'

Just for a second or two, Rose didn't seem quite so confident, and the smile faded to be replaced by a more sombre expression.

'Kim? Murdered? Good God. I knew she had gone AWOL again, but murdered?'

'You knew she was missing?'

'Greg's a mate. He told me. Are you sure you've got this right, and there hasn't been some sort of mistake?'

'I'm afraid there's no mistake,' said Norman. 'Mr Lawrence identified the body just a couple of hours ago.'

'Poor Greg. Is he all right? I should go over and see if he needs anything.'

'I'm sure he'll appreciate that, but can we just ask a couple of questions first?' asked Southall.

'Of course.'

'Greg Lawrence says he was with you on the night Kimberley disappeared.'

'That's right. He often comes over when the girls are on their night out. I have a snooker table set up in the garage.'

'Was anyone else here?'

'Alan Evans. He's another one who can't seem to cope at home alone when his wife goes out.'

'Can you confirm when this was?'

'It was the Monday before last, which was what, the fourteenth?'

'Can you tell us what time Mr Lawrence left?'

'Ten thirty.'

Norman was taking notes, and now he looked up.

'That's an exact memory,' he said.

'I remember it very clearly because Greg was drunk, and we had to take him home.'

'Drunk?'

'Yes. He and Kim had had another big bust-up before she went out. He always hits the bottle when it happens. This time he hit it a bit too hard.'

'Did they have a lot of arguments?' asked Southall.

'You could say that. Kim's one of those who always want more, you know? More money, a bigger house, a faster car. Whereas Greg's quite the opposite. As a result, he doesn't deliver what she wants, and so she gives him a hard time. Between you and me, he's a bit of a loser. I've never quite figured out how they ever got together.'

'A loser? But didn't you say he's a mate?' asked Norman.

'Oh, yes, he's a lovely guy. We've been mates for years, but even so.'

'So, you took Greg home, and then what?' asked Southall.

'Alan and I put the poor guy to bed, then I took Alan home and came back here.'

'What time did you get back here?'

'I dropped Alan off at about quarter past eleven, then came back here, so I suppose I got here at about eleven twenty, or thereabouts.'

'And Kimberley didn't come home while you were at Greg's?'

'No. The idea was to get him to bed before Kim got home so she wouldn't know what state he was in.'

'But wouldn't she have noticed when she got home?'

'Ah. No. They have separate rooms, you see.'

'Any particular reason for that?' asked Norman.

The smug smile was back on Rose's face now.

'I don't know, Sergeant. I've never asked.'

Rose looked from Norman to Southall.

'Look, is there anything else?' he asked. 'I feel I should get over to Greg's place.'

'No, thank you. That's all for now, Mr Rose,' said Southall, 'but we will need to speak to you again.'

'Yes, of course. I'll help in any way I can.'

* * *

'Is it just me,' asked Norman, when they were back in the car, 'or is that guy difficult to like?'

'How do you mean?'

'I always try to give people the benefit of the doubt—'

'Is that right?' asked Southall. 'So how come you already have Greg Lawrence lined up as your prime suspect?'

'That's an exaggeration,' said Norman. 'You know very well he has to be a person of interest simply because he's the husband of the victim. Anyway, I'm talking about liking people, not suspecting them. I mean, I suspect Lawrence, but I don't dislike him whereas I couldn't like Nick Rose, even if I wanted to. I told you the guy was going to be an arse.'

'I have to agree he's not exactly what you'd call instantly likeable.'

Norman turned the car around and stopped, then he fumbled his mobile phone from his pocket and took a photograph of Rose's car.

'What are you doing?' asked Southall.

'When I have some time to kill, I'm going to run his car registration number through the database.'

'On what grounds?'

'Because he's a smug arsehole and needs taking down a peg or two. Maybe I'll find some sort of traffic violation against him.'

'My, you really don't like him, do you?' said Southall.

'And the way he spoke to you. I could have happily smacked him for that.'

Southall stared at Norman.

'That's very gallant of you, but I can take care of myself, you know.'

'I'm not suggesting you can't,' said Norman. 'I'm just saying I know how hard it must be for a woman to get where you are, and it annoys me when people don't show a bit of respect.'

'The thing is, Norm, people don't respect the police these days. And men like Nick Rose still live in the dark ages where women are concerned. So, he's got two reasons to disrespect me: one, because I'm a woman, and two, because I'm a police officer.'

'And now I suppose I've offended you by defending you.'

Southall laughed.

'Oh, please,' she said. 'I'm not one of those women. I won't complain if you hold a door open for me, either.'

'Thank God for that,' said Norman, 'because I'm old-fashioned enough to do that. It's how I was raised.'

'You can still be a modern woman and appreciate good manners.'

'I'm glad to hear it. Anyway, where to next?'

Southall looked at her watch, then reached for her phone.

'It's half five,' she said. 'Let me call the others and tell them to go home. I don't believe in having people work late just for the sake of it. Kim Lawrence will be no more dead in the morning, and I like my team to get enough rest to stay fresh.'

'Okay, so what about me?'

'You and I are going to the King's Head,' said Southall.

'The pub? Now that's an offer I can't refuse.'

CHAPTER 17

'Ted Granger? I'm DS Norman from Llangwelli Station, and this is DI Southall. We want to ask you some questions.'

'It's a bit inconvenient,' said Granger. 'This is a busy pub.'

Norman looked around the almost deserted bar.

'Yeah, all right,' said Granger. 'So, it's early now, but the place will be heaving later.'

'If you'd prefer, we can come back later, and then, if it's as busy as you claim, it really will be inconvenient,' said Norman.

'I don't have a lot of time for idle chat.'

'That's good,' said Southall, 'because we don't deal in idle chat. As DS Norman said, we'd like to ask some questions.'

'Questions about what?'

'You must have heard about Kimberley Lawrence. We found her body on the beach.'

Granger showed no emotion whatsoever.

'And why should that concern me?'

'Because she was in here the night she died. She was with three other women.'

'We get lots of people in here. As I said, it's a busy pub.'

'Was it busy on Monday the fourteenth?'

'That's over a week ago! How am I supposed to remember who was here that night?'

Norman began thumbing back through his notebook.

'Apparently, these four women meet up here every month, always on a Monday night,' he said, finding the page he wanted. 'Here we go. Their names are Pippa Roberts, Abbey Moore, Ruth Evans, and of course Kimberley Lawrence.'

Granger seemed to come to a decision.

'Yeah, I know who they are, but I don't know them well if you see what I mean.'

'Can you confirm they were here that night?'

'Yes.'

'You're sure?' asked Norman. 'Only a minute ago you said you didn't know.'

'I remember now because it was the night my barmaid didn't turn up, so I had to do it all myself.'

'Oh, that's such a shame,' muttered Norman.

'Can you confirm what time they left?' asked Southall.

'They usually stay until closing time.'

'And did they leave at closing time that night?'

'I can't say for sure. Like I said I was behind the bar, rushed off my feet.'

'Did they all leave together?'

'I don't know. Why don't you ask them?'

'Oh, don't worry, we're going to,' said Southall. 'I wonder if they'll remember it being as busy as you say it was.'

'Look, they were in here from about eight o'clock, and when I closed up, they were gone. Did I clock them all out? No, I didn't. Did they all leave together? I don't know. What more can I say?'

'Do you have CCTV in here?' asked Southall.

'Not inside, but there is a camera overlooking the car park.'

'Can we look at it?'

'You can if you want, but it only records for seven days.'

'And then it records over itself?' asked Norman.

'It's an old system,' said Granger. 'I know I should update it, but well, I never got around to it.'

'Why am I not surprised?' asked Norman.

Granger stared at him for a few seconds, then turned to Southall.

'Is there anything else?' he asked. 'Only I've got things to do.'

She gave him an icy smile.

'Yes, that'll do for now,' she said. 'But we'll need to speak to you again.'

'You know where to find me,' said Granger. 'I'm not going anywhere.'

Southall nodded to Norman and headed for the door.

'If the landlord wasn't such a shit I might well have bought us a drink,' said Southall, as the door swung closed behind them and they began walking towards their car.

Norman smiled.

'I thought you told Nick Rose you don't drink.'

'I don't drink with men like him.'

'Oh, right. I see what you mean.'

'We will have a drink,' said Southall.

'That's okay,' he said. 'I was planning on washing and styling my hair tonight anyway.'

Southall studied Norman's hair and smiled.

'That's a style?'

'My hair and I have never agreed on a style,' said Norman. 'And I'm much too long in the tooth to worry about it now.'

CHAPTER 18

Thursday 24 October 2019

When Southall pulled into the car park on Thursday morning, she immediately spotted a car she hadn't seen before. A man was sitting in the driver's seat. As she parked her car, he climbed from the car and walked across the car park, timing his walk to arrive just as she closed her car door and locked the car.

'DI Southall?'

'That's right.'

The man extended his hand.

'I'm DS Marston.'

'Ah, Marston. Are you feeling better now?'

'Much better, thank you. I understand you've been busy. I'm sorry I wasn't here when you arrived.'

'These things happen,' said Southall. 'DS Norman seems to have everything under control.'

'DS Norman? Does this mean I've got my transfer?'

'You'll need to speak to Superintendent Bain about that.'

'But why else would there be a replacement? Anyway, what's this DS Norman like?'

'Why don't you come inside and meet him?'

Marston followed Southall into the building and into the inquiry room, where the three younger team members were already at their desks.

'If it's all right, I'll go and speak to Superintendent Bain now,' said Marston.

'There's something I need to speak to you about before you go anywhere,' said Southall. 'In my office.'

As she spoke, the door burst open and Norman backed in carrying two small cardboard boxes.

'Okay, everyone,' he said. 'I can't start my day without decent coffee, so, until we get a machine in this place that produces something that tastes like the real thing, I've decided to treat you all.'

He carefully placed the boxes on his desk and peeled back the tops.

'Here you go. Help yourselves. There's coffee in this one, and doughnuts in the other one.'

Only now, as he stepped back from the desk, did he notice Southall had company.

'This is DS Marston,' she told him.

Norman looked awkwardly at Marston and then at the box of coffees.

'I'm sorry I only got five coffees. I didn't know you were going to be here.'

'That's okay,' said Marston. 'You weren't to know.'

'I'm just going to speak to DS Marston in my office,' Southall told Norman. 'I'd like you to join us.'

'Sure.'

Norman collected a coffee for himself, and one for Southall then followed them to her office. He set one of the coffees on her desk then stepped to one side.

'I don't know how this is going to work,' said Marston.

Southall raised an eyebrow.

'How what's going to work?'

'One Inspector, two Sergeants, and three DCs. It's a bit top-heavy, isn't it? Especially when all the good stuff goes to Region.'

'How it's going to work is for me to worry about,' said Southall. 'And, for your information, all the good stuff doesn't go to Region anymore.'

'It doesn't? How did that happen? These kids can't cope. They don't know their arses from their elbows.'

'Maybe that's because no one ever gives them a chance,' said Norman. 'From what I've seen so far they don't lack many skills, they just need experience.'

Marston smirked.

'You're joking.'

'Do I look like I'm laughing?'

'If you'd spent as long with them as I have, you'd know—'

'I figure maybe that's the bigger part of the problem,' said Norman. 'I'm guessing you don't let them have responsibility for much.'

'Can't trust the buggers not to mess everything up.'

Norman's face smiled, but deep inside this guy was beginning to get under his skin.

'Yeah, I thought so. That explains why they seem so surprised when we ask them to do anything. How d'you expect people to learn if you treat them like that?'

'But they're all useless; that's why they're here.'

Norman looked at Southall. She had been sipping her coffee, but now she put it down on her desk.

'Yes, well, we'll see about that,' she said. 'Anyway, since you raised the subject of people being incompetent, that's what we need to talk about.'

'I don't know what you mean,' said Marston.

Southall smiled a humourless smile and pointed to a chair.

'Sit down, Marston. I'll explain.'

Marston sat down while Southall walked around her desk and sat in her chair, which was raised high enough to make her taller than him. Norman smiled. He was beginning to take a shine to DI Sarah Southall.

'What's this about?' asked Marston.

'Were you on duty last Friday?'

'I wasn't feeling well, but I came in as usual. I had a bad stomach. I thought it would wear off, but it just got worse, so I went home at about two p.m.'

'You know we've got a murder case?'

'I've heard, yes.'

'The victim's name is Kimberley Lawrence. Does that ring a bell?'

'Should it?'

'Her husband, Greg, says he came in to report her missing.'

'Oh, yes, that's right. I was just about to go home when the front desk called me.'

'So you admit you spoke to him?' asked Southall.

'Why wouldn't I admit it?'

'But there's no missing person report logged for Kimberley Lawrence.'

'I didn't log it. I didn't see the point. I was in a hurry to get away, and the case would go to Region anyway, so I passed it straight on to them.'

'What exactly do you mean when you say you passed it on?'

'I called in there on the way home and reported it directly to them.'

'That's a bit unorthodox, isn't it?'

'Well, yes, I suppose. But I was desperate to get home, and as I said, I was passing there anyway.'

'Can you prove any of this?'

Marston pulled his notebook from his pocket and passed it to Southall.

'It's all in there,' he said.

Southall thumbed through the notebook until she found what she was looking for, then carefully began reading his notes. Suddenly she stopped and looked up at him.

'Why have you made a note saying, "serial runaway", and underlined it?'

'Kimberley Lawrence had form for running off and wasting our time.'

'So, you knew her?'

'I knew her husband. He's been in before. The first time I passed it on to Region, and it turned out to be a waste of time. She came back.'

'What do you mean "the first time"? Is this a regular thing?'

'Region don't go much on anyone wasting their time. After I got my balls chewed off that first time, it was obvious she was just some sort of tart who did this sort of thing for fun. Sure enough, it happened again, and again, and each time she came back.'

'So let me get this straight,' said Southall. 'You're saying that you, at the rank of Detective Sergeant, have the authority to decide which cases we investigate. Does Superintendent Bain know about this?'

'No, of course, I don't think that. I was just saving everyone a lot of time and trouble. What's the point in going to the expense of setting up a major investigation when the woman always comes back!'

'She didn't come back this time,' said Norman.

Marston squirmed in his seat.

'Look, you can't blame me for this. I took notes and passed a report on to Region. If nothing happened after that, it's down to them, not me. I did what I was supposed to do.'

'But, if she always comes back, why did you report it to Region this time?' asked Southall.

'Because she had been missing longer than usual.'

'I see,' said Southall. 'And then you went home, right?'

'Yes.'

'When you went to Region to file the report, who did you speak to?'

'I can't recall.'

'You can't recall?'

Southall turned her attention back to the notebook.

'This is exactly why we use notebooks,' she said, after a few seconds.

Marston looked puzzled.

'You say you can't recall,' she continued, still looking down at the notebook. 'Now I'm not sure if that's the truth, or if you don't want to tell me who it was because you don't want to get someone into trouble. But it doesn't matter because, much to my surprise, you keep quite good notes.'

Now she looked up at him and smiled another mirthless smile.

'Are you friends with DS Hickstead?'

'We have a pint now and then.'

'Keep him informed about what's going on here, do you?'

Marston didn't know where to look.

'We exchange stories, as you do.'

'As you do,' repeated Southall. 'And are you careful what stories you share?'

'There's nothing here worth keeping secret, is there?'

'When did you find out we'd found a body?'

The question took Marston by surprise.

'You did know, didn't you?' insisted Southall.

Marston sighed.

'Morgan called me the morning she found it. She called me first. I told her I was off sick and I couldn't help her. I told her to call you.'

'And then what did you do?'

'I'm not sure I know what you mean?'

'Okay, let me make it easy for you. Did you call DS Hickstead, and tell him we'd found a body?'

'Well, yes, I did as it happens. I didn't know if you'd be up to it, and anyway Region always take over anything—'

Southall sat bolt upright.

'You didn't know if I'd be up to it?' she asked. 'Are you suggesting you're in a position to question my ability? How the hell do you think I got this rank?'

'Er, well, er, that probably didn't come out as I intended. What I mean is—'

'Marston,' said Norman. 'I've got to hand it to you. You're an even bigger idiot than I first thought.'

'What?'

'Have you ever heard the expression, "when in a hole, stop digging"? You probably should have stopped before you even started, but hey, what do I care?'

'Superintendent Bain told me you had applied for a transfer,' said Southall. 'Is that right?'

'Yes,' said Marston. 'As I said, I live near Region.'

'Oh, you've applied to go to Region?'

'Yes. The work there is a bit more interesting.'

Southall pulled a face.

'That may be true,' she said, 'but there won't be quite so much of it now we're here. Do you think you'll get the job?'

'I hope so.'

'So do I,' said Southall. 'So do I. You'd better go and see Superintendent Bain now. Perhaps he'll have some news for you.'

Marston stared at her, unsure if the interview was over.

'Well, go on,' she said, 'before I change my mind.'

'Oh. Right. Yes, of course.'

Marston scuttled from the room as quickly as he could.

'Jeez, what an idiot,' said Norman.

'I can see why he and Hickstead get on,' said Southall. 'They both belong in the dark ages.'

'D'you know if he's got that job?' asked Norman.

'I hope so. The boss suggested as much. I certainly don't want him here.'

'D'you think he's the mole you're looking for?'

'I think so, don't you?'

Norman nodded.

'For sure,' he said. 'So, does this mean you think Catren Morgan's in the clear?'

'On reflection, I think Hickstead was probably grooming her so she could take Marston's place.'

She took a mouthful of her coffee.

'This is damned good coffee, Norm. Where did you get it from?'

'There's a guy with a mobile kiosk. He was parked down by the harbour. He says he intends to be there every day. He'll get my business, that's for sure. Anyhow, what's the plan for today?'

'I want to speak to Kimberley's three girlfriends, and then I want to visit Greg Lawrence and see if he'll let us have a look through Kimberley's things.'

'D'you want me to get a search warrant?'

'We'll get heavy if we need to, but let's try the softly, softly, approach first. At the moment he seems to be cooperating, so let's use that to our advantage. And one more thing. Can you get someone to find every shop with a CCTV camera within a hundred yards of the King's Head? We might just get lucky and find one that shows where Kimberley went after she left the pub.'

'I'll get Morgan and Thomas on that,' said Norman.

CHAPTER 19

'Phillipa Roberts?'

The woman who had just opened her front door looked at the warrant card Norman held up in front of her.

'I'm DS Norman, and this is DI Southall.'

'Is this about Kim?'

'You mean Kimberley Lawrence?'

The woman was upset, but she nodded.

'We understand you were friends. We'd like to ask you a few questions if that's okay?'

The woman stepped back and swung the door open.

'You'd better come in.'

'So, Phillipa, had you known Kim long?' asked Norman once they were settled.

'It's Pippa,' she said. 'I met Kim about seven years ago. We were in the same aerobics class at the gym, and just seemed to hit it off, you know.'

'The night Kim disappeared, you were on a girls' night out, is that right?'

'Yes. There are, sorry, were, four of us. We used to meet during the first week of the month.'

'Was it always the King's Head, on a Monday?'

'Always the King's Head, but usually it would be a Wednesday, but one of the other girls, Abbey, couldn't make it, so we changed to Monday.'

'So it was you, Kim, Abbey Moore and Ruth Evans. Is that right?'

'That's right.'

'And you didn't get together any other time?'

'Oh, yes. We'd celebrate birthdays together. And if one of us were having a party, we'd all be there.'

'And when you're on these nights out one of you picks the other three up on the way?'

'That's right. It was Abbey's turn to drive.'

'But Kim didn't leave with you?'

Pippa looked guilty.

'Kim was a good friend. She was lots of fun, you know? But she had what I call a darker side. She would arrive with us, but she didn't always leave with us.'

'Can you be a bit more specific about this darker side?' asked Southall.

Pippa was wringing her hands.

'I don't like to speak ill of the dead.'

Southall smiled encouragingly.

'I understand, Pippa, but I'm afraid we need to know as much about Kimberley as we can if we're going to catch whoever did this to her. And you can't hurt her now, can you?'

Pippa considered for a moment.

'She sometimes got these moods, and when she was like that, she liked to play the tart.'

'D'you know what triggered these moods?'

'Usually, it would be an argument with Greg.'

'Her husband? Did they argue a lot?'

'She was very demanding. The poor guy adored her, but he couldn't do much right, no matter how hard he tried.'

'What do you mean, he couldn't do much right?'

'He was one of those people who didn't have much confidence. He was always trying some new way of making money, but they never came to anything, and the more he failed, the lower his confidence got.'

'I thought he was a builder.'

'He's not a builder; he's an odd-job man and not a very good one. That's why he's always trying to find the magic bullet, you know? He's convinced there's something out there online that will make him a fortune, but so far it just seems to have cost him a fortune.'

'And Kim didn't like it, right?'

'She worked with people who earned six-figure salaries. She wanted him to be like that, and it used to frustrate her that he didn't match up to them.'

'Why didn't she leave him?'

'I don't know, I never asked. I always got the impression she stayed with Greg because she could walk all over him and do whatever she liked. Being with him meant she could present this facade of being the happily married wife.'

'But you all knew it was a lie, right?'

'All their closest friends did, but it was the colleagues at work she wanted to impress the most, and I got the impression they didn't know the truth.'

'Tell us about that last girls' night out.'

'It was just a normal night, except Kim was in a shitty mood. That usually meant she'd had another bust-up with Greg.'

'That must make it hard to enjoy your night?'

'We knew to ignore the mood and carry on as usual. I suppose we put up with it because when she was normal, she was such fun to be around.'

'So, what happened at the end of the night?'

'There were two guys at the bar talking to the landlord. Towards closing time she went over and joined them.'

'And this was normal behaviour for her?'

'Normally she's a bit more subtle, but that night it was like she didn't give a damn who knew what she was doing.'

'That must have been awkward for the rest of you.'

'Embarrassing is the word.'

'Was she more interested in one particular man?'

Pippa looked away for a moment.

'Look, she could be so nice, and she was, most of the time . . .'

'I understand this must be difficult for you, Pippa, but we wouldn't ask if we didn't need to know. You understand that, don't you?'

When she looked up at Norman, she had tears in her eyes.

'The answer is no; she wasn't interested in one in particular. It didn't seem to matter who it was, as long as they were willing. And if she was desperate, there was always Ted Granger.'

Norman exchanged a look with Southall, who merely raised her eyebrows.

'You mean Ted Granger, the landlord of the King's Head?' asked Norman.

Pippa nodded.

'Okay, so, Kimberley went off to the bar. Then what happened.'

'When she's like that, we know what's probably going to happen, but we'd rather not know, if you see what I mean. Rather than watch the show, we finished our drinks and left.'

'What time was this?'

'I was home by eleven, so it must have been about ten forty-five.'

'And you just walked off and left her?'

'Oh, no. We told her we were leaving and tried to get her to come with us, but she was adamant she was staying and said to go without her.'

'And you were happy with that?'

'Of course not, but we couldn't force her to come, could we? She's done it so many times before, and she's never come to any harm . . .'

There was an awkward silence as Pippa's voice faded away to nothing.

'Can you remember what these guys looked like?' asked Norman gently. 'Were they regulars?'

'I've never seen them before but, as I said, we normally go on a Wednesday night. They could easily be Monday night regulars.'

'And you can't describe them?'

'They just seemed like regular guys, but to be honest, I was too embarrassed to look at them, so I didn't see their faces. I know it's not much help. I'm sorry, I can't tell you more.'

'You've probably been more helpful than you realise,' said Southall. 'One last question: did Kimberley have her mobile phone with her?'

'She always had the damned thing with her.'

'One more thing,' said Southall. 'Can you tell us what Kim was wearing? Her husband doesn't recall.'

'I think she was wearing her blue jacket, with a white top and skirt. She had great legs, and she liked to show them off.'

'What about her shoes?'

'Red, with killer heels about four inches high. She used to say they were the reason she had great legs.'

'I don't suppose you know what size?'

'She was a size four, the same as me.'

* * *

'We seem to be surrounded by liars,' said Southall when they were back in their car. 'Didn't Greg Lawrence tell us the girls' night out was always on a Monday?'

'He certainly did,' agreed Norman as he started the car. 'And Granger claimed he hardly knew our victim.'

They went on to interview Abbey Moore next, but her story added nothing to what they already knew. She did offer one thought that stuck in Norman's mind when he asked her what she knew about the Lawrences' marriage.

'I know they didn't have to get married, so I assume they were once like any other normal, happy couple. On that basis, I would have to ask the question: did she make him the way he is, or did he make her the way she is? It's hard to say . . .'

* * *

Ruth Evans wasn't at home, and they had no idea where she might be, so Norman pushed a card through her door, asking her to call them as soon as she could.

CHAPTER 20

Southall kept her smile, but couldn't hide the disappointment from her voice, when Nick Rose opened the front door of Greg Lawrence's house.

'Oh, Mr Rose.'

Rose gave them a smile that lacked any pretence of warmth.

'Can I help you?'

'We'd like to speak to Mr Lawrence.'

'He's a bit fragile.'

'We realise that,' said Norman. 'We wouldn't expect anything else, but we're investigating a murder, and I'm afraid we need his help.'

Briefly, it looked as if Rose was going to argue, but then he stepped back and swung the door open.

'You'd better come in. Greg's in the kitchen.'

Norman followed Southall through to the kitchen. Greg Lawrence was sitting on a stool at the breakfast bar, staring out through the window at nothing in particular, an untouched cup of coffee before him.

'Good morning, Mr Lawrence,' said Southall. 'How are you?'

Lawrence turned a bleary-eyed gaze in their direction. It was apparent he still wasn't sleeping, and the empty bottles standing on the windowsill bore testament to how well he was, or perhaps wasn't, coping.

'I'm afraid we need to ask you some questions,' said Southall. 'And we'd like to look through Kimberley's things if that's okay?'

'What questions?'

'About you and Kimberley, mostly.'

Nick Rose had followed them into the kitchen, and now he spoke.

'Do you people have no respect?' he asked. 'The poor guy's just lost his wife, and now you want to start digging for dirt?'

Southall turned to Rose.

'We're investigating a murder, Mr Rose. No matter how unpleasant you may think our questions are, we intend to do the job properly. You suggested you knew a few detectives when we spoke before. I'm sure if you ask one of them they will tell you we're just following procedure.'

'It's okay, Nick,' said Lawrence. 'They're just doing their job.'

'Do you want me to stay?' asked Rose.

'No, I'll be fine,' Lawrence told Rose.

'Well, if you're sure. I'll call in again later.'

'Yeah, thanks, Nick. I'd appreciate that.'

They stood in silence as Rose made his way from the house.

'He's all right when you get to know him,' explained Lawrence when Rose had gone. 'He's just looking out for me.'

'Have you known him long?' asked Norman.

'Since we first moved here, about ten years ago. We went down the pub one night, he was there, and we got talking. We hit it off straight away.'

'Is he married?'

'No, he never has been as far as I know. He says he's too independent to share his life with anyone else and prefers to live alone.'

'Is he a good friend?'

'Yes, he's here for me now, isn't he? He didn't have to be.'

'We've been speaking to some of Kim's friends. They suggest you and Kim didn't always have the happiest of marriages.'

'There's no doubt she could be difficult to please. I can't argue with that.'

'Difficult to please in what way?'

'She worked with a lot of people who were high earners.'

'And you couldn't match that?'

'I don't do so bad.'

'Our investigations suggest you barely break even, and without Kim's money, you'd struggle to pay your way. That sort of thing is bound to cause friction between a couple, right?'

Lawrence's eyes narrowed.

'It's just a temporary thing. The building trade's tough at the moment.'

'Judging by the state of your vehicle, I'd say you hadn't worked in weeks,' said Norman.

'I'm sorry?'

'You have a puncture, and I don't need to be an expert to see it's been like that for some time.'

'Oh, that. Yes, I do have a puncture, and yes, it has been like it for weeks.'

'But you're still working?'

'I have a friend who has an old 4x4 run-around he hardly uses. He lets me borrow it. The thing is the puncture is the least of my problems where that van's concerned.'

'Go on,' said Norman.

'I managed to break the gearbox on the damned thing. D'you know how much it's going to cost for a new one?'

'And you don't have the money, right?' asked Norman.

'As I said, it's tough at the moment.'

'Looking at your bank statements I'd say it's been tough for two or three years, at least.'

'Look, what is this?'

'We're just trying to establish some background,' said Norman. 'It might help if we can establish what state of mind Kim was in.'

'State of mind? You make it sound like you think she committed suicide.'

'One thing we know for sure, Mr Lawrence, is that Kim did not commit suicide.'

'So where are you going with this?'

'We've been told that when the other girls left the pub, Kimberley was chatting up a couple of guys at the bar in the pub. Is that normal for her?'

'Jesus! What sort of question is that?'

'Look, let's stop playing games here, Greg. We know Kim has disappeared on several occasions, and we know every time she goes, there's another guy involved. You even said as much yourself. Her friends say it was almost a regular thing. We're just trying to establish if that may have been what happened on the night she disappeared.'

Lawrence hung his head and released a long, heartfelt sigh.

'We had a big argument before she went out. That always seemed to be like a trigger.'

'A trigger?'

'We'd have a row, and she would disappear with another guy. It was her way of punishing me.'

'You must have been pretty angry when that sort of thing happened.'

'Disappointed is the word I would use.'

'It didn't make you angry? I think everyone would understand if you were.'

'No, not angry, just disappointed.'

'If I'm honest, Greg, I have to say that's hard for me to believe.'

'You'd be surprised what you can accept when you love someone as much as I loved Kim.'

Norman nodded. He knew from personal experience there was a certain amount of truth in that remark.

'Can we go back to the night Kim disappeared?'

'What about it?'

'You say you were playing snooker with Nick Rose.'

'That's right.'

'Was anyone else there?'

'Alan Evans.'

'You're sure?'

'Yes, I'm sure.'

'And how did you get home?'

'I can't recall.'

'You can't recall? Now, why is that? It wasn't that long ago.'

'I was a bit pissed if you must know.'

'A bit pissed? According to Nick Rose, you were paralytic. He says he and Alan Evans had to drive you home and put you to bed.'

Lawrence glared at Norman.

'Well, there you are then. If you already know, why are you asking me?'

'I'm just doing my job, Greg. You wouldn't want me to cut corners, would you?'

Southall had been quiet during Norman's questions, but now she spoke.

'Before we go, do you mind if we have a look at Kimberley's things?'

'Sure. I don't know what you think you'll find but go ahead.'

'Where do we go?'

'At the top of the stairs, turn right and go past the bathroom. It's the only other door on that side of the house.'

'You have separate rooms?'

'Have done for a couple of years.'

Southall knew she had to ask the question.

'Were you and Kimberley still intimate, Mr Lawrence?'

'If you mean did we still have sex, yes we did. Sometimes.'

There was a sullen silence which Lawrence didn't appear to want to break.

'Right, well, we'll take a look at Kimberley's room now if that's okay. Do you want to come up with us?'

'I don't know where she keeps stuff so I can't help you, and if I can't trust the police, who can I trust?'

Norman followed Southall from the room, and up the stairs to Kimberley's room, checking to make sure Lawrence hadn't followed them. Then they began to search the room, careful not to make too much mess.

'I've found her diary,' said Southall.

She sat on the bed and thumbed through a few pages.

'Anything interesting?' asked Norman.

'I can't tell yet. It'll take some time to go through. She seems to make a lot of notes and uses lots of initials. We'll ask him if we can take it with us.'

'You'd think he would have got rid of it if anything was incriminating in there.'

'Or maybe he was telling the truth, and he really doesn't poke around in her stuff.'

'I don't buy that,' said Norman.

'It's possible, though.'

They had been through everything, but the diary was the only item of interest they found.

'No laptop, or tablet?' asked Southall.

'I was hoping we might find her mobile phone, but there's nothing like that.'

'Okay. That's enough for now,' said Southall

Lawrence was waiting for them in the hall.

'Did your wife have a laptop or a tablet?' asked Southall.

'No, just her mobile phone. She used to say she spent enough time on a computer at work, and she came home to get away from the damned things.'

'I found her diary. Do you mind if we take it with us? We'll give you a receipt for it, of course.'

'You can take whatever you want. I've got nothing to hide.'

* * *

111

'I take it you'd like another word with our favourite pub landlord before we call it a day?' asked Norman as they climbed into their car.

Southall smiled.

'I think it would be rude not to, don't you?'

CHAPTER 21

Ted Granger was standing behind the bar, talking to two customers perched on stools at the bar. He had the sort of face that made it hard to tell if he was smiling or grimacing, but Norman was confident the expression that darkened his face when he saw them enter wasn't a smile.

'What do you two want now?' he demanded. 'Can't you see I'm busy?'

Norman beamed a smile at him as they approached the bar.

'Well, I guess I would have to concede you have twice as many customers today, but busy? I don't think so.'

'It's not just about the number of customers. I've got loads to do to prepare for tonight. For a start, I have to go down into the cellar.'

'That's fine,' said Norman. 'We can do the steps. We'll come with you. You can talk while you work, can't you?'

'I don't want you down in my cellar.'

'You don't? Why is that? Have you got something to hide? You don't water down your beer, do you?'

One of the customers picked up his glass and held it up to the light, prompting a snort of dismay from Granger.

'Don't take any notice of him,' he snapped at the man. 'He's just trying to cause trouble. Coming in here, stopping a man from doing his job. It's not right.'

'I'm just doing my job, asking you to answer a few questions,' said Norman. 'That's all you have to do, and then we'll go away. It's not difficult.'

'This is harassment,' said Granger.

'Don't talk rubbish, Mr Granger,' said Southall. 'If you had answered our questions truthfully the first time, we wouldn't be back here.'

'I don't know what you mean.'

'You know exactly what I mean. So, let me give you a choice. You can stand here and answer our questions in front of your two friends. We can go and sit down away from the bar, or we can have a couple of constables arrive in a car with nice, blue flashing lights and drag you down the station. Take your pick.'

Granger tried to outstare Southall, but quickly realised she had much bigger balls than he did. He licked his lips, eyes darting between her and Norman. Norman yawned expansively, then reached a hand into his pocket.

'I'll call the guys,' he said, producing his mobile.

'No! Wait. There's no need for that!' Granger protested loudly.

Norman smiled. The two men sitting at the bar had turned to watch the proceedings and were enjoying Granger's discomfort.

'I tell you what,' said one, winking at Norman. 'Why don't Bill and I go and play a couple of games of darts, then you can have your cosy little chat, right here where you are now.'

The two guys made their way across the bar to the dartboard. Granger was fuming, but what could he say?

'Right,' said Southall. 'You know why we're here, so let's not mess around any longer.'

'I answered your questions yesterday.'

'Yes, you did,' admitted Southall, 'but today you're going to answer them truthfully.'

114

'I did—'

'Do I look stupid, Granger?' snapped Southall.

Granger swallowed hard but said nothing.

'We're conducting a murder investigation. It's a grave business, and by the same token misleading our investigation is also a grave offence. Do you understand what I'm saying?'

Granger swallowed again, but this time managed to nod his head.

'So, tell me about you and Kimberley Lawrence.'

'Me and Kimberley?'

'This is your last chance,' warned Southall. 'If you persist in buggering around I'll drag you down to the police station myself.'

'But what about my pub?'

'You can close it, can't you?'

'Yeah, but—'

'Jeez, Ted, you need to quit stalling and start thinking,' said Norman. 'D'you think we'd be here if we didn't already know you've been spouting bullshit? If I were you, I'd quit annoying the DI here, and start talking, because she doesn't have endless patience, and trust me, things can get real messy when it runs out.'

'What d'you want to know?'

'Did you know Kimberley Lawrence?' asked Southall.

'Yes, I suppose I did.'

'Were you in a relationship with her?'

'Now, hang on a minute—'

'Yeah, we thought it sounded unlikely too,' said Norman, 'but then we heard Kim wasn't fussy and it made a bit more sense.'

'Are you saying you weren't in a relationship?' asked Southall.

'It wasn't a relationship.'

'You were having sex with her. What would you call it?'

'It wasn't like that.'

'So, what was it like?'

'It was casual.'

'How casual?'

'If she was in here, and she was in the mood, she would stay behind after I closed the pub.'

'Was this a regular thing arranged in advance?'

'No. I told you. It was casual, just something that happened now and then.'

'You mean like when she was desperate?' asked Norman.

Granger looked daggers at Norman, but he didn't rise to the bait.

'I mean, it happened now and then. We were both adults. We knew what we were doing.'

'D'you know her husband?'

'Who? Greg? Of course, I do. He drinks in here sometimes.'

'But you don't find that awkward?'

'Why should I? Like I said, we're all adults.'

'So, he knew about you and Kim?'

'I don't know. You'll have to ask him.'

'Oh, we will, don't worry.'

'He never said anything to me that suggested he knew. Look, don't make me out to be the villain here. I'm not the only one. Half the blokes in town have been there.'

'So, this casual thing that just happened now and then, did it happen on Monday fourteenth?' asked Southall.

'No.'

'You seem very sure.'

'I am very sure.'

'We have witnesses who saw Kimberley in here at around ten forty-five chatting with you and two other guys up at the bar. So, if she didn't stop here with you after the pub closed, what did happen that night?'

'I don't know. I was clearing tables and washing up. I'll admit I was hoping Kim was going to stay behind, but she didn't.'

'What time did she leave?'

'I don't know. One minute she was here, then the next time I looked she was gone.'

'Was this before closing time, or after?'

'I can't say for sure because I was in and out from behind the bar, but I know I'd rung the bell and called last orders.'

'And that would have been at ten minutes before eleven, right?' asked Norman.

'Yeah.'

'Did she have another drink when you rang the bell?'

'Gawd, I dunno. I can't remember.'

'What about the two guys she was chatting with?' asked Southall.

'What about them?'

'Did you know them?'

'They've been in once or twice before, but I don't know them.'

'Have they been in since?'

'I don't think so?'

'Did one of them buy her a last drink?' asked Norman. 'I mean, wouldn't you, if you thought you were in with a chance?'

'Now you come to mention it, yeah, I think they all had one last drink.'

Southall looked at Norman.

'Allow twenty minutes from the bell, to drink up,' she said.

'So, we're looking at her leaving here around eleven fifteen,' suggested Norman.

Southall nodded.

'These men,' she said to Granger. 'Did they leave with Kim?'

'I didn't see them leave so I can't say for sure.'

'Did you see them without her, or her without them?'

'No, I don't think so.'

'Then we can probably assume they left together,' said Southall, thoughtfully. 'Can you describe them?'

'You're joking.'

'I don't joke about murder, Mr Granger. Kimberley died the night we're talking about, and you've just told me she left with two men. Do I need to fill in the blanks?'

'Yeah, but a lot of people come in here. I'm not—'

'You already told us they had been in here once or twice before,' said Norman. 'And you admit you were chatting to them at the bar. I think you can do better than "I'm not sure", don't you?'

'How old are they?' encouraged Southall.

'Twenty-five, thirtyish.'

'Tall? Short?'

'One's a bit taller than the other.'

'Too vague,' said Norman.

Granger snorted impatiently.

'All right, the shorter one is about your height, and the other one is three or four inches taller.'

'Hair colour?'

'Brown, both of them.'

'Eye colour?'

'Aw, come on. Does it look like I gaze into the eyes of every bloke who comes in here?'

Norman conceded the point, and he could see for himself that the light in here wasn't exactly bright.

'How were they dressed?' asked Southall.

'I dunno. Like any other bloke, I guess. I don't take much notice of what men are wearing.'

'Let me put it another way,' said Southall. 'Would you describe them as well dressed, or scruffy.'

'Tidy clothes, I suppose, but not expensive.'

'Is there anything else you can tell us? What about voices? Was there a distinctive accent, or are they local?'

'Local, I think, but—'

'—you can't be sure, right?' asked Norman cynically.

'Look, mate, I'm trying to help, but how's it going to look if everyone thinks I'm some sort of grass who talks to the police all the time?'

'Don't worry about that, Mr Granger,' said Southall. 'I'll be only too happy to tell anyone interested just how unhelpful you've been in assisting us with our murder inquiry.'

'What are you talking about? I am being helpful.'

'That's a matter of opinion,' said Southall.

She stepped back from the bar and began to walk away, but then stopped, turned and directed an icy glare at Granger.

'Don't think this means you've heard the last of this,' she warned. 'I don't forget people who lie to my face. As far as I'm concerned, you're still a suspect.'

Granger thought about a smart remark, but there was something about Southall's face that convinced him it would be best if he kept it to himself.

'Come on, Norm, let's get out of this place.'

Only when Southall turned and began walking away, did Granger feel brave enough to speak.

'I've told you all I know,' he called after them. 'You have no right to keep on hassling me.'

'You're sure about that, are you?' asked Norman.

'I know my rights.'

'I wouldn't count on it,' said Norman. 'As the lady said, if this turns out to be more bullshit, we'll be back, and next time we'll be taking you away with us.'

* * *

It was after six thirty when they got back. Southall headed off to find Bain to bring him up to date with their progress so far, and Norman made his way to the inquiry room. He had figured on spending some time catching up with his notes and then going home. What he hadn't expected was to find his young charges still working at their desks.

'What are you guys still doing here?'

'No one told us we could go home, and we weren't sure where we stand on leaving when we felt like it,' explained Morgan.

'Okay, that's fair enough,' said Norman. 'But no one's going to have a problem with you going home at the end of your shift.'

'That's what we thought, but we weren't sure.'

'Okay, well now you know,' he said. 'And if you two are here, where's Thomas?'

'We did rock, paper, scissors, and he lost. So, he's got the job of checking all the riverside sites.'

'How's he getting on?'

'We came up with dozens of possible sites and he's working his way through them.'

'He's also getting soaked for his trouble,' said Lane, 'so we told him to go home and soak in a hot bath.'

Norman wandered across to his desk, fished his notebook from his pocket and placed it down.

'Norm? I think I've found something.'

It was Morgan. She was staring at something on a TV screen at the spare desk.

As he walked over to join her, she began to explain what she was doing.

'I've been canvassing the area around the pub, looking for CCTV cameras. I managed to find seven. Most of them have nothing useful, but here, take a look at this.'

Norman stopped by her chair.

'Here you go,' she said. 'This was taken from a camera outside that funny little Italian restaurant. They don't open on Mondays, but the camera is running 24/7. The timestamp says 23.20. Now watch this.'

Norman watched over her shoulder as she pressed play.

On the opposite side of the road from the camera, a woman walked into view.

'That's Kim Lawrence,' said Morgan. 'She's walking away from the pub.'

'She still has her handbag,' said Norman. 'I wonder where she lost that.'

As he spoke, a car came into view. Like Kimberley, it was coming from the direction of the pub, and it slowed to stop alongside her. As Norman watched, the car stopped, the passenger door opened, and Kimberley eased herself inside. Then the door closed, and the car drove off.

'Holy shit!' said Norman. 'I don't suppose we have a registration number for that car?'

'Not from this camera,' said Morgan. 'It's always the side view. I can tell you it's a dark coloured Renault Clio, possibly blue, or dark green, but that's all.'

'Crap,' said Norman. 'Even so, there can't be that many of those registered locally. We need to get onto—'

Morgan had ejected the disk she was playing, and now placed another in the tray and pressed it home.

'Hang on,' she said. 'I only said I couldn't get a number from that camera. Lucky for us, there's another one just around the corner. When the car turns right, we get a full-frontal view. Like this . . .'

On the screen, the car turned onto the road from the left and then headed straight towards the camera. As Morgan had said, the registration number was in full view. They could also make out two figures in the front seats, but the focus wasn't good enough to make out their faces.

'Dammit,' said Norman, squinting at the screen. 'If I hadn't just seen Kim get into the car, I would never have known that was her in the passenger seat.'

'Yeah, it's hopeless,' agreed Morgan. 'I can't even tell if that's a guy or a girl in the driver's seat. But at least we have the reg number, and that's as clear as a bell.'

'Can you find out who owns that car?'

'I'm just about to make that call.'

'That's a great day's work,' he said. 'Well done. The boss is going to be over the moon when she sees what you've achieved today.'

Morgan beamed a smile in his direction, grateful for the praise, but Norman noticed Judy Lane was keeping her head down and focusing on the paperwork before her on the desk as she typed away at her keyboard. He shuffled quietly over to see what she was doing.

'How are you doing there, Judy?'

She looked up, embarrassed.

'I'm afraid I can't offer anything that's going to solve the case,' she said.

'Hey, don't worry,' said Norman. 'Catren got lucky today. Your turn will come. What are you up to anyway?'

'Everyone seems to be bringing in evidence and taking statements,' she said, 'but no one is keeping track of it all. I know that's your job, as the DS, but you're busy with the boss, and it's the sort of thing I'm good at, so I thought I'd make a start, just to help out.'

'Can I have a look?'

She moved aside so he could see what she had been doing. Norman studied her work for a couple of minutes before he spoke.

'Have you done investigation management before?'

'I helped out once or twice before I came here,' she said uncertainly. 'I know it's a job for a trained DS, and I'm sorry if I've stepped out of line, but it's the sort of thing I do quite well. It's just everyone else seems to have a job to do, and I wanted to help . . .'

Her voice trailed off into silence as Norman continued to study her work.

'You know how long it takes to train for this job?' he asked.

Lane shook her head.

'I'm sorry if I've messed up.'

'Not at all,' said Norman. 'This is very good. And you say you enjoy doing this? Jeez, I hate it.'

'So, you don't mind that I've done this?'

He smiled down at her.

'Do I mind that you've used your initiative and saved me several hours work? Heck, no.'

'Oh. Cool. I wasn't sure if you'd think I was trying to steal your job or something.'

'I would have got around to starting eventually, but then I would have been struggling to catch up, and I would end up working nights on top of my day shift and, well, you can imagine, right?'

'I suppose you're going to take it over now,' said Lane.

Norman studied her face.

'You say you enjoy this, right?'

'Yes, I do.'

'And you realise that strictly speaking this job has to be done by a DS?'

She sighed.

'Yes, I know. I'll copy it all across to your desk. Is it okay if I do it in the morning?'

'That's not what I mean,' said Norman. 'As I said, "strictly speaking", it should be a DS, but I get the impression our boss is more interested in competence than regulations. Besides, if a sergeant is keeping an eye on your work, I don't see a problem.'

For a moment he thought Lane was going to burst into tears, then she seemed to catch on to what he was saying, and her face broke into a huge smile.

'Oh, thank you,' she said.

'Let's not get carried away,' he said. 'I need to run it past the boss first, but I think once she sees what you've done so far, she'll be happy to let you carry on.'

As Norman turned away from Lane's desk, Southall walked into the room. The surprise on her face was clear to see as she joined Norman.

'What are they all doing here? Why haven't they gone home?' She looked around again. 'And why do they all look so pleased with themselves?'

'Because they're keen,' said Norman, 'and because they've been waiting to report their progress to you.'

'What progress?'

'You're going to love this. I'll let Catren show you what she's found.'

Southall watched as Morgan played the CCTV from the restaurant, then switched to the other footage that showed the car registration number.

'Have we got an address?'

'Just got it a minute ago, boss,' said Morgan, handing Southall a slip of paper with a name and address.

Southall looked at Norman.

'Norm? I want this guy brought in, and I want SOCOs all over his car.'

'Yeah, no problem,' said Norman.

Now Southall turned to Morgan.

'Do you want to go with Norm and help bring this guy in, Catren? You found him, so it's only right. Unless you want to go home.'

'To an empty flat? No thanks, boss. I'll go with Norm.'

'Before we go,' said Norman, 'can Judy show you what she's been doing? I think we might have discovered a natural, but you need to approve it.'

As Norman watched Southall walk across to Judy Lane's desk, he reached for his phone to let Forensics know they had a car to collect. A small sigh of contentment escaped him as he waited, and he realised he felt happier than he had in a long time. Finally, he had a sense of purpose, and he wondered if life could get any better than this.

CHAPTER 22

Southall peered through the two-way mirror at the frightened young man sitting at a table in the interview room. His name was Alex Cousins, and they now knew he was twenty-eight years old, and he had lived at his current address for just over a year.

'After hearing Granger's vague description, I was half-expecting a blond-haired midget,' said Southall.

'Yeah, I was quite surprised,' admitted Norman. 'But I guess it was vague enough to cover a wide spectrum of possibilities.'

'Has he said anything?' she asked Norman.

'He admitted it was his car.'

'Does he know why he's here?'

'We told him we'd like him to help with our enquiries, that's all.'

'Did you arrest him?'

'We didn't have to. He volunteered to come. Says he has nothing to hide. He knows SOCOs are all over his car, too.'

'Has he asked for a lawyer?'

'He hasn't mentioned one.'

'And he does know which crime we're talking about?'

'He didn't ask, so I didn't specify.'

'Do you think he knows? He must, surely?'

'I got the impression he thinks we're talking about a motoring offence.'

Southall couldn't hide her surprise.

'What?'

'When we asked about the car he said there must be some mistake, and that it couldn't have been him, because he hardly ever uses the car.'

'His flatmate was adamant the car hadn't moved in over a week, and that we've got the wrong guy, but I got the feeling that was like a reflex phrase, you know? Anyway, he says he's on his way down.'

'Who's his flatmate?'

'His name's Jay Bartham. It turns out they've been sharing the flat for about a year. They work from home, running a small software business.'

'Does he match the description, too?'

Norman grinned.

'Vaguely, yeah.'

Southall had another look at the suspect through the mirror.

'I'm not sure what I was expecting,' she said, wistfully, 'but whatever it was, he's not it.'

'Me too,' agreed Norman. 'But it takes all sorts to make a murderer.'

'Come on, let's see what he has to say. Where's Catren?'

'I told her she could watch from here, but she says she has some more CCTV footage she wants to go through.'

* * *

Above the table, Alex Cousins was doing his best to appear confident, but below the table his nervous foot-tapping told the truth.

'This is Detective Inspector Southall,' Norman told him, as they settled at the table. 'She wants to ask you some questions, okay?'

'Is it okay if I call you Alex?' asked Southall.

Cousins nodded.

'Can someone tell me why I'm here?' he asked.

'This is a small community, Alex. You must be aware we found a body on the beach.'

At the mention of the body on the beach, Cousins's eyes widened, and he swallowed hard.

'No one said anything about that. I thought this was about a speeding offence.'

'I didn't say anything about a motoring offence,' said Norman.

'But you said you wanted my car. I thought—'

'We want a forensic team to look at your car because we have CCTV footage of the murdered woman getting into it the night she died.'

Cousins looked horrified. He slammed his fist down on the table.

'What? Never. This is bullshit!'

'You might want to calm down, Alex,' said Norman, quietly. 'This could be a long night, and we don't want to be fighting with you.'

'This is some sort of joke, right?'

'We never joke about murder, Alex. Are you saying the CCTV footage is wrong?'

It was as if a switch had turned on in his head, and he was suddenly calm.

'When was this?'

'The night of Monday fourteenth.'

'That's like a week and a half ago.'

'That's correct. Can you recall where you were that night?'

'We were in the King's Head.'

'Who's we?'

'Me and my flatmate, Jay Bartham.'

'Was there any particular reason you were there or is that a regular Monday night thing?'

'We're business partners as well as flatmates. We were celebrating because we had landed a contract earlier that day.'

'Is that where you usually celebrate?'

'What, the King's Head? Once in a while maybe, but no, I wouldn't say it was somewhere we usually go.'

'So, you don't know the landlord?'

'Not really.'

'Okay, so you were in the King's Head, celebrating. How long were you in there?'

'We got there about nine o'clock, I suppose.'

'What time did you leave?'

'Closing time.'

'Can you be more precise?'

'I'm not sure. About quarter past eleven, I guess.'

'Can you recall if the pub was busy?'

'We were sitting on bar stools at the bar, so we had our backs to the room. I tend to say hello to anyone who stands next to me at the bar, so I probably would have spoken to most people who came up to order a drink, but I don't think it was many. So, I would say it wasn't packed, but there were a few people in there.'

'Did you notice a group of four women? They were sitting at one of the tables.'

'That's right.'

'What did you think of them?'

'I thought they were probably young mums on a quiet night out.'

'Anything else? Did they approach you, and start talking to you?'

'One of them did. She had been making eyes at me from the minute we walked in.'

Southall opened the folder on the table in front of her. She took the morgue photograph of Kimberley Lawrence's face and placed it on the desk in front of Cousins.

'Is this her?'

Cousins recoiled in horror.

'Jesus! Is that her? Is she dead?'

'I'm sorry, I should have warned you. That's the photograph taken in the morgue after she was cleaned up. Is it her?'

'It could be her. It's a bit hard to tell . . .'

Southall produced another photograph, this time of Kimberley when she was alive.

'This is the same woman before she died.'

'Yes, that's her,' admitted Cousins, quietly.

'When did she approach you?'

'It was near closing time. She just marched over and started talking to me.'

'Was she drunk?'

'She'd had a few, but I got the impression she could handle it. I'd say she was tipsy, not drunk.'

'Do you recall her name?'

'D'you know, I don't think she told me.'

'What did you do?'

'She was fit, you know? And it was obvious what she wanted, so I started chatting to her. Why wouldn't I?'

'So, you thought your luck was in, right?' asked Norman.

'To be honest, when her mates got up to leave, I expected her to go with them. I thought maybe she might give me her phone number, and we'd connect later, you know?'

'Connect later,' echoed Norman. 'No, I'm not sure I do know.'

'And did she leave with them?' asked Southall.

'No, she didn't. She told them she was fine and she'd find her own way home.'

'What did you think?'

'I was surprised. I mean, come on, whatever happened to subtlety? It was so obvious, in front of all her friends, it made me feel like she'd be scoring me afterwards and telling them what I was like.'

'So, you turned her down?'

'Ah, well, no. The thing is, I had the car, and I was taking Jay home, but he could see what was in the cards, so he said he'd walk and I should offer her a lift.'

'Do you always drive your car when you go celebrating?'

'We'd been to Carmarthen and were on the way back home. Anyway, I hate alcohol. I never touch the stuff.'

'Okay, so this lift — where?'

'Wherever she wanted to do it.'

'What happened to being nervous?'

'Look, we only live once, don't we? It occurred to me I might never get the chance again, so why not?'

'As it happens you were right, you won't get that particular chance again,' said Southall, quietly.

'What?'

'Never mind, it doesn't matter. Tell me what happened next.'

'Jay finished his drink and set off home, and that left me with her.'

'So, you took her out to your car.'

'We were just leaving when her mobile phone started to ring. She looks at the number, tells me to go on ahead, and she'll catch me up.'

'Who was calling?'

'No idea, and I didn't ask. She made it obvious she wasn't going to answer it while I was there, so I headed for the car park. I assumed it was her husband or the babysitter.'

'She didn't have any children.'

'How am I supposed to know that?'

Southall sighed. Cousins had got over his earlier nerves, and his growing confidence was becoming irritating.

'Go on,' she said. 'What next?'

'I went to the car park, got in the car, started it up, and waited. But then I saw her emerge from the pub, turn the other way, and walk out onto the street.'

'So, what did you do?'

'I thought whoever had been on the phone must have made her change her mind about me.'

'I bet that made you angry,' said Norman.

'I was pissed off, but no, not angry. You have to see it from her point of view; it could have been her husband, or the babysitter. If it was her husband, she could hardly tell him she was going to be late home because she was about to shag some bloke she'd just picked up, could she? It's the

130

downside of going with married women, but it's not worth getting mad about it. There's plenty more to choose from.'

'So, you're saying she walked off, and you drove home. So how come we have CCTV—'

'I didn't say that,' said Cousins. 'What happened was, she walked off towards the street, and then I caught her up in the car and stopped to offer her a lift.'

'So, she did get in your car?'

'Yes.'

'Okay, so where did you take her?'

'Well, that's the thing. She said she was feeling sick and wanted to go home. Then, no sooner had we set off, her phone started ringing again. I don't know who it was on the other end, but whoever it was, and whatever they said, made her decide she wanted to get out of my car.'

'What did you do?'

'I told her I thought she shouldn't be walking on the streets on her own and that I was happy to drive her wherever she wanted to go. I thought that was fair enough, but then she went on about how she could look after herself, and how men were so condescending, and all that sort of crap.'

'So, on top of playing around with your libido, she was now ranting at you?' asked Norman. 'That's enough to try anyone's patience. Is that when you lost it with her?'

'As I said, you have to see it from her point of view. She was pissed at the person on the phone, not me. I was just the nearest person she could take it out on.'

'So, you took her off somewhere and—'

'No, I didn't take her anywhere. I stopped and let her out.'

'Do you seriously expect us to believe that?'

'It's what happened.'

'How long would you say she was in your car?' asked Southall.

'No more than two, maybe three, minutes.'

'And where did she go after you let her out of your car?'

131

'I don't know. All I can tell you is the last time I saw her she was standing where I had left her and she had the phone to her ear.'

'What time was this?'

'I don't know exactly, but it would have been no more than five minutes after we left the pub.'

Southall stared at Cousins for a good minute. He licked his lips nervously, and his foot tapped furiously, but he didn't drop his gaze.

'Look, I said I'd help, and I have, so can I go home now?'

'I'm afraid that won't be possible yet,' said Southall. 'You were probably the last person to see Kimberley alive, so until I can corroborate your story, I'm afraid I'm going to have to ask you to stay.'

'Speak to Jay, he'll tell you. He's probably here somewhere.'

'You've had ten days to agree on your stories,' said Norman.

'Oh, I see. So I'm already guilty. Am I under arrest?'

Southall gathered the photos into the folder and closed it.

'You will be if you try to leave before I say you can.'

'Ah. Right. Well, can I at least have a drink?'

'I'll get someone to bring you a cup of tea.'

'Thank you.'

* * *

Norman followed Southall back to her office.

'What d'you think?' he asked.

She sighed as she placed the folder on her desk.

'Either he's incredibly confident he's got away with it, or he's telling the truth, and I can't decide which it is.'

'I can't believe he volunteered all that and didn't ask for a lawyer,' said Norman.

'That's what makes me think he's telling the truth,' said Southall. 'Once he got over his nerves, he started to get a bit cocky, but at the same time, he seems too naive to be lying. Find this flatmate and see if he can corroborate his story.'

132

'They've had ten days to learn it off by heart,' said Norman.

'Yes, maybe they have, but speak to him and see what he says.'

'Okay, I'll see what I can do.'

'I'd better send the others home; I don't want them dead on their feet tomorrow.'

CHAPTER 23

Half an hour later, Norman was back. Southall was standing by the monitor where the CCTV had been playing.

'How did it go?' she asked.

'Unless forensics can come up with something from the car, I think we'll have to let Cousins go.'

'The stories match?'

'Yeah. Not a perfect match but close enough to ring true. Bartham says it's a ten-minute walk home, and Cousins got back just after him at around eleven thirty. Even Lewis Hamilton couldn't have driven Kimberley out of town, bashed her head in, dumped her body, and then got back that quick.'

'Yes, you're right, but I already knew that.'

'You did? How come?'

'Here, watch this.'

She pressed a button, and the monitor came to life.

'This is more footage from another camera a bit further from the pub. Remember the last time we saw Kimberley she was getting into Cousins's car? Now watch what happens.'

Norman watched the jerky image on the screen as a car, clearly the same one they had seen Kimberley climb into earlier, pulled into the side of the road and stopped. A few seconds later, the passenger door opened, and a figure emerged from the car and stepped onto the pavement.

The car then pulled slowly away, and now Norman could see for sure it was Kimberley standing on the pavement. As the car pulled away, she reached into her handbag for her mobile phone. She thumbed the screen for a moment, then held the phone up to her ear. Norman looked at the timestamp. It said 23.25.

'Look at her,' said Southall. 'She doesn't look the least bit stressed, and she's still got her bag, and her mobile phone.'

'I wonder who she's calling?'

'Get the guys to call all the taxi firms in the morning. Maybe she wanted a lift home.'

'I have to admit that footage is pretty conclusive,' said Norman. 'That's just how Cousins described it.'

Southall sighed.

'I suppose I'd better go and tell him the good news.'

Norman looked at his wristwatch. It was nine p.m.

'D'you need me for anything?' he asked.

'No. You get off home. I have to update Superintendent Bain, and then I'm going to take Kimberley's diary home.'

Norman smiled.

'Reading in bed, huh?' he said. 'Don't stay awake all night. You need to sleep as much as the rest of us.'

CHAPTER 24

Friday 25 October 2019

'So how was your bedtime reading?' asked Norman next morning. 'Did it tell us anything?'

'Kimberley Lawrence should have written a book,' said Southall. 'I'm sure it would be a best-seller!'

'It was that good?'

'I never realised how dull and boring my life had become.'

'So, she led a colourful life?'

'I'll say. I lost count of the number of conquests she mentions.'

'You have a list of names?'

'Wouldn't that be something? But I'm afraid she tended to use expressions like "a nice boy with blond hair and blue eyes", or "well-muscled young man". My favourite was "a surprisingly virile old dog, for such a miserable person, but sometimes it's a case of any port in a storm". She refers to the "port" several times.'

'She had a way with words, then?'

'Yes, we've got numerous vague descriptions, if you fancy trying to make sense of any of them. The only clue that might help us is someone she referred to as, "N". It seems there was a period where she was having a proper affair with him, but then four months ago he ended it.'

'D'you think the "N" stands for Nick Rose?' asked Norman.

'I don't know. I got the impression he rather despised her.'

'Maybe an affair that didn't last made him feel that way.'

Southall frowned.

'I could understand that if she had ended it, but it doesn't fit quite so well when it's the other way around.'

'Maybe she was playing around behind his back,' suggested Norman. 'Sort of cheating on the cheat. I reckon he's the sort of guy who would hate that.'

'The entries in the diary suggest she didn't do that. They seemed to be at it all the time. There's an entry that says, "who would have thought of having sex at lunchtime? It's the perfect cover. Even though Greg suspects something is going on, he'll never think of a lunchtime bonk — it just wouldn't occur to him."'

'Bonking in the lunch break, and then going back to work?' said Norman. 'Jeez, these people have some stamina! So, she does mention Greg, then? Anything about him that helps us?'

'Oh yes, she says he's, "as much use as a chocolate teapot," on more than one occasion. She also wishes she had never married him, and thanks God she doesn't have to rely on him for decent sex and how she would die of frustration if it weren't for "N".'

'She was doing all that, and he knew she was doing it, and yet he says he still loved her! He must have been blind or stupid.'

'Don't they say love is blind?'

'Well, if you want to believe that, I suppose he's the proof,' said Norman. 'What happens after this guy ends the affair?'

'She says she's devastated and doesn't know what she's going to do. But then her libido seems to go into overdrive, and she starts recording conquests left, right and centre.'

'So "N" dumps her, and her reaction is to throw herself at every man and his dog?'

'Up until about six weeks ago, when she mentions having sex with someone she never expected, and how amazing he was. She adds it's a pity he's so unlikable.'

'Maybe that's Granger.'

'I agree he's unlikable, but I'm pretty sure he's, "any port in a storm", and he goes way back. It's not him.'

'Perhaps "N" isn't Nick Rose, but this new guy is. He's about as unlikable as they come. Was this an ongoing thing, or a one-night stand?'

'It's hard to say. He isn't mentioned again, but the diary entries get less frequent after that.'

'Perhaps she had to slow down to recharge her batteries,' said Norman. 'I'm getting worn out just listening to this.'

'No, it's nothing like that. It's because things had taken a sinister turn.'

'They had?'

'Apparently, she was frightened of someone.'

'You mean she had a stalker? Was it Greg?'

'There isn't a single passage in this diary that suggests she was frightened of Greg, or that she thought he would do her any harm, even if he caught her red-handed. If anything, I think she did care for him; she just found his complete lack of ambition frustrating.'

'They were in a downward spiral, weren't they?' suggested Norman. 'The more he lacked ambition, the more frustrated she got with him and the more she cheated on him. And the more she cheated on him, the more his enthusiasm dried up.'

'Yep, and I believe she made sure he knew enough, without ever being careless enough to get caught. It was her way of punishing him.'

'I'm beginning to think he could have caught her out, but he didn't want to,' said Norman. 'It's like he was trying to kid himself it wasn't happening.'

He sighed and shook his head.

'Jeez, what a mess. I suppose it never occurred to Kim that her behaviour was sucking all the confidence out of the guy.'

'Whatever was going on between them, she showed no sign of being frightened of him.'

'Okay, so if it's not Greg, perhaps one of her conquests wanted to take things further and didn't want to take no for an answer.'

Southall smiled.

'Now we're on the same page! That's my guess, but how do we work out who it is when all we have is the initial "N", and a load of vague descriptions?'

'Making calls to a mobile is often a favourite way of stalking. We should get her phone records today. Maybe we'll get lucky and find a number that helps.'

'I have to attend a meeting later this morning to support the boss,' said Southall. 'Apparently, I've started an argument between us and Region over the missing person report that never was. Marston and Hickstead are trying to blame everyone but themselves, and DCI Davies at Region is going bananas because two of his sergeants are at the centre of it all.'

'Why does that involve you? No one here was to blame. Marston and Hickstead screwed it up between them.'

'Region wants us to take the blame.'

'That's not going to happen,' said Norman, confidently. 'Nathan Bain won't accept that sort of crap from anyone.'

'Oh, he's confident they can't pin it on us. I'm sure he's only attending because he's looking forward to the fight.'

Norman smiled knowingly.

'Yeah, that sounds like him. He never ducked a fight when I worked with him. I reckon the two of you together will make a formidable team.'

'I like to think I can stand my ground,' said Sarah.

'Yeah, I don't doubt you can,' said Norman. 'I wish I could be a fly on the wall. It should be fun.'

'I'm not sure fun's the word I would use. I'd much rather be looking for our murderer. Anyway, there's no need for things to grind to a halt just because I'm going to be away for a couple of hours. I'd like you to interview Kim's secretary this morning. Take Catren Morgan with you.'

Norman grinned.

'Sure,' he said. 'Enjoy your meeting.'

* * *

As Norman and Morgan walked to their car, he tossed her the keys.

'As you're the junior partner here, I'll enjoy the luxury of being chauffeured.'

'You want me to drive? Oh, right on,' said Morgan, keenly, as she climbed into the driver's seat.

'This isn't an opportunity to show me how fast you can drive,' Norman warned, as he settled in next to her. 'I'm not impressed by stunt driving, and we only use the blues and twos in an emergency, not because we're late for lunch, okay?'

'Aw, that's not fair,' said Morgan. 'I was planning on trying to break the sound barrier.'

'Yeah, well, you can forget any ideas like that. The people we want to speak to will still be there if it takes us two minutes or two hours.'

'Seriously, have you tried going fast around here?' asked Morgan.

Norman thought for a few seconds.

'Now you come to mention it; the roads are pretty narrow, and—'

'If you can find a stretch where you can go faster than thirty miles an hour there's usually a bloody tractor up ahead, or some doddery old fart who's forgotten their car has more than two gears,' said Morgan, finishing Norman's sentence for him.

'Hey, let's have a bit of respect for the old farts of this world.'

'Sorry, Sarge. I forgot you are one.'

Norman smiled. He'd let her win that one. There would be plenty of opportunities to get his own back.

'Just drive, Catren, just drive.'

Morgan drove slowly out of the car park and turned left. Norman was carrying a folder with their notes, and Morgan kept quiet while he skimmed through them but, as soon as he had finished, she spoke.

'Can I ask a question?'

'Sure.'

'What d'you know about DI Southall?'

'How d'you mean?'

'What's her background? Where did she work before this?'

'Didn't you guys research her before she arrived?'

'We did our research on the guy we were told was coming. Southall was a late replacement. We didn't even know she was coming until she arrived. Then I found that body, and we've been so busy since I haven't had time to do it.'

'I know Superintendent Bain believes in her,' said Norman. 'That's good enough for me.'

'And you're not curious?'

'Why should I be?'

'But she's a DI, and she's a woman, and she's not even forty. That's good, isn't it?'

'It's terrific, but it doesn't matter how old you are, it's your ability that counts.'

'But she's done well for a woman, right?'

'I can't deny it's harder for women.'

'That's what I mean,' said Morgan. 'She must have worked her arse off to get that position.'

'It's not just about hard work. You have to be a bit special to be a DI, and you have to be very dedicated.'

'Exactly,' said Morgan. 'She's a go-getter. So, why did she come here?'

'I'm not sure what you mean.'

'No one volunteers to come here, especially someone with high ambition,' said Morgan. 'This is a dumping ground for those who screw up. I'm just wondering how she screwed up.'

Norman aimed a deliberate stare in her direction.

'Jeez, I must have missed the memo that told me I had screwed up,' he said.

Morgan squirmed in her seat.

'Ah, shit! Sorry. I didn't mean you.'

'But you just said no one comes here unless they've screwed up.'

'Yes, but—'

'Look, if you're going to exempt me, you've just disproved your all-encompassing theory about screw-ups,' said Norman. 'That means you can't continue to use it to explain why DI Southall is here.'

Morgan was struggling to come up with a response.

'Well, have you screwed up?' she asked, finally.

'I'm not exactly proud of the way my personal life has turned out,' confessed Norman, 'but I haven't screwed up at work. Don't forget; I'm a Rejoiner. They hardly would have invited me back if I was in the habit of screwing up, would they?'

Morgan didn't have an answer for that.

'So why are you here?'

'I told you before. Superintendent Bain offered me the opportunity to come and help train you guys. It seemed like a great offer, and I fancied a change of scenery anyway, so it was a no-brainer.'

Morgan quietly digested this news, but Norman could see she still wasn't convinced about Southall.

'Maybe it's because I've been around a long time,' he continued, 'but I believe I'm a pretty good judge of people. I'm not always right, but probably nine times out of ten, I am.'

'And she passes your test?'

'With flying colours,' said Norman. 'I also believe Nathan Bain is an even better judge than I am and, as I said before, he rates her. That works for me. As for why she chose to come here, I don't know, but I do know she loves the idea of giving you guys a chance and building a team.'

'But don't you wonder why?'

'No.'

'Seriously?'

'I'm sorry, Catren, but if you think I'm a source of juicy gossip, you're going to be disappointed. I'm sure the DI has her reasons for choosing to come here, and if she wanted me to know I'm sure she would tell me. But the fact is, she hasn't mentioned it, and I respect her privacy. I suggest you should, too.'

'Don't you guys talk?'

'About the case, yes.'

'You mean to say you spend all that time together and you don't know anything about each other?'

'I know she can do her job, and she knows I can do mine. What else do we need to know?'

They drove on in silence for a minute or two until Morgan turned right and pulled into the car park of the company where Kimberley Lawrence used to work.

'We both know Avril has already spoken to the boss,' Norman reminded Morgan, 'and we know what she said. But, for the purposes of this interview anything we hear is new to us, okay?'

'Make sure the story is still the same, right?' asked Morgan.

Norman grinned.

'Exactly,' he said.

CHAPTER 25

Avril Fisher was a small, timid, fifty-something. She reminded Norman of a mouse, and he was finding it challenging to get that image out of his head. Despite his best attempts to help her relax, she seemed to almost cower before them. This merely served to reinforce the image in Norman's head.

'I understand this must be very upsetting for you, Avril,' he said, gently, 'but we need to ask you a few questions about what happened, and then we're hoping you can help us build a better picture of Kimberley. We have an idea of what she was like at home, but people can be quite different at work, so maybe you can tell us something we don't already know.'

She nodded her head.

'I'll do my best,' she said.

'Tell us what happened the week she disappeared.'

'She came into work as normal on Monday, but then on Tuesday morning, she didn't show. This wasn't like her at all. In the five years I worked for her she had never been late, so I knew something must be wrong.'

'So, what did you do?'

'At first, I thought perhaps her car had broken down. She had been complaining about it for days, so it seemed quite possible. But she would have phoned if that was the case, and she didn't. By nine thirty, I decided I should call her at home and see if she was all right. I was worried about her, you see.'

'And you're sure it was nine thirty?' asked Morgan.

'Oh, yes. I had decided I would wait half an hour, and that's exactly what I did.'

Norman had no doubt this was correct. He felt sure Avril was that precise in everything she did.

'So, what happened when you called?' he asked.

'That man . . . I mean, Mr Lawrence, answered the phone.'

Morgan, who was taking notes, glanced sharply at Norman, who nodded in response. Yes, he had noticed it, too.

'And what did Mr Lawrence say?' asked Norman.

'At first, he seemed confused.'

'In what way confused?'

'As if he didn't believe what I was saying. He insisted I must be wrong and that Kim must be at work.' She looked guiltily at Norman. 'I don't like to speak ill of people, but I believe he has a drink problem. I can't prove it of course, but I think he may have been the worse for wear.'

'You mean he was drunk?'

'I would say he had a hangover.'

'So, let me get this clear,' said Norman. 'You're saying Greg Lawrence seemed to think his wife had gone to work as normal?'

'At first, yes. Then he seemed to come to his senses, and that's when he said he would go and look for her and let me know. He seemed to think her car may have broken down too.'

'Okay,' prompted Norman. 'Then what happened?'

'After about an hour he turned up here.'

'You saw him?'

'Oh, yes. He came into the office. He was hoping Kim would be here.'

'But you still hadn't heard anything?'

145

'Not a word. It was as if she had vanished off the face of the earth.'

'What did Greg say?'

'He said he had driven the route she normally takes to get here, but he hadn't found her, or her car, anywhere. When he realised she wasn't here, he said he was going to go back home, by another route, and would let me know if he found her. He also said he was going to check with the police and hospitals in case she had had an accident.'

'Did he get back in touch?'

'He called just before lunch to tell me Kimberley was at home after all, and that she was sick.'

'So, she had been at home all the time? Did he explain how he had managed to miss her?'

'He said she had got halfway to work, felt ill, turned around and gone back home. He says he must have missed her on the way.'

'You sound as though you didn't believe him,' suggested Norman.

'It sounded unlikely to me, but I had no reason to suspect he was anything other than stupid.'

'You didn't like him much, did you, Avril?'

'I never really met him. Most partners support each other at social functions, but he rarely made an appearance. Kim always had to come alone.'

'So, you don't think they had a happy marriage? Did Kim ever say as much?'

'Let's put it this way,' said Avril, carefully. 'I can't recall her ever running him down specifically, but I never heard her praise him either.'

'She wasn't proud to call him her husband?'

'I think not. Kim rarely spoke about her private life, but whenever she did, it was because she was disappointed about something.'

'So, what about Kim, the person? What was she like?'

'Very hardworking.'

'Yeah, I was told that by your HR manager, but I got the feeling she was just giving me the corporate viewpoint. You were closest to her, right? You would know what she was really like as a person.'

'I'm not sure what you're getting at.'

'I mean, was she popular among the other staff?'

'I think most people liked her.'

'C'mon, Avril, that's pretty non-committal. You were here with her for five years; you can do better than that.'

'Well, I suppose there were one or two women who seemed envious of her position.'

'Right. What about the men? Did she get on with them?'

'I don't know what you're suggesting—'

'I'm not suggesting anything, but you have to admit, she was an attractive woman, and you just told us she was unhappy at home. These things happen at work sometimes.'

For the first time, Avril began to show some passion.

'Have you no respect for the poor woman? She's been murdered, and all you can do is come here making accusations like that. Shouldn't you be out looking for her killer?'

'Hey, look,' said Norman. 'I'm not trying to cause trouble here—'

'I don't know what you're suggesting, but I can assure you there was nothing untoward going on here!'

Avril got to her feet and began tidying her desk.

'If you've no more questions, I have work to do.'

Morgan glanced at Norman.

'Yeah, sure,' he said. 'I think we have all we need for now, but we may need to speak to you again.'

'Well, you know where to find me, don't you?'

* * *

'Wow!' said Morgan as they made their way down the stairs at the back of the building. 'Did you touch a nerve, or what?'

Norman smiled.

'You noticed?'

147

'It would have been hard to miss.'

'She was never going to tell us anything definite,' said Norman, 'but the reaction told its own story.'

'Do you think she knows she gave the game away?'

'I don't know. You have to admire her loyalty. A lot of people would have been happy to dish the dirt in that situation, especially knowing the person they were talking about couldn't do anything about it.'

'So, does this mean there's a relationship at work?'

'Maybe. Or perhaps it's just common knowledge Kim liked to share the love with all and sundry.'

'That's not exactly a clear lead, is it?'

'No, but we should have Kim's phone records today, and we can compare that with a list of staff names, plus the boss has Kim's diary. If we put it all in the mix who knows what might come out. And we can always come back and lean on Avril if we have to.'

The sun was shining as they emerged through the back door of the building. A paved path led across a lawned area and on to the car park. About halfway along the way, a partly roofed seating area had been provided for those members of staff who smoked. A lone woman was sitting at the table, enjoying the autumnal sunshine as she looked out at the fields beyond the car park.

As they approached, she exhaled a vast cloud of smoke and then turned towards them.

'Are you the police?' she asked.

'That's right,' said Norman.

'Are you asking about Kimberley Lawrence?'

Norman and Morgan stopped walking.

'That's right,' said Norman. 'Did you work with her?'

'I didn't, but my boss did.'

'Who's your boss?'

'Mike Gordon. He's the Finance Director. I'm his secretary.'

'And you are?'

'Ruby Davies. Do you want to speak to me?'

'We've already spoken to Avril Fisher,' said Norman. 'She was pretty close to Kim.'

Ruby smiled.

'Ah, yes, Avril, the timid little mouse who wouldn't say boo to a goose.' She winked at the two detectives. 'The problem with speaking to Avril is she can only see her boss through rose-tinted glasses.'

Norman nodded at Morgan and gestured her towards the table.

'I'm DS Norman, and this is DC Morgan,' said Norman. 'D'you mind if we join you? We haven't had a break this morning, and it would be a shame not to make the most of the sunshine.'

They settled at the table opposite Ruby.

'What is it you want to tell us?' asked Norman.

'I bet Avril didn't tell you Kimberley Lawrence was having an affair with my boss, did she?'

'Really? And you have proof of this?'

'Are you going to tell him I told you? I don't want to lose my job.'

'That's not usually how we work,' said Norman. 'So, do you have proof?'

'I haven't caught them going at it if that's what you mean.'

'But?'

'But, why does she call him "Nookie"?'

'Nookie?' echoed Norman. 'Wasn't he a bear?'

Ruby and Morgan both looked mystified.

'I'm sorry?' said Ruby.

'Ignore me,' said Norman. 'You're both too young to remember. Sorry, you were saying Kim used to call him Nookie.'

'That's what she used to call him when she thought no one was listening. And, another thing, why do they go to lunch together every Tuesday and Friday?'

'Going to lunch with someone isn't quite the same as having an affair,' said Morgan.

'Ah, yes, but what if they go to lunch at his house on those days, and they just happen to be the days when his wife is at work, and he knows the house will be empty?'

'Okay,' said Morgan. 'That's a bit more suspicious. How long has this been going on?'

Ruby smiled.

'A couple of years, at least.'

'Does he live far away?'

'Five minutes' drive. He was clever enough to head in the other direction when he left here, but it was just a ridiculous charade. He drove in a circle back to his house. If you went the other way, you'd pass them. Everyone knew — it was an open secret.'

'This happened often?'

'Let's just say he was a frequent flyer if you get my drift. And, talking of flying; why did the Finance Director make a habit of turning up at hotels where the IT Director was staying?'

'They went abroad together?'

'This company does a lot of business abroad. As IT Director Kim often did follow-up trips in support of the sales team. They travelled all over. My boss is away right now. He comes back on Sunday, and she would have been there too if she was still alive.'

'So, your boss is part of the follow-up team?'

'No. But he makes a habit of going anyway.'

'But if she's not there, why go this time?'

'Because it was already booked, and it might look suspicious if he didn't go.'

'But surely the other members of the team would know, wouldn't they?'

'But this isn't with the sales team. This is the follow-up. Often it was just Kim, and him. Even if anyone else were there, they wouldn't dare mention it anyway because my boss is a mighty powerful man in this company. People who work here are extremely well paid, and they don't want to rock the boat. The last person who suggested something was going on was looking for a new job the very next day.'

'And you can prove this happened?'

'I'm his secretary, but it's also my job to book flights and hotels for everyone in the company. I can prove they were on the same flights, and staying at the same hotel, on frequent occasions. I'll send you a list if you don't believe me.'

Morgan fished a card from her pocket.

'My email address is on there,' she said, as she passed it to Ruby. "Send it to me.'

'So, how come Avril doesn't seem to be aware of this affair?' asked Norman.

'Because Avril thinks the sun shone out of Kim's arse,' said Ruby.

'Why does she think that?'

'Because Kim filled her head with this idea that she was the loyal wife, supporting her husband through thick and thin, while he's an ingrate who took all she had to give and gave nothing back in return.'

'And that's not true?'

'I'm not saying he's not useless, but if she's so loyal, how do you explain her and Mike Gordon? And, according to all the gossip I've heard, my boss is not the only guy stoking her fire. If that's being loyal and supportive, I need a new dictionary.'

* * *

'Well, that saved us some time,' said Norman, as they walked to their car. 'Now we not only suspect she was having an affair, but we also have the name of the guy she was supposedly involved with.'

'You're not convinced?' asked Morgan.

'I would have to say I'm more or less convinced, but I'm trying to keep an open mind. You never know, maybe Ruby has some sort of axe to grind. It's not as if Kim's here to defend her reputation, is she?'

'It sounds like she certainly enjoyed putting it around,' said Morgan. 'She must have had some energy.'

'You sound envious.'

Morgan grinned.

'I can't even find one guy I like enough to keep jumping into bed with at the moment,' she said. 'Besides, I don't have the time, and I certainly don't have the stamina she must have had!'

Norman smiled but didn't quite know what to say.

'Of course,' continued Morgan, 'if it's true, and she was playing fast and loose behind this guy's back, maybe he got fed up sharing.'

'It's a possibility we can't ignore,' admitted Norman. 'Let's wait until he gets back from his trip and then we'll ask him.'

They drove in silence for a minute or two, then Morgan spoke.

'Who is Nookie Bear?'

'What?'

'When Ruby said the name Nookie, you said something about a bear?'

'Oh, that's right I did. There used to be a ventriloquist who had a dummy called Nookie, and Nookie was a bear. I remember seeing him once. It must be thirty years ago now. He was funny, but the language. Jeez, that bear was bluer than blue.'

'It sounds hilarious,' said Morgan, doubtfully.

'I enjoyed it,' said Norman. 'But it wouldn't work nowadays. I suppose you could say it was of its time. It was one of those things where you had to be there, you know?'

CHAPTER 26

They were nearing the harbour on their way back to the office.

'Pull in by that coffee kiosk,' said Norman. 'I think we deserve a drink.'

Morgan parked as close as she could, and Norman climbed from the car to get two coffees.

Morgan watched as Norman joked comfortably with the guy serving him. He was quite different from the sergeants she had worked with before who seemed to regard her as nothing more than a gofer. She realised she was beginning to admire her new sergeant, with his wild hair, untidy suit, and his apparent ability to relate to everybody.

'Latte, right?' he asked, as he passed her coffee through the window.

'That's right.'

He made his way around the car and slipped in next to her.

'Can you help me with something?' he asked.

'Of course,' she said, and sipped at her coffee.

'I'm thinking of learning Welsh.'

A broad smile creased her face.

'Really?'

'Yeah, why not?' asked Norman.

'But why? Everyone speaks English around here.'

'Not everyone does,' said Norman. 'I think it would be handy when the locals slip into Welsh because they think I can't understand what they're saying.'

'But isn't that what we locals are for?'

'Yeah, but what if you're not with me?'

Morgan nodded.

'Okay, that's a fair point, but I still think it's unnecessary.'

'I feel it's the respectful thing to do if I'm going to live here, and I think it would be good to be able to pronounce the place names properly, don't you?'

'What place names?'

'Llangwelli Station for a start.'

He pronounced it 'Langwelly'.

'I think you'll find most of the people around here pronounce it the same way you do.'

'But it's not correct, is it?'

'Strictly speaking, it's not correct, but they do it because most of them are English. There's a good reason this area is known as little England.'

'Oh, yeah, I forgot that.'

'But you're right; the Welsh pronunciation is quite different.'

'Yeah, I've been practising,' said Norman. 'D'you wanna hear it?'

Morgan rolled her eyes.

'You're serious, aren't you?'

'Absolutely.'

'You don't have to do this.'

'I know, but as I said, I feel it's the respectful thing to do.'

Morgan sighed.

'Okay. Go on, then, let's hear it.'

She took a mouthful of coffee as Norman prepared himself.

'Okay, here we go,' he said. 'I can do both. So, the English say, Langwelly, and the Welsh say, Clangoolly.'

Morgan spluttered as she tried to contain her laughter. But then she lost control and the coffee she had been trying so hard not to spray everywhere was suddenly snorting out of her nose. It was a couple of minutes before she could speak.

'Jeez, there's coffee all down your front,' said Norman.

'Oh, I'm sorry, Sarge' she said. 'It's just the way you—'

'Yeah, I get it.' said Norman. 'I didn't pronounce it right.'

'At least you tried,' she said.

'So it was a little off the mark. I'll get better with practice.'

'I thought you said you had been practising.'

'Was it that bad?'

'I'd say it was a typically English pronunciation.'

'No, shit. Really? It was that bad?' asked Norman sulkily. Morgan nodded her head.

'I'm afraid so.'

'It's a stupid language anyway,' said Norman. 'I saw a village name the other day that had at least ten letters, but there were no vowels. I mean, how does that work?'

'It's a different alphabet, that's all. There are actually seven vowels in Welsh.'

'But how can there be? It's the same letters!'

'And that's why the English have such a problem learning Welsh. Just because the letters in the alphabet look the same, it doesn't mean they are the same. You would have the same problem if you went to Russia or China.'

'Russia and China use completely different letters. In fact, there are no letters in Chinese; they use characters instead. Anyway, they're both thousands of miles away from England, so I expect them to be different. Wales is just over a bridge, for God's sake, but language-wise it might as well be on another planet.'

'Are you saying the Welsh should give up their language?'

'Good God, no. I think the fact you have your own language is awesome. I just wish it was easier to understand. And another thing; why do they insist on putting place names in two languages? When I first arrived here, I spent hours trying to find Abertawe on a map. I knew it must be some-where near Swansea because they were on the same signpost, but d'you think I could find it?'

Morgan was laughing again.

'Yeah, exactly,' said Norman. 'They're two names for the same place, but how was I supposed to know that? They don't even start with the same letter!'

'You would have found it easily enough if you weren't using an English map.'

'But no one tells you this when you come over the bridge, do they?'

'It's a cunning plan to confuse the English invaders,' she said, with a wry smile.

'Yeah? Well, you can tell whoever dreamt up the plan that it's working perfectly,' said Norman.

Now it had started to rain.

'And another thing,' said Norman. 'It always seems to be raining here. How d'you people cope with it?'

'You get used to it,' said Morgan. 'And, of course, it helps that we all have webbed feet and gills.'

CHAPTER 27

'So, how was the meeting?' asked Norman.

'Heated,' said Southall. 'Superintendent Bain doesn't mince his words, does he?'

'He never did when I worked with him,' said Norman.

'He used a few swear words too.'

'Only a few? Well, he must have mellowed, because he used to use hundreds, and lots of them began with the letter f.'

'I didn't realise just how passionate he is about this project,' said Southall.

'Oh, he is, for sure,' said Norman. 'I feel kind of flattered that he came looking for me to join.'

'I can understand why. He speaks highly of you,' said Southall.

'He does?'

'He tells me you're someone who wouldn't give in. He says you just kept getting up every time you were knocked down. That makes you a great example for these guys here.'

'He means I can be stubborn.'

'Being stubborn doesn't have to be a bad thing,' said Southall. 'If I weren't stubborn, I'd never have got to DI. I would have given up a long time ago.'

'Sounds like you've had your share of shit from above, too. It makes you wonder why we keep coming back for more. I guess we must be masochists.'

'I can't really complain about work,' said Southall. 'It was everything else that blew up in my face. If I'm honest, it was only the decision to focus on my job, and the support from my boss, that kept me sane. Mind you, going through all that shit has made me a much better police officer.'

'Yeah, it tends to do that,' agreed Norman.

For a moment, he thought she was going to open up and tell him her story, but instead, she became lost in her thoughts. Respectful of her privacy, he turned to his notebook.

'Anyway,' she said after a short while. 'You don't want to hear about that. Did we get anywhere with the taxis?'

'Lane's called every taxi within ten miles and got nothing.'

'Oh well, we knew it was a long shot. How did you get on with the secretary?'

'She more or less confirmed Greg Lawrence's story about what happened on Tuesday morning after Kim disappeared. And she definitely doesn't like Greg, although I believe that's based on what Kim told her about him. I don't think she ever got to know him.'

'Did we learn anything we didn't already know?'

'Not from Avril, she's much too loyal to her old boss to let anything slip. But on the way out we had a fascinating conversation with a lady called Ruby Davies. She's the secretary to Mike Gordon, the company Finance Director. According to Ruby, Kim and Mike were having an affair. She claims it had been going on for a couple of years.'

'How on earth did she find the time to fit an affair in?'

'Apparently, they liked a little sport at lunchtime.'

'That confirms what was in Kim's diary.'

'Ruby says he lives five minutes from the office. His wife works a couple of days a week, so the house is empty.'

'I can't imagine doing that and then coming back to work!'

'Yeah, me neither, but I suppose it takes all sorts.'

'Have you spoken to him?'

'We couldn't. He's away until Monday. They also both travelled a lot for work, and liked to share the same hotel room.'

'Do their bosses know?''

Norman shrugged.

'I have no idea.'

'Does he know about her other conquests?'

'That's what we were thinking.'

'It would be motive enough for a lot of men,' said Southall, thoughtfully. 'Especially if it had been going on for a long time.'

'So now we have two suspects,' said Norman.

'Does this mean Mike Gordon is "N" in the diary?'

Norman smiled.

'Actually, it does,' he said. 'According to Ruby Davies, Kim had a pet name for Mike Gordon. She called him Nookie.'

'Wasn't he a bear?'

Norman stared at Southall.

'Jeez, you know Nookie bear?'

Slowly her face broke into a grin.

'To be honest, I'd never heard of him until Catren mentioned him in the ladies a few minutes ago. She said you'd be surprised if I said that.'

Norman was impressed.

'Ha! Right, gotcha,' he said. 'I can see I'll need to be on my toes if you're going to be working as a team against me.'

'We've got to have a little fun occasionally.'

'I couldn't agree more,' said Norman. 'Murder is too serious a business without a laugh here and there. But, getting back to the serious stuff, we haven't found Kim's car yet, have we?'

'We've not been looking for it,' admitted Southall. 'Is it relevant? All the evidence suggests she didn't use it.'

'Yeah, but what if we're wrong about that?'

'How d'you mean?'

'Well, we're assuming she left the pub, got into a car, and was driven off to the murder scene, right?'

'And you think that's wrong?'

'Well, maybe there's an alternative idea we might consider.'

'I'm willing to consider anything within reason.'

'Okay, so we know from the CCTV footage that she got into Alex Cousins's car, but then got out again. And we saw she then made a phone call.'

'Yes, and if we had the damned phone records, we might know who she called.'

'We're assuming that call was to ask someone to come and pick her up, right?'

Southall nodded.

'That's the theory.'

'But what if we're wrong?' asked Norman. 'What if she was calling someone to ask if she could visit them? What if they said yes, and then she went home, got in her car and drove there?'

'How did she get home to collect the car?'

'She could have walked. It's only about fifteen minutes.'

'She was drunk.'

'Yeah,' said Norman, 'but she wasn't falling down drunk, was she?'

'What about Greg? Wouldn't he have heard her?'

'Not necessarily. I mean you were there when I was hammering on his door the other day. And if he'd been drinking . . .'

'Could she have driven, like that?'

'Why not? We both know there are still plenty of people who won't let being drunk stop them driving. Anyway, even if she was usually sensible about it, maybe this time she wanted whoever it was badly enough not to care.'

Southall was thinking.

'I think you could be on to something,' she said finally. 'Let's step up the search for the car. Perhaps, if we find it, we might find the crime scene, too.'

'I'll get onto it,' said Norman. 'What's the plan for the weekend?'

'Ruth Evans is expecting someone to interview her tomorrow morning. Would you mind doing it? I've got to catch-up on mountains of paperwork. Take Catren with you.'

'Sure,' said Norman. 'But first I have to sit with Judy Lane for a while. I told her I'd look over what she's done so far.'

'I can do that,' said Southall.

'Are you sure? I mean it's my responsibility really.'

'Of course, I'm sure,' said Southall. 'You take the interview, and I'll do the supervising. It's called teamwork. And another thing; I'd like everyone to finish as early on Saturday afternoon as possible, and then I don't want to see anyone until Monday morning.'

'That sounds fair enough to me.'

CHAPTER 28

Ruth Evans had called in response to the card Norman had pushed through her letterbox. An attractive forty-something with a ready smile, she had the door open before they even reached it.

'Please come in,' she said as Morgan made the introductions on her doorstep. 'My husband has taken our two sons to play football, so we should have some peace for a while.'

She led them into a pristine lounge and indicated the armchairs.

'I'm sorry I wasn't here the other day,' she said, as they settled into their seats. 'It's a terrible business. I'm only too happy to help in any way I can.'

'We'd like you to tell us what you can remember about the night out with Kimberley and the other girls,' suggested Norman. 'Then, perhaps you can give us your impression of Kimberley as a person, just to help us form a complete picture of her.'

'Yes, of course. So, on that Monday night, Abbey picked me up a little after half past seven, then we called for Kim and Pippa on the way to the pub . . .'

* * *

Ruth confirmed everything they already knew about the night in the pub but was unable to add anything new. At first, she was reluctant to speak about Kimberley's private life, which Norman hoped meant she had something to hide. However, after a lot of encouragement and some skilful questioning, she did loosen up, but again could only confirm what they already knew.

Norman was disappointed, but at least Ruth had confirmed the story as they knew it, so it wasn't a complete waste of their time.

'So, if you left the pub at quarter to eleven, what time did you get back here?' he asked.

'It's not a long journey. I've walked it before now, but it's a bit chilly at this time of year. I was here before eleven.'

'I understand your husband was playing snooker with Nick Rose and Greg Lawrence,' said Norman.

'Yes, that's right. Alan likes a game of snooker now and then.'

'Do you normally go out and leave your two boys home alone?'

'They weren't alone. We have a babysitter.'

'So, the babysitter was here when you got back?'

'My husband got back before me. The babysitter had gone home. She only lives next door.'

'Your husband was here? What time did he get back?'

'You'd have to ask him,' said Ruth. 'He was in bed when I got home, so he must have got home at least a few minutes before me.'

Morgan looked up from her note-taking and caught Norman's eye, but his face was deadpan.

'Is your husband going to be long?' asked Norman.

Ruth smiled.

'Now that depends on the game,' she said. 'Sometimes if they win, the dads take the boys down the pub and buy them lunch as a treat. If that happens, he might not be back until early afternoon.'

'What about if they lose?'

'Ah, well, in that case, they'll be home by midday. Did you want to speak to him?'

'We still need a statement from him,' said Norman. He fished a card from his pocket. 'Perhaps if you could ask him to give me a call on that number.'

'I can call him now if you like.'

'I wouldn't want to interrupt the boys' football match,' said Norman. 'When he gets home will be fine.'

'Yes, of course.'

Norman looked at Morgan.

'I think that's about it for now,' he said.

'I'm sorry I can't be more help,' said Ruth.

'If you remember anything else, you have my number,' said Norman. 'Feel free to call me anytime.'

* * *

'I was right, wasn't I?' asked Morgan as she drove them away.

Norman turned to look at her.

'Right about what?'

'There's a discrepancy about times, isn't there?'

'We haven't taken a statement from Alan Evans yet. He might say the same as her.'

'But the timeline you and the boss drew up says Nick Rose dropped him home at eleven fifteen.'

Norman was impressed she had remembered a detail like that.

'Yes, you have got that right,' said Norman. 'There is a discrepancy between what Ruth Evans just told us, and what Nick Rose told us. We'll check it out when we get back.'

'I didn't think you'd noticed.'

'Of course I noticed,' said Norman, 'but I didn't think I should draw attention to it in case she changed her mind.'

'Oh. I didn't. Did I?'

'She had her eyes on me, so I don't think she noticed your reaction, but you need to try not to give yourself away so easily. Even if someone tells you where the smoking gun is, you need to try and look unimpressed.'

'Oh. Sorry.'

'Don't apologise for being human. Just remember it for next time. Anyway, it's not necessarily a big deal. Maybe someone has made a genuine mistake, and it's not significant in the grand scheme of things.'

'Can I tell the boss?'

Norman smiled indulgently. He couldn't fault her enthusiasm.

'Sure, you can tell her. After all, you spotted it, and it's written in your notebook.'

Morgan's smile began to fade.

'In my notebook. I suppose that means I'm going to have to type up the report.'

Norman sighed happily.

'I'm afraid so,' he said. 'I've seen your handwriting, and I'm not sure I could accurately decipher your notes.'

'Crap!' said Morgan. 'My writing's not that bad. Is it?'

'Actually, it's not bad at all, but you still have to do the report. And look on the bright side; at least you can do it on a computer where you can correct errors with ease. When I was your age, we were still using typewriters and correcting fluid.'

'What's correcting fluid?'

Norman looked at Morgan and shook his head.

'Jeez, sometimes I feel as if I must have gone through a time warp when I crossed that bridge from England.'

'What?' asked Morgan.

'Just drive, Catren. I think I hear the rest of the weekend calling me.'

CHAPTER 29

As Morgan parked the car, Norman's mobile phone rang.

'It's Alan Evans. My wife told me you'd like to speak to me.'

'We need to take a statement from you about the evening of Monday fourteenth. Is it possible to arrange that?'

'Do I need to come to the police station?'

'That would make life easier.'

'It won't take long, will it? I can come down now if you like.'

'Really? Your wife said you might be taking the boys for lunch. I don't want to spoil their treat.'

'No one's going to the pub today, so we're back home. I can be with you in ten minutes. It's no trouble.'

'Thank you. That would be helpful,' said Norman. 'We'll be waiting at the front desk.'

* * *

If Norman had created a picture of what he thought Ruth Evans's husband would look like, Alan Evans was precisely it. Good-looking, six feet tall, and clean-cut, he had a ready smile and a firm handshake.

As they began the interview, it soon became apparent his attitude was the polar opposite of Nick Rose, and Norman couldn't help but wonder how these two men could be friends. He figured it must be a classic case of opposites attract.

'So, you left Nick's at ten thirty?' asked Norman. 'Do your snooker nights normally end that early? Last time I played snooker, it took hours to complete just one game.'

'Sometimes they can go on until midnight. We play a sort of round-robin event, and then the best two play a final game, but that relies on all three of us being capable of playing.'

'I'm not sure I understand.'

'Greg was pissed. He kept bleating on about how Kim didn't love him and never had loved him. It doesn't exactly make for a happy atmosphere, you know? Nick didn't want to see his snooker table ruined so he wouldn't let Greg play, and that just made him whinge even more. In the end, we gave up, and I went home.'

'So, Greg was still there when you left? How did he get home?'

'I believe Nick took him.'

'In that nice Maserati? Wasn't he worried Greg might throw up on the way?'

'I wouldn't have let him in my car, but Nick's a lot more patient with Greg than I am.'

'You don't like Greg?'

'It's not that I don't like him, I get frustrated hearing him whining all the time. I told him, if he was that unhappy with his wife, he should do something about it.'

'Do something about it?' asked Norman.

'Well, you know, leave her, not keep complaining to us. He's the only one who can change the situation, isn't he?'

He looked guilty as he realised what he'd said.

'Well, of course, he can't change it now, but he could have done if you see what I mean,' he added awkwardly.

'That's okay,' said Norman. 'I understand. It can be difficult to get used to the idea of someone not being here anymore. Did you get on with Kim?'

'I tended to steer clear of her.'

'You didn't like her?'

'Let's say I didn't approve of her morals.'

Norman nodded. He thought he would have agreed had he known Kim.

'How did you get home, Alan? Did you drive?'

'I don't take my car. It's only a ten-minute walk.'

'And you got home when?'

'I can't give you the exact time, but it must have been ten forty-five or a couple of minutes before.'

'What happened then?'

'I paid the babysitter, saw her home, and then went to bed. When I say I saw her home, what I mean is I stood at the front door and watched her until she reached her front door and went inside. I do it every time. I'm sure nothing's going to happen to her, it just seems the right thing to do.'

'Was your wife home by then?'

'She came in about fifteen minutes after me. I was in bed by the time she got home.'

'And you didn't go out again after that?'

'Look, am I a suspect, or something?'

Norman sighed.

'Let me be honest with you, Alan. At the moment, for elimination purposes, we're trying to establish where everyone was, and when. We don't have a particular suspect but, by definition, that means everyone is a suspect until we can eliminate them. Some people take offence at this, and I understand why, but it's nothing personal, it's just how we have to work.'

Evans thought about this for a few seconds.

'I see what you mean. It can't be easy.'

'It is what it is,' said Norman. 'Dealing with people's hostility goes with the job.'

'Well, if there's anything else I can do to help.'

'I think that's about it for now,' said Norman. 'But if you think of anything else . . .'

* * *

Norman knocked on Southall's office door, even though it was open. She looked up from her paperwork and smiled.

'Come in, Norm,' she said. 'Catren Morgan tells me we have a discrepancy.'

'We certainly do,' he said, 'and Alan Evans has just confirmed it. According to him, he left Nick Rose's house at ten thirty, to walk home, and Greg Lawrence was still there.'

'Oh, dear. Does this mean Mr Rose has told us a pack of lies? Now, why would he do that?'

'If you want to ask him, you'll have to wait until Monday. He's away for the weekend.'

'In that case, I suggest we take a break now and reconvene on Monday. Then, we'll speak to Mr Rose.'

'That sounds like a plan I can work with,' said Norman.

CHAPTER 30

Monday 28 October 2019

Rose didn't look pleased to find Southall and Norman on his doorstep, but he quickly managed to turn his frown into a smile.

'Good morning, Inspector Southall, Sergeant Norman. How nice to see you again.'

'Is it?'

Rose looked puzzled.

'I'm sorry?'

'We haven't come for a friendly chat,' said Southall.

The smile on Rose's face faded to a frown, and he stepped outside, pulling the front door closed to make it clear he had no intention of letting them into his house.

'Your attitude makes your intentions abundantly clear, Inspector. I'm sure the Chief Constable will be delighted when I tell him how belligerent you can be.'

'And I'm sure the Chief Constable will be even more delighted when I tell him you obstructed our murder investigation.'

'I beg your pardon?'

'You told us you and Alan Evans took Greg Lawrence home at ten thirty p.m. Yet Alan Evans says he left here at ten thirty to walk home, and that Greg was still here, with you, when he left.'

The condescending smile was back on Rose's face again.

'Ah, yes. I have an explanation for that.'

'Good. I can't wait to hear it,' said Southall.

'Do I need my solicitor to be present?' asked Rose.

'I don't know,' said Norman. 'Do you?'

'You're not under caution,' said Southall, looking him straight in the eye. 'At least, not at the moment but, if you want to play games, we can always do this down at the station.'

Rose did his best to outstare Southall, but it wasn't long before he realised he was wasting his time.

'I'm sure that won't be necessary,' he said, finally. 'There's a simple explanation.'

'Which we're still waiting to hear,' said Norman.

Rose sighed.

'Okay. Look, I know how these things work. As Kim's husband, Greg is automatically the number one suspect. But he's a fragile guy, and I don't believe he killed her. I just thought if I gave him an alibi, it would steer you guys away, at least until he gets himself together. It hasn't done any harm, has it?'

'So why bring Alan Evans into it?'

'You're right; I shouldn't have done that. I didn't think it through.'

'So, you think it's okay for you to decide whether a man is guilty of murder?' asked Norman. 'And this is based on what? A hunch? We tend to prefer something a little more tangible than that. And, of course, there's also the fact you involved a third person in your little conspiracy.'

'I'd hardly call it a conspiracy,' said Rose.

'Really? What would you call it?' asked Norman.

'You see, from where we're standing, Mr Rose,' added Southall, 'you're playing with the law about perverting the course of justice.'

'I've known Greg Lawrence for years. He wouldn't do that sort of thing. Besides, he was drunk, and he was with

171

me. He couldn't have done it. He was sleeping like a baby when I left him.'

'And what time did you leave him?' asked Southall.

'Around eleven, I suppose.'

'And you think he couldn't have woken up after you left?' asked Norman.

Now Rose looked sheepish.

'Oh, wow!' he said. 'Do you really think he might have done that? I never thought. I just assumed. You know, now you come to mention it, we did have a conversation about this once. I remember it quite clearly because I thought it was such an extraordinary thing for him to say. I don't recall the exact words, but he was saying how frustrating it was when you love someone so much, and they keep kicking you when you're down. Then he said, "I probably shouldn't admit this, but there are times when I could quite happily murder her." He was talking about Kim, of course.'

Southall studied Rose's face.

'You're sure about that? He said he'd like to murder her?'

'Well, yes, but I'm sure he didn't mean it. It was just in the heat of the moment, after a couple of beers. I think they'd argued about something before he came around here.'

'We'll talk again, Mr Rose,' said Southall. 'When we do, you might want to have your solicitor with you. I may well charge you with obstructing a police inquiry, and if I do, I don't think your friend, the Chief Constable, will disagree that it's the right course of action for me to take.'

* * *

'I knew that guy was going to be trouble,' said Norman, as they drove away. 'Now I'm wondering what else he's covering up.'

'Yes, well, we can deal with him later. Right now, I want another word with Greg Lawrence.'

As Norman turned the car towards Lawrence's house, Southall's phone rang.

'Yes, Catren.'

She listened for a minute.

'Okay, we're on the way. Wait a little down the road from the car. We'll meet you there.'

'Good news?' asked Norman as she ended the call.

'Uniforms have found Kim's car.'

'Now we might be getting somewhere,' said Norman. 'Where is it?'

'Catren's just sending me a text with the location.'

There was a notifying ping from her phone.

'Here we go. I'll just whack it into the satnav.'

She tapped the address into the satnav then sank back into her seat with a sigh.

'How are we going to play this?' asked Norman.

'Uniforms have found the car, but they haven't been near it. They're watching from a distance until we get there. We'll meet Catren and decide how to play it from there.'

CHAPTER 31

'Kimberley's phone records have finally arrived, boss,' Morgan told Southall when they met up with her.

'Has anyone had a look at them?'

'They came in as I was leaving. Judy was just opening the envelope when I left.'

'Okay, let's get this car sorted first. Which one is it?'

They looked across the road at a small car workshop which bore the names, 'Dennis & Swann'. Several cars were parked on a small forecourt in front of the building.

'The red one,' said Morgan.

'Who would have guessed someone like Kimberley would have a bright red sports car?' said Norman, ironically.

'Yes, it does seem rather appropriate,' agreed Southall. 'What do we think? Is it here for repairs, or is it a coincidence that it was dumped outside a small car servicing workshop?'

'Avril Fisher said Kim had been complaining about the car for days,' said Norman. 'My gut tells me that's why it's here.'

'It's a rather conspicuous hiding place,' said Morgan.

Southall sighed. 'Yes, that's what I think, too.'

'Why don't I go inside and suss the place out?' suggested Norman. 'If I think there's anything funny going on, I'll come back out, and we can call for back-up.'

'D'you think we'll need it?' asked Southall.

'No, but better safe than sorry, right?'

'If you're sure.'

'I'll be fine,' he said.

'Be careful, Norm.'

Norman thought Southall was rather melodramatic considering he was just going to make enquiries about car servicing, but he nodded okay and headed for the workshop entrance.

Just inside the main door, there was a scruffy little cubicle that served as an office. No one seemed to be in attendance and Norman began to think he was wasting his time, then the sound of tuneless whistling accompanied by the clicking of a ratchet spanner led him to a small man in blue overalls working underneath a car up on a lift.

'Hi,' said Norman. 'I'm sorry to creep up on you like this, but there's no one in the office.'

The man smiled at Norman and came out from beneath the car.

'Sorry about that,' he said. 'That's the trouble with being a two-person business when your mate's on holiday. You have to be all things at once.'

'At least you're your own boss, though,' said Norman.

'Yeah. I wouldn't have it any other way.'

Norman flashed his warrant card.

'I'm DS Norman. Are you Dennis, or Swann?'

'Tony Dennis. What can I do for you?'

'The red Alfa outside. Is it yours?'

'Why, d'you want to buy it?'

'Is it for sale?'

'It will be if the owner doesn't come and collect it. She owes us nearly five hundred quid for the work my mate did on it. We're not a charity; we can't afford to work for nothing.'

'So you know whose car it is?'

'Yeah, of course I do, although I can't think of her name off the top of my head. Kim, is it? Something like that. Nice looking woman. We've worked on her car three or four times.

I told her it's a heap of crap, and she should get rid of it, but she seems to think it's the bee's knees, and we're happy to take her money if she's daft enough to keep shelling out.'

'You don't keep up with the news, then?'

'I've been away myself, mate. I only got back yesterday. Why, have I missed something?'

'I take it you keep a record of your bookings and work?'

'We keep a diary, and proper accounts, if that's what you mean. Here, I'll show you.'

The mechanic led Norman back to the tatty little office. The desk was more of a shelf, really, but it was enough to hold a large desk diary.

'Here we are,' he said. 'Are you looking for anything in particular?'

'When did the Alfa come in?'

The mechanic shuffled back through the pages until he found the right one.

'There. Monday fourteenth. I wasn't here, but I expect she dropped it off on her way home from work; that's what she usually does.'

'How did she get home?'

'She usually books a taxi.'

'And you didn't think there was anything funny about the fact she hadn't collected it?'

'As I said, I've been away. I didn't even know it was here until I came in this morning.'

'But you know she owes you money.'

'I'll be on the phone chasing her up at lunchtime, don't you worry.'

'I wouldn't bother with that if I were you.'

'What? You want me to let five hundred quid go down the Swanee? You m—'

'Kimberley can't pay you, Tony. She's dead.'

Tony sat down slowly.

'What? No! She can't be dead.'

'I'm sorry, but I'm afraid it's true.'

'Jesus! What happened to her?'

'I'm afraid it's an ongoing investigation. I can't tell you anything.'

* * *

Five minutes later Norman made his way back to join the others.

'Where the bloody hell have you been?' snapped Southall.

She took a step towards him, and Norman took a hasty step back. Catren Morgan looked distinctly embarrassed.

'It's okay,' said Norman. 'Kim dropped the car off here on the Monday she died. It had been playing up, and these two guys repaired it.'

'It's not bloody well okay,' roared Southall. 'You were supposed to suss the place out and come back to us, not carry out the whole operation on your own. What if the guys had attacked you?'

Norman had raised his hands in surrender now.

'No one was going to attack me. There was only one guy there, and he was happy to speak to me. He showed me the booking in the diary. It was all above board. He was shocked to hear she was dead.'

'It's not bloody good enough,' hissed Southall, her face reddening. 'I will not have anyone, not even you, going off-piste like that.'

'Off-piste?' said Norman, his irritation beginning to get the better of him. 'I wasn't off-piste. I made a judgement call based on thirty years of experience. I'm here because of my experience, so let me use it.'

'I'm going back to the office to look at those phone records,' said Southall.

'What do you want me to do?' asked Norman.

'Take DS Morgan with you and find Greg Lawrence. I want to hear his version of events on the night of Monday fourteenth, again, and I want to know why he didn't tell us about her car.'

* * *

177

'Jesus,' said Norman to Morgan, as Southall drove away. 'What was that all about?'

'I think she has history,' said Morgan.

'What?'

'Well, you know what you said about checking out the new boss?'

'I think I said to leave it alone.'

'Yeah, well, I wanted to know, so I did little digging over the weekend, called a couple of friends from training, you know the sort of thing.'

'And?'

'It turns out she did mess up. I told you she must have or she wouldn't have ended up down here.'

'And this makes you feel better: how?'

'Hey, look, if there's something we should know . . .'

'And? Is there something we should know?'

'Her first job as DI went tits up.'

'Is that it? Jesus, Cat, we've all had jobs go tits up.'

'But someone got shot.'

'Ah. I see. Do we know how this guy got shot?'

'With a gun, of course.'

'Yeah, I know it would have been with a gun, but what were the circumstances?'

'Oh. I'm not sure. Rumour has it the guy decided to ignore orders and do his own thing.'

'So that's hardly Southall's fault, is it?' said Norman.

'But she got the blame. They wouldn't have blamed her if she wasn't responsible.'

'Are you kidding me?' asked Norman.

'But doesn't it go with the job? If you lead any sort of operation it has to be your responsibility in the end, doesn't it?'

'Was the guy who got shot an adult?'

'Of course he was.'

'And did he disobey orders?'

'So I'm told.'

'In my book, an adult is responsible for his, or her, own actions,' said Norman. 'So, yes, as head of the operation,

Southall is going to get the blame if it goes wrong, but is she responsible for an idiot who does his own thing, and gets himself shot? I don't think so, do you? It's a flaw in the system, not in the person who ends up taking the blame.'

'Wow! Did I touch a nerve, or what?' asked Morgan.

'I know only too well how the system favours those whose face is a good fit. I also know how it works against those who don't go with the flow and speak their mind. Nathan Bain will tell you the same thing. He's a classic example. So yeah, it is a sore point with me.'

'Oh. Right. That's told me, then,' said Morgan.

'Sorry,' said Norman. 'I didn't mean to chew your head off. It's just that things aren't always what they seem. I tell you what; let's go and get a coffee on the way to Greg Lawrence's house, right?'

'Who's buying?'

Norman sighed.

'I suppose I am. Again.'

'Actually, my mum always told me not to accept things from strange men, so perhaps I'd better buy.'

'I take exception to the "strange men" comment, but I'm happy to let you buy for a change,' said Norman.

CHAPTER 32

The sun had put in a rare appearance, so Norman and Morgan walked to a bench with a view of the sea.

'Growing up in London I've always been something of a city boy,' said Norman, as he gazed out to sea. 'But I have to say, I'm enjoying the slower pace of life here, and just being near the sea is strangely therapeutic.'

He sighed happily as he breathed in the sea air, and felt the warmth of the sun on his face. Sitting alongside him, Morgan thought this must be a sign Norman was getting old.

'This might be the perfect place for an old codger like you,' she said, 'but, I could do with a bit more excitement in my life. I think London would suit me down to the ground.'

'Excitement is overrated,' said Norman, 'and trust me, you'd miss this place much more than you think. In the words of the song, "you don't know what you've got till it's gone".'

'What song's that, then?'

Norman turned to Morgan in dismay.

'Seriously? You've never heard of "Big Yellow Taxi" by Joni Mitchell?'

'Is this another old person thing?' asked Morgan. 'Because I have no idea what you're talking about.'

'If you're going to keep on about the fact I have a few years on you, I'm not going to waste my breath trying to educate you,' said Norman, and returned his gaze out to sea.

Morgan kept quiet for a minute or two, but she wasn't good at silence.

'Can you advise me on something?' she asked.

'Why would I do that?' asked Norman, still gazing at the view.

'Because you always seem to know what to do in any given situation.'

'Oh, so now my being older is a good thing?'

'You said you were here to pass on your experience.'

'That's true, and I'm happy to do it, but you should understand I don't always know what to do. Sometimes I make it up as I go along.'

'Okay, whatever. I'd still like your advice. In fact, I need your advice because I have no idea what to do.'

Now Norman turned his full attention on her.

'You're not in any trouble, are you?'

'No, it's nothing like that. It's to do with the boss.'

'What about the boss?'

'Well, you know I said I'd been doing some research?'

'And I told you it means nothing.'

'Yes, but I didn't just ask around, I googled her, too. And now I wish I hadn't.'

Norman sighed. 'Do I want to hear this?'

'Are you seriously telling me you don't already know?'

'Know what?' asked Norman.

'That she's a walking tragedy. Honestly, you couldn't make it up.'

Despite himself, Norman was now intrigued enough to want to know more.

'In what way?'

'Well, did you know that another detective killed himself over her?'

'What?'

'According to the newspapers, this detective murdered two people and then hanged himself. And he did it all to impress her!'

'That sounds like tabloid crap to me,' said Norman.

'There's more,' said Morgan. 'The story goes that she got pregnant, and this detective might have been the father.'

'What do you mean, he might have been the father? Either he was, or he wasn't.'

'Whatever, her husband left, but then got part-custody of the baby!'

'I can't imagine a guy would leave his wife, and then seek custody of the baby if someone else was the father, can you?'

'Oh. I hadn't thought of it like that,' admitted Morgan. 'What d'you think it means?'

'I think it means the detective who hanged himself wasn't the baby's father, don't you?'

'That doesn't mean there wasn't an affair, though.'

'Well, yeah,' conceded Norman, 'but is this any of our business? Anyway, people have affairs all the time. It's only tragic for the people who find out their partner has been cheating on them.'

'Oh, no, the tragic bit isn't the affair. Twelve months later, the ex-husband, his girlfriend and the baby were out in their car when they collided with an articulated lorry. They all died.'

'Holy shit!' said Norman.

He was horrified for Southall but, at the same time, in awe of the fact she had managed to keep going after such a tragedy. He gazed back out to sea, not quite sure what he should do next.

'I told you it was tragic,' said Morgan.

'Yeah, you got that right,' said Norman. 'Have you told anyone else about this?'

'No, I haven't, but the thing is, what do we do now?'

'What do you mean, what do we do now? We do nothing, of course.'

'But it must be terrible for her. I mean, how do you deal with something like that?'

'I guess she dealt with it by throwing herself into her work and studying to become a DI,' said Norman.

'But what do we say to her?'

'We don't say anything. If she has chosen to deal with it by keeping it inside, we have to respect that. As far as we're concerned, we know nothing about it.'

'But I won't be able to look her in the eye.'

'Yes, you will.'

'I won't.'

'Catren, you have to. You can't tell her you know. It's an invasion of her privacy. If she wanted us to know, she would have told us.'

'Yes, but—'

"Have you finished your coffee?' asked Norman.

'Yes.'

'Then, come on, let's go. We have to speak to Greg Lawrence.'

'Right. Okay.'

'And you don't mention any of what you told me about the boss to anyone, right?'

Morgan could see Norman was serious about this.

'Yes, of course.'

'And, as of now, you try to forget it, right?'

'I don't know if I can.'

'Well, try, Catren, for God's sake, try.'

CHAPTER 33

'Hi Greg,' said Norman, as Lawrence opened his front door. 'Glad we caught you.'

Lawrence was wearing a sweater with the sleeves pushed up to his elbows, revealing a bandage around his right forearm, just above the wrist.

'That looks nasty,' said Norman. 'What happened?'

Lawrence hastily pulled his sleeves back down.

'It's nothing. I caught my arm on a stray piece of barbed wire. I did it at work a couple of weeks ago, replacing some old fencing.'

Norman stared into Lawrence's eyes, but he didn't look away. Instead, he asked a question.

'Have you got some news about Kim?'

'I'm afraid not. But we do have another question we were hoping you could answer.'

'Sure. I said I'd help if I can.'

'We finally found Kim's car.'

'Is that a good thing? Does it help find her killer?'

'We don't know yet. We found it in a workshop owned by a couple of mechanics called Dennis & Swann. Does that mean anything to you?'

'Should it?'

'Why didn't you tell us it was in for repairs?'

'I'm sorry? In for repairs?'

'That's what the mechanic told us. According to them, Kim dropped the car off at their workshop, on the way home from work on the day she died. Did you know she was having problems with it?'

'It's not unusual. She was always having problems with it, but I didn't know it was in the workshop.'

'You didn't know?'

'Why would I?'

'Did you two tell each other anything?'

'I've already told you; that day when she got home from work, we had a big bust-up. She was too busy shouting at me to tell me something as mundane as the fact her car had broken down again.'

'But didn't you notice if the car was missing when you went out that night?' asked Morgan.

'No, I didn't,' said Lawrence, indignantly. 'She normally keeps the car in the garage. I had no reason to go in there that night, so why would I notice it wasn't there?'

'But the next morning—'

'As I told you before, the next morning, I got up late, and Kim wasn't here,' said Lawrence, belligerently. 'I looked in the garage, and the car wasn't there, so I assumed she had gone to work and left me sleeping off my hangover, right? That's why I then got Nick Rose to drive the route from here to her office, in case the car had broken down, or she had had an accident. You already know all this!'

Norman held his hands up.

'Okay, Greg, calm down. I'm sorry, we didn't mean to upset you, but we have to check these things. You can see that, can't you?'

Lawrence sighed.

'I'm sorry,' he said. 'I just wish you could get this finished. I haven't even been able to arrange Kim's funeral, yet.'

Norman patted his arm.

'I know it's difficult for you,' he said, kindly. 'I can't make any promises, but I'll see if I can hurry things along with the coroner for you.'

He turned to Morgan.

'Come on, Catren. Let's leave Greg in peace.'

* * *

'What do you make of that bandage on his arm?' asked Morgan as she put the car into gear and started driving. 'Didn't the pathologist say she had broken nails which might suggest she'd tried to fight off her attacker?'

'If you mean, do I think Kimberley scratched him before he killed her? Yes, of course, it's possible, if he's the killer.'

'You said all along it would be the husband.'

Norman sighed.

'Statistics say it's almost always someone the victim knows, and often it is the husband, but it's not a dead cert. Besides, unless there's some conclusive DNA evidence like his skin under her nails, we're going to need a bit more proof than a scratched arm.'

'You're not going to dismiss it, are you?'

'Of course not,' said Norman. 'We'll add our observation to the evidence log, bear it in mind for now, and see what else we can find to go with it.'

CHAPTER 34

Norman was pleased to see Southall was in a much better mood when they got back.

'Greg Lawrence says he didn't know her car was in for repairs,' he told her.

'Do you believe him?'

'Yeah, I think I do. One thing we did notice, though; Greg has a bandage on his right arm, just above the wrist.'

He pointed to the same place on his arm.

'Oh, really? Did he explain how it happened?'

'He says he caught it on some barbed wire while he was doing a job replacing a fence.'

'I think we should check that out at some stage. According to the financial records, he didn't exactly get many jobs. He certainly doesn't pay much into his bank account, and looking at the state of his credit record, he's not getting cash in hand either.'

'Okay, I'll get onto it,' said Norman.

'Hang on a minute; we've got something a bit more interesting to check out first.'

She handed him a sheaf of papers.

"This is a printout of Kim's phone records.'

'Jeez,' said Norman. 'She liked her phone then.'

'She was a heavy user with lots of contacts, but look at the last few calls she made on the night she died.'

Norman studied the last page.

'Do we know whose number that is?' he asked.

'It's Mike Gordon.'

'The guy who worked with her? The one she was having an affair with?'

'That's the one,' said Southall.

'Wow! That puts him well up among the frontrunners. Are we going to visit him?'

'He's volunteered to come here later this afternoon.'

Norman smiled.

'We all love a volunteer, right?'

Southall smiled.

'Look, about this morning,' she said.

'This morning?'

'I was a bit snappy.'

'Think nothing of it,' said Norman.

'No. I owe you an apology and an explanation.'

'You're the boss. You don't need to explain.'

'Yes, I do. The fact I'm the boss shouldn't mean I can bite your head off without good reason.'

'Well, in that case, you must have had a good reason, and I'm okay with that,' said Norman.

'Well, you shouldn't be. And you're going to hear it whether you like it or not.'

Norman nodded.

'Okay. I'm listening.'

'In my last position, I had an operation go wrong.'

'We've all been there,' said Norman.

'Someone got shot and ended up in hospital. I got the blame, of course, as I was leading the operation—'

'But the guy disobeyed your orders, and it was his fault he got shot,' finished Norman.

'Oh,' said Southall. 'So, you know?'

Norman nodded.

'Do they all know?' she asked.

'Actually, they told me,' he said. 'Because of the culture in this place, they all believe no one comes here unless they screwed up, so they did some research on you to see where you went wrong.'

'Shit!' said Southall. 'That's embarrassing.'

'I wouldn't worry about it,' said Norman. 'To be fair, we all used to do it when there was a new boss on the way. Didn't you? And anyway, from what I can make out they all agree with me, that the guy was a prize idiot and you weren't to blame.'

'Seriously?'

'I think you'll find you're doing great. They've never enjoyed their work so much, and that's down to you trusting them to do their jobs.'

'I don't think it's just me, but thank you for having my back, and I'm sorry about this morning.'

'No worries,' said Norman. 'It's why I'm here. And I accept your apology.'

CHAPTER 35

'Thank you for coming in to speak to us, Mr Gordon.'

'Not at all. This is a terrible thing to happen. I'm not sure how I can help, but I'll do my best.'

Southall beamed a smile at him.

'We've been asking as many people as we can for their view of Kimberley. It helps us to form a more fully rounded picture of her. So, what can you tell us about her?'

'I didn't really know her that well.'

Really?' said Southall. 'We were led to believe you and Kim often worked together doing follow-ups with new clients.'

'Ah, well, yes, that's true, but that was business.'

'And you often travelled abroad?'

Gordon shifted uncomfortably.

'Er, well, yes, that did happen now and then.'

'Now and then,' echoed Southall. 'I see. And how long would these trips usually last?'

'Usually, we'd be there and back in a day, or sometimes we'd stay over if it was far away.'

Southall opened the folder before her on the desk and sorted through the papers inside. Then she placed three sheets of paper, side by side, in front of Gordon.

'Do you know what these are, Mr Gordon?'

Gordon studied the sheets of paper and licked his lips nervously.

'Where did you get these?' he asked.

'Can you tell me what they are?' insisted Southall.

'They look like receipts,' he said.

'That's correct,' said Southall. 'They're receipts for trips you and Kimberley made abroad, together.'

'As I said, it happens.'

Norman, looked, slowly and deliberately through his notes and then looked up at Gordon.

'What you actually said, Mr Gordon, is that it happens now and then, and usually lasts for just a day.'

'Yes, that's right,' said Gordon.

'But these three receipts occurred during a period of just five weeks,' said Southall.

'We get busy sometimes.'

'And each of these trips lasted at least three nights. One of them covered a whole week.'

'I'm not sure what you're suggesting,' said Gordon.

'You told us you didn't know Kim very well,' said Southall. 'I'm suggesting that if you spent several nights on location with one other person, the chances are you would have spent a lot of time together. I don't believe you would only have discussed business.'

Gordon said nothing, his eyes flicking from Southall to Norman. Finally, he managed to summon up something approaching anger.

'I don't know what you're suggesting, Detective Inspector, but I can assure you I'm a happily married man!'

'Maybe you are,' said Norman. 'But that doesn't seem to have stopped you having an affair with Kimberley Lawrence, does it?'

'This is outrageous, I—'

'I suggest you cut the crap and stop wasting our time,' said Southall. 'You book a double room, for God's sake. D'you seriously expect us to believe nothing is going on?'

'I'll tell you something else,' added Norman. 'Everyone, where you work, knows about your lunchtime trysts.'

Gordon looked as if he had been slapped.

'Come on, Mike,' said Norman. 'Do you think the people you work with are stupid? It's an open secret. They all know. The only one who chooses not to believe it is Avril Fisher, but that's because she thought Kimberley was some sort of saint. Everyone else knows better.'

Gordon's mouth opened and closed, rather like a fish stranded out of water, but it was a good few seconds before he could speak.

'All right. So I admit I had a fling with Kim.'

'A fling? From what I heard, it lasted over two years,' said Norman.

'Look, we were both consenting adults. It was just a bit of fun. It meant nothing.'

'I've read Kim's diary, Mr Gordon,' said Southall. 'It might have meant nothing to you, but that's not how she saw it.'

Gordon didn't look convinced.

'Or should we call you, Nookie?' asked Norman.

Now Gordon knew they really had read Kim's diary.

'Okay. I admit we had an affair, and it lasted a couple of years. But I stopped it four months ago because I felt Kim was getting too involved. It started as a bit of fun, but in the end, she started suggesting she was going to leave her husband, and I should leave my wife, and we should set up home together. I didn't want that.'

'Moving on,' said Southall. 'Can I ask you where you were on the night of Monday, fourteenth October?'

'Don't you know? You seem to have been poking around in my private life—'

'Do I need to remind you this is a murder inquiry?' asked Southall.

'No, of course not. I'm sorry,' said Gordon sheepishly.

'Nothing's off the table as far as we're concerned,' added Norman. 'And the more bullshit you feed us, the worse it will get, so just answer the question.'

'I was hosting a dinner for some potential new clients at the Midway Hotel.'

'Where is that exactly.'

'It's twenty miles north of here.'

'That's convenient,' said Norman.

Gordon flashed an angry look in his direction, but Southall spoke before he could say anything.

'How long did the dinner go on for?'

'It was all over by ten thirty.'

'And did you come back home afterwards?'

'No. I knew I'd be having a few glasses of wine, so I booked a room for the night.'

'So what did you do after dinner?'

'I went to my room and went to bed.'

'And you didn't go out again?'

'No.'

Southall studied Gordon's face for a few seconds before she continued.

'Did you hear from Kimberley that night?'

'I'm sorry?'

'Kimberley. Did she contact you that night? I should warn you before you answer that we have her telephone records.'

Gordon sighed.

'Then you already know she called me.'

Southall smiled but said nothing.

'What time did she call?' asked Norman.

'If you already know, what's the point?'

'The point is we want to hear it from you,' insisted Norman.

I don't recall the exact time. It was after eleven.'

'Did she call just the once?'

No, I think it was three times in all, but as I said I don't recall the time.

'Eleven fifteen,' said Norman.

'Well, there you are; this is a waste of time if you already know it all.'

'What did she say?'

Gordon sighed again.

'That she was sorry. If we could just have one more night together, then she would accept it was all over, and never bother me again.'

'And that was it? What did you say to her?'

'I said it was too late for that, and she had to get used to the idea it was all over.'

'Then what happened?'

'She called again, and we had much the same conversation.'

'Are you sure? Only according to the records, you called her at 23.19, not the other way round.'

'If you say so.'

'It's the records that say so, Mr Gordon, not me,' said Norman. 'So why did you call her?'

'Because she had threatened to do something stupid. I didn't want that to happen.'

'Stupid? You mean like suicide?'

'Yes, but only after she had told my wife.'

'Ah, now I get it. It wasn't the suicide bit that bothered you. You didn't want Kim to speak to your wife.'

Gordon glowered at Norman but said nothing.

'Then what happened?' asked Norman.

'I put the phone down, and five minutes later she called for the final time.'

'And?'

'She said she would kill herself if I refused to see her one last time.'

'She was that desperate?' said Norman. 'Or did she threaten to speak to your wife again?'

'You can believe what you like,' said Gordon. 'That's what she said.'

'And what happened after that?'

'I went to sleep.'

'Someone threatened suicide because of you, and you managed to go off to sleep? Jeez, you must be one cold fish.'

There was a knock on the door. Southall nodded to Norman who paused the interview, then they both left the room.

194

'We'll be back shortly,' said Southall.

Judy Lane was waiting outside the door.

'Any news from Thomas?' asked Southall.

'Oh, yes,' said Lane. 'The hotel CCTV shows Mike Gordon driving out of the car park in a dark blue Jaguar at eleven thirty-five, and he didn't return until one in the morning. I checked with DVLC, and the car is registered in Gordon's name.'

'Excellent,' said Southall. 'Call Thomas back and ask him to get a copy of the CCTV and then he can come back here.'

'Those invoices Ruby Davies sent have proved to be handy,' said Norman.

'They certainly gave us a head start here,' agreed Southall.

'I've got something else, boss,' said Lane. 'Once I'd heard from Thomas I thought I'd carry on checking the CCTV footage from the town cameras. I found footage of a car cruising slowly up and down just before midnight. It was a dark blue Jaguar.'

Southall gave Lane a high five.

'Got him!' she said. 'Let's see him explain this one away.'

CHAPTER 36

'Well, now, Mr Gordon,' said Southall as they settled back into their seats.

'Is this going to take much longer?' he asked. 'When I volunteered to come in to answer a few questions, I didn't think I'd be here all night.'

Norman smiled at him.

'Yeah, well, sometimes things can take a bit longer than expected,' he said. 'And then sometimes we find we have more questions than we originally planned.'

'What the hell does that mean?'

Southall flashed a humourless smile in Gordon's direction.

'It means we have one or two more questions,' she said. 'But I'm sure you'll have a simple explanation.'

'Explanation for what?'

'For why the hotel CCTV shows you driving your car out of the car park at eleven thirty-five on the night of four-teenth October. I could have sworn you said you didn't go out once you'd gone to your room.'

'It'll be right there on the recording,' said Norman, 'and I even made a note of it here.'

He pointed to his notebook in case Gordon should be in any doubt.

'There must be some mistake.'

'You think?' asked Southall. 'Is it also a mistake that we found CCTV footage of your car cruising around Llangwelli later that same night? Perhaps you'd like to explain.'

Gordon licked his lips, and then licked them again, but said nothing.

'Let me tell you what we think happened, and then you tell me if we got it right,' said Southall. 'We think you got so scared that Kimberley might speak to your wife that you decided you had to make sure she couldn't. We think that last call you made to her was to tell her you were going to come and collect her. She would have thought you were going to take her back to the hotel, but you didn't, did you? You made sure she could never speak to your wife, or anyone else.'

'What?' said Gordon in disbelief. 'You think I killed her? That's ridiculous.'

'You've just seen all the evidence,' suggested Norman. 'Don't you think it all adds up?'

'Yes, I mean no. You've got it all wrong. That's not what happened.'

'Okay, so tell us, what did happen?'

'The last time Kimberley called me she begged and begged for us have one last night together, and finally, I agreed.'

'But your hotel was twenty miles away, and she had no car,' said Norman.

'That's right, so I offered to drive over and collect her.'

'I thought you booked a hotel room because you knew you'd be drinking?' asked Norman.

'Yes, I did, but in the end, I only had one or two glasses of wine so I thought I'd be all right.'

Southall couldn't help but smile.

'So, you want us to believe that having just told Kim it's all over and that she's wasting her time, five minutes later you're arranging to get out of bed and drive twenty miles to pick her up?'

'Why is that so hard to believe?'

'Actually, you're right,' said Norman, sarcastically, 'it's quite easy to believe when we remember she had threatened to tell your wife about the affair, and you needed to make sure she didn't.'

'Now you're just trying to make your theory fit my story,' said Gordon, angrily.

'No,' said Southall. 'We're still waiting for you to tell us what actually happened.'

'I drove over to Llangwelli, went to the pub where she said she would meet me, and she wasn't there. The reason you have CCTV footage of me driving around the town is that I was looking for her.'

'And that's it?'

'Yes. I drove around for about half an hour, but I couldn't find her anywhere, so I went back to the hotel.'

'Can anyone corroborate this story?' asked Southall.

'I hardly think so. I was on my own. I thought you said you had CCTV footage.'

'Yes, we have,' said Norman, 'but we don't have that many cameras we can cover every inch of town for every second you were there. Did anyone see you?'

'If they did, I didn't see them.'

'What time did you get back to the hotel?'

'I don't know, probably about one a.m.'

Southall and Norman exchanged a look.

'And that's it?' asked Southall. 'Didn't you wonder what had happened to Kim?'

'Of course I did.'

'But you didn't think to find out where she got to?' asked Norman. 'If that were me, wasting my time, and losing my precious sleep, I would have wanted to know where the hell she had got to!'

'I was hardly going to call her home, at one a.m., was I?'

'Why would you? Your favourite form of communication with her was via her mobile phone, yet we can see from the records that you didn't call it again after that night. Not once.'

'Why would I? I already told you: the affair was over. I didn't want to encourage her to think otherwise.'

'Or maybe you knew she wouldn't answer, on account of the fact she was dead!'

Gordon banged his fist on the table.

'Right! That's it! I've had enough. I came in here of my own free will to try and help, and all you've done is try to get me to confess to a murder I didn't commit. I'm not saying another word until my solicitor is here. And that's another thing; why wasn't I given a chance to call him?'

'You volunteered to come in, Mr Gordon. You could have brought a solicitor with you, but you chose not to.'

'So, does that mean I'm free to go?'

'You can go home,' said Southall, 'but don't even think about going far, or leaving the country.'

'Do you think I'm stupid?' asked Gordon. 'You already think I'm guilty, so running away will only make me look even more so. I'm not going to give you that satisfaction. I'm innocent, whatever you might think.'

CHAPTER 37

It was eight thirty p.m. by the time Gordon left.

'There is a way we can check out his story, you know,' said Southall as they walked back to the incident room.

'There is?'

'That posh Jaguar of his must have cost a fortune. A fancy car like that comes fitted with telematics.'

'You'll have to forgive me if I'm a little rusty on some of the latest technology,' said Norman. 'We didn't have much call for it where I've been working.'

'You know how you can track a mobile phone from mast to mast? Well, telematics uses the same sort of principle. It's like having a SIM card built into the car, but instead of telephone masts, it uses GPS to track and record the car's movements. The idea is that the information can be used to find a car if it's stolen, but that same information can also show us a vehicle's movements at a given time.'

'No kidding?' said Norman. 'I didn't realise it was that sophisticated.'

'Depending on the specifics of the system, it can even tell you if any of the doors opened. It should show us where Gordon picked up Kim, and it might even tell us if she opened the passenger door or one of the back ones.'

'Wow! That sort of evidence would be pretty hard to argue with.'

'What you might call an open and shut case,' said Southall.

Norman gave her an approving look, and she smiled back.

'As I'm the boss, I'm allowed to use the pun,' she said.

'It seems only right,' agreed Norman. 'Now, much as I hate to admit it, I've never had to access this information before, so—'

'That's okay. If Region has always handled the big cases, I don't suppose anyone here has ever done it either. Leave it to me. I'll send in a request tonight, and then we can set up a proper procedure that will allow anyone to do it next time.'

'That sounds like a plan,' said Norman, as he pushed the doors open for her.

He was surprised to find Thomas still at his desk and headed across to speak to him as Southall made her way to her office.

'Why are you still here, Dylan? You know what the boss said about making sure you get plenty of rest. Why haven't you gone home?'

'Well, I would have gone by now,' said Thomas, 'but I've got this report to finish.'

'What report?'

'Well, I know you probably think I've been out every day wasting time, but I believe I may have found the spot where the body was dumped.'

'Really? Wow, the boss is going to love you if you have. Can you show me on the map?'

Thomas walked across to the map, studied it for a second, and then pointed to a spot by the river.

'Just there,' he said. 'It's a small clearing by the riverbank, but it would be a perfect spot. It's down a track, so away from the road. No one passing would see a car down there. The grass is pretty long, but I'm sure a vehicle has been down there at some stage.'

'Have you informed forensics?'

'Er, no, I only got back five minutes ago, but I have cordoned off the area with police tape.'

'Okay, so what do you think we should do now?'

'Leave it until morning?'

'What if the guy who dumped the body drives past and sees your tape?'

'Ah, I see what you mean. He could go down there and mess up the scene, right?'

'There could be any number of possibilities,' said Norman. 'Better to be safe than sorry, right?'

'Should I call them, now?'

'You've got it,' said Norman.

'Do you want me to go out there and meet them?'

Norman looked at his watch.

'Can you handle it on your own?'

Thomas seemed to stand taller.

'Sure I can, Sarge.'

'Okay, call them, and off you go,' said Norman. 'I'll drive out there when I finish here to see how you're getting on.'

Beaming happily, Thomas hurried back to his desk and reached for the phone.

* * *

'Right, that's all done,' said Southall, twenty minutes later. 'I'm going home. Are you going to be here much longer?'

'I think I'm about done,' said Norman. 'I just have to go out and check up on Thomas.'

'Why, what's he done?'

'He thinks he might have found the site where the body was dumped.'

'Excellent! Can you show me where?'

He led her across to the map and pointed out the site.

'It's right by the river, down a lane. It would be out of sight of the road. Thomas is out there now waiting for SOCOs to arrive.'

'They're going to love him. It's pitch dark and pouring with rain.'

'Oh, crap, is it? I didn't realise.'

'And, of course, the site's two weeks old. They will be very lucky to find any evidence now. I suspect they'll take one look at the site and suggest they come back in the morning.'

'Yeah, you're probably right,' said Norman. 'It was my idea to get them out there tonight, but I didn't know it was raining.'

'I'd go home,' she said. 'The site will still be there in the morning.'

'I can't. I told Thomas I'd go out there when I left here, and see how he's doing.'

'Rather you than me,' said Southall. 'I hope you have an umbrella.'

CHAPTER 38

Norman had genuinely been unaware it was raining, but as he walked out to his car, he could see Southall hadn't been joking. It wasn't the usual heavy rain, but the sort of slow, persistent stuff that creeps up on you without you realising how wet you're getting. And then, suddenly, you're soaked.

It was pitch dark with no chance of the moon breaking through. Norman thought, knowing his luck, there probably wouldn't be a street light within miles of the site, either.

'Bollocks,' he muttered as he started his car. 'Just what we need.'

It took barely ten minutes to reach the location, and Norman said a silent thank you to his satnav. Not knowing the area, he would almost certainly have been driving around for hours without it. A white van and a solitary patrol car parked at the side of the road were a sure sign that he had found the correct place.

It was only when he climbed from his car and opened the boot that he realised his coat was still at home drying from the last soaking. He still hadn't got round to buying a pair of wellington boots, and he now decided, if he was going to live here, they were a necessity he couldn't do without. And, of course, as if to round things off, the battery in his torch was dead.

Muttering numerous curses against the Welsh rain, he headed down the grassy path towards a dim light that appeared to be coming from a pop-up tent that had been erected by the forensic guys. He found Thomas huddling under the tent.

'Have you got a signal on that thing?' asked Norman.

'Yeah, and it's quite a good one, considering we're so far off the beaten track.'

'Where is everyone?' asked Norman.

Thomas pointed down a grassy path.

'Down there.'

'So why are you up here playing on your phone?'

'They're just securing the site before calling it a day. They say it's too dark, the rain's not helping, and stumbling about in the dark could destroy any evidence that is out here.'

'Do they think it's the site?'

'They won't commit, but they did admit they think it's worth checking out more thoroughly. On the downside, they're saying it's already been two weeks since the murder, and we've had plenty of heavy rain in that time, so the chances are they won't find much.'

'What d'you think?' asked Norman.

'About working here tonight? I wouldn't want to work out in this weather. And no one's likely to come out here tonight, are they? They said they'd cordon the area off properly, and then they're going home. The night shift guys have agreed to drive past a couple of times.'

Norman looked at the foul weather and thought Thomas was right. No one in their right mind would come out here tonight.

'You've lived here all your life, right?' asked Norman.

'Not right here, but in this part of Wales, yeah.'

'Does it always rain like this?'

Thomas laughed.

'No, Sarge, not always like this. Mostly it pisses down.'

'What, all year round?'

'It's worse this time of year, but yeah, it rains a lot, that's why everything is so green.'

'No shit,' said Norman.

'You get used to it.'

'That's what Catren said. I suppose it's easier when you've had over twenty years to get used to it.'

'It's not so bad. At least it doesn't get cold.'

Norman thought he could quite happily accept some severe cold spells if it meant he didn't have to get soaked all the time.

'How are you getting back?' he asked.

'Patrol car. They're going to give me a lift back when they've finished.'

'Go and tell them you've got a lift. I'll take you. There's no point in standing out here for nothing.'

CHAPTER 39

'What do we do now?' asked Norman. 'I suppose we just need the telematics to prove Gordon's car was here on the night Kim died, and it's a wrap.'

'I was thinking about that at home last night. Gordon was adamant he was innocent and very confident we wouldn't be able to prove otherwise,' said Southall.

'You mean you think he's telling the truth?'

'I'm sure some of the things he's told us aren't true. For instance, does what we've heard about Kim make you think she's the type to beg? From what I can make out, it's more the other way around. She's the sort of woman certain men would beg to sleep with.'

'Yeah, I must admit I found it hard to believe she would be begging Gordon to sleep with her one last time, but to be fair we've never met her, so maybe we're wrong about that.'

'So, hold that thought, and ask yourself: what if he is telling the truth? I mean we have no concrete evidence to prove he's not, do we? And he admits he left the hotel to come looking for her. Would he have done that if he had killed her?'

'But he couldn't deny it, could he?' said Norman. 'We had the CCTV footage to prove it.'

Southall sighed.

'It's just that it all feels a bit too convenient, a bit too easy. Does that make sense?'

'I think you're trying to say your instincts are telling you it's not him,' said Norman. 'Am I right?'

'Yes, I suppose so.'

'I've always been one to take notice of my hunches,' said Norman. 'If it's worrying you that much I think we should assume it's right. So, can I make a suggestion?'

'Yes, please, go ahead.'

'We have to wait for the telematics, right? And we know they will be enough to show us if he's telling the truth, or not.'

'Right so far,' said Southall.

'And how long will we have to wait?'

'I don't know. Superintendent Bain is putting as much pressure on as he can, to support us. He's optimistic we won't have to wait too long.'

'So, let's assume we have to wait a couple of days and then, when they arrive, they prove we're wrong. If we just wait, we'll have wasted those two days, right? And all the time those idiots at Region are watching and waiting, for us to mess up.'

'Oh yes, there's nothing they would like better.'

'Also, I might be wrong, but I reckon waiting around isn't really in your DNA, is it? I think it will drive you crazy.'

'I don't know what you mean,' said Southall, with a cheeky grin.

'Yeah, I thought so,' said Norman. 'So, why don't we cover our backs, assume Gordon is innocent, and carry on looking elsewhere while we wait?'

'Good thinking,' said Southall. 'To be honest, I haven't ruled out Greg Lawrence yet.'

'We've never pressed him about that injury to his arm, have we?' said Norman. 'And we never actually did a proper search of his house.'

'Good thinking, Norm,' said Southall. 'Those are a couple of loose ends we can tie up while we're waiting.'

As if on cue, the phone began to ring on Norman's desk.

'DS Norman.'

'Sarge? It's Thomas.'

'Hi Dylan, what can I do for you?'

'I'm out here with the SOCOs. They reckon this is probably the right place.'

'Brilliant! I'll tell the boss. I expect she'll want to come out there and take a look. Well done.'

He rushed across to Southall's office.

'Are you busy?' he asked.

She surveyed the growing pile of paperwork on her desk.

'No more than usual.'

'It looks like Dylan has found the place where the body was dumped. Do you want to come and take a look?'

'Now?'

'I can handle it myself if you're busy.'

'I wouldn't miss it for the world,' she said. 'I'll be right there.'

* * *

Norman parked his car as close as he could get to the scene. Then he led Southall down the grassy lane which was becoming muddy due to the rain and the amount of foot traffic up and down it during the last few hours. Even so, it was clear from two wheel tracks that a vehicle had been down the path at some time.

Southall stopped and studied the tracks for a moment.

'They look too smooth to get tyre tread patterns,' said Norman. 'The wheels must have been spinning in this mud. Mind you, with the rain they get here I'm not surprised.'

'Yes, you'd need a four-wheel drive to get down here, and back out again,' said Southall.

'Yeah, for sure,' agreed Norman. 'A Jag just like Gordon's would be perfect for the job.'

They followed the track around a bend, and suddenly they were alongside the river. Norman stopped and looked back along the lane.

'You'd never be seen from the road,' he said.

Southall followed his gaze.

'You're right. You couldn't find this place by accident, could you? You would have to know it was here.'

Thomas had seen them coming, and hurried over to speak to them.

'Good morning, Dylan,' said Southall. 'How on earth did you find this place?'

'I tried all the tourist spots, but none of them seemed right somehow. Most of them are too close to the road, or not close enough to the river. Then I had the idea of asking a guy I know who's a keen fisherman. I told him what I was looking for, and he suggested I come here.'

'Initiative, I like that. Good work, Dylan,' said Southall. 'Do a lot of people come here?'

'I don't think so. My friend reckons the fishing community keep it to themselves, so tourists don't spoil it for them.'

'So, in your opinion, unless someone stumbled across it by chance, they would need to be a local, and a keen angler to know it was here?' asked Southall, thoughtfully.

'I'd say so,' said Thomas.

'Good. That's very helpful. Have they found anything?'

'They're not optimistic,' said Thomas. 'They were hoping they might get some tyre marks, but what with the grass growing back through, and then the rain, there's nothing left that's usable. They're searching around hoping to find something that might help us.'

There was a shout from away to their left, and about fifty yards away, one of the SOCO team raised his hand. A photographer rushed over to record his find.

Five minutes later the SOCO made his way back through the undergrowth to bring his find over to show them.

'It looks like a red shoe,' said Norman, as the man approached.

'With a four-inch heel?' asked Southall.

'It looks that way,' said Norman.

The technician had reached them now, and he held up the shoe.

'Is it a size four?' asked Southall.

The technician nodded.

'Size four, right foot.'

'Well done,' said Southall. 'Our victim was wearing a pair of shoes identical to that the night she died.'

'We'll keep looking for the other one,' said the technician.

'Thank you,' said Southall. 'I know you'll do your best.' She turned to Thomas.

'Well done, Dylan. I think we can assume this is where Kim's body entered the river, and it may well be where she was attacked. As you did all the legwork to find the site, I'd like you to stay with these guys, if that's okay.'

'No problem, boss. I'm happy to do that for you.'

'You see,' said Norman, as he and Southall walked back up the track towards their car. 'I told you they were happy with the way you trust them to do their jobs. Thomas is as happy as Larry. I bet he's never been praised like that before.'

'I'm always happy to give praise where it's due. It's only right.'

'Oh, I agree,' said Norman. 'But not everyone thinks like that. I think it's probably easier to give praise to others when you're confident in yourself, and your ability.'

Southall accepted the compliment without comment. She'd had her doubts about Norman at the beginning, but she thought he was proving to be a great asset to the team. She certainly found him a reassuring presence.

* * *

When Southall got back to the incident room, Judy Lane had some excellent news for her.

'The telematics for Mike Gordon's car has just come in by email,' she said.

'Already?' said Southall. 'Superintendent Bain must have more influence than I thought.'

'Shall I print them off?'

'Oh, yes, please. This could solve the case for us.'

By the time the printer had finished, Norman had joined them. Lane spread the print-out on a desk, and they huddled around it.

'This is a map of the area on the night in question,' she explained. 'The markers show where the car was, and at what time.'

'Wow! This is so cool,' said Norman. 'We can see exactly where Gordon was for the whole hour.'

Southall wasn't quite so happy with the result.

'But, according to this, he didn't stop anywhere. How could Kimberley have got into the car if he didn't stop? Are we saying she dived through a window as he passed by?'

In his excitement, Norman had missed Southall's meaning.

'Look, he even passed the site Dylan identified, twice,' he said.

'Yes, Norm, he passed the site, but he didn't go to it, did he? And he didn't stop.'

'Crap! There must be some mistake,' said Norman, the disappointment evident in his voice.

'The mistake is ours for thinking Gordon was lying,' said Southall. 'This proves he did exactly what he said, and drove around for the best part of an hour before going back to his hotel.'

'Bugger!' said Norman. 'I was convinced he wasn't telling the truth.'

'He was lying about something, for sure,' said Southall, 'but it wasn't about cruising around for an hour without finding Kimberley.'

She sighed.

'Oh well, back to the drawing board. We're not going to be beaten that easily.'

CHAPTER 40

Once again, it was Nick Rose who opened Greg Lawrence's front door, and once again, his face showed just how unhappy he was to see them.

'Unless you've you come to tell Greg he can finally bury his wife I can't see why you're bothering him, yet again.'

Southall offered a fake smile.

'And good morning to you, Mr Rose,' she said. 'Is Mr Lawrence here?'

'Yes, he is, but he doesn't want to speak to you.'

Southall brandished a search warrant.

'That's a pity, but we don't need to speak to him to carry out a search.'

'What? This is crazy. The guy's still in mourning. You've no right to carry out this campaign of persecution.'

'Campaign of persecution,' echoed Norman, thoughtfully. 'That's very eloquently put, but you're wasting your breath; we're going to search the house whatever you think.'

Rose seemed to puff himself up with anger and made sure he filled the doorway as best he could. Then he began to speak.

'This is an outrage, I—'

'I haven't got time for this bullshit,' said Southall loudly. 'Sergeant Norman, please explain the situation to Mr Rose; he seems to have a problem understanding how this works.'

'It's like this, Mr Rose,' said Norman. 'We could have brought a small army of police officers to search the house, but out of consideration for Mr Lawrence there are just the three of us detectives, and a uniformed PC, as you can see. Now, you can step out of the way and let us in, or we can call the troops in and have you arrested. It's your choice.'

'But this is so—'

'Unfair?' asked Norman. 'Yeah, perhaps it is, but so was what happened to Kimberley. Now, we feel everyone should be trying to find out who was responsible, don't you?'

'Well, yes, of course, but we all know Greg's not responsible.'

'But do we?' asked Norman. 'The only alibi he has is your claim that you left him here at eleven p.m., and as you know, we have reason to doubt that.'

'I've already explained why I said that.'

'I'm sure you consider yourself a fine, upstanding member of the public, who always does the right thing,' said Norman. 'That would certainly explain your self-righteous attitude, but I'm afraid once doubts surface about what someone has told us, we have to consider if even one word of it was true.'

'But of course, the rest of it was true. I wouldn't lie to the police.'

Norman spread his arms and shrugged his shoulders.

'And yet you did.'

The attitude Nick Rose had been displaying seemed to seep from him like a deflating balloon, and suddenly he wasn't quite so sure of himself.

'So, how about you get out of the way and let us get on with our work?' suggested Norman.

Unseen by everyone, Greg Lawrence had come to the door, behind Rose.

'What's going on?' he asked.

214

Rose stepped aside so he could see.

'It's the police. They want to search the house.'

'Well, let them in,' said Lawrence.

He stepped forward and addressed Southall.

'What are you looking for? Perhaps I can help.'

'That's okay, Mr Lawrence. I'm afraid in this instance we must ask you to leave it to us.'

'Oh, right. Okay. Do I have to leave the house, or can I just carry on having my breakfast in the kitchen?'

'The kitchen will be fine, but I must ask you to stay there. PC Brunswick will accompany you,' said Southall.

'Well, I'll let you carry on, then.'

'Are you sure about this, Greg?' asked Rose doubtfully.

'Why not? I've got nothing to hide, and if it helps them find out who killed Kim, I'm all for it.'

'Yes, but—'

Lawrence ignored Rose's protest, turned on his heel and headed back to his breakfast.

'Mr Rose. If you wouldn't mind letting PC Brunswick through,' said Southall, pointedly.

Rose sighed and stepped aside to let the PC into the house.

'I'm sure you're wasting your time,' he said.

'Yes, well, it's our time, and I decide how we use it,' said Southall, then she turned to Norman and Morgan.

'Right, come on, then, let's get started.'

Rose followed them inside, found his jacket, made his excuses, and left.

* * *

It was Catren Morgan, poking around in the garage, who made the discovery. Realising what she had found she made her way back into the house. She found Southall in the lounge.

'Boss? I think you'd better come and see this.'

Southall followed Morgan back out to the garage where Morgan pointed to three carrier bags filled with clothes. With her gloved hand, she lifted the top layer from one of the bags.

There was a sharp intake of breath from Southall.

'Oh, my, Catren. I didn't expect us to find that,' she said.

Carefully Morgan lifted the red shoe from the bag and held it aloft.

'Would you agree that's a four-inch heel?' asked Southall.

'I would,' said Morgan. 'And from the muddy state of it, I would even go so far as to say it's the left shoe that goes with the right one found earlier.'

'It looks like a match to me,' said Norman, who had come to see what Morgan had found.

'We'll have to get forensics to see if the mud matches, but I think we're all agreed there's not much doubt,' said Southall. 'Let's go and see if Greg can explain how it got here.'

Lawrence had spread a newspaper across the kitchen table to read. He didn't look up when Southall marched in, followed by Norman and Morgan.

'Mr Lawrence,' said Southall. 'Do you normally keep carrier bags full of clothes in your garage?'

'That'll be Kim,' he said. 'She buys so many clothes she . . .' his voice faded, and he stopped speaking for a moment. 'Sorry. I should say she used to buy so many clothes she had to keep making room for them. About once a month she would take the stuff she threw out to the charity shop in town.'

'Did she ever throw shoes out?'

'I expect so. She had a thing about buying shoes. I could never understand it myself. I mean, how many pairs of shoes does one woman need? But you've seen her bedroom, and the overflow shoe store in the smaller spare room.'

'We found this in one of the bags out there.'

Southall held the red shoe up for Lawrence to see. If they had expected him to be shocked he'd been found out, he didn't show it.

'One of many I expect,' he said and returned to his newspaper.

'Your wife was wearing a pair of shoes just like this on the night she died.'

'I expect she had more than one pair like that. She even bought two pairs of identical boots once.'

'But this isn't a pair. It's just a left shoe.'

Now Lawrence looked up, confused.

'I'm sorry, I don't see what you're getting at.'

Southall looked at Norman and nodded her head.

'We believe we have found the site where your wife was attacked,' said Norman. 'Earlier this morning a search of that site revealed a right shoe just like this one. So, unless we can find a shoe to match this one here in this house, we're inclined to believe this one goes with the one we found earlier.'

Lawrence looked even more confused.

'Kim was wearing that shoe when she died?'

'That's what we think,' said Norman.

'But how could it be here, if she was wearing it when she died?'

'We were rather hoping you could tell us that,' said Southall.

'Me? How would I know?'

They were all staring at him now, but no one answered the question. He stared back for what seemed like an age and then finally, he realised what they were implying. Panic flashed across his face.

'Now, wait a minute,' he stuttered. 'You can't think I had anything to do with Kim's death. I mean, yes, she was far from perfect, and she could be a bitch when she wanted to be, but I loved her. I wouldn't hurt her. Why do you think I put up with the affairs all this time?'

'I think you put up with the affairs because without her you would have had nothing, Greg. We've been through your finances. You were as good as broke and have been for years. It was Kim who brought the money in, wasn't it?' said Southall.

'But eventually, even you couldn't take it any longer,' continued Norman. 'We don't know what triggered it, probably the bust-up you had that night, but whatever, it was enough to push you over the edge.'

'No!' shouted Lawrence. 'That's not true. I didn't see her after she went out that night. I went around to Nick's, got hammered, and then came home. I don't remember anything more until I woke up the next morning. You have to believe me!'

'The thing is we don't "have to believe" anything,' said Norman. 'We work with evidence, and right now, the evidence seems to be pointing at you.'

'I think we should continue this interview down at the station,' said Southall. 'Catren, can you and PC Brunswick take Mr Lawrence down to the police station, and book him in. In the meantime, we'll get some more bodies down here and do a thorough search of the house and garden.'

Brunswick reached for Lawrence and helped him to his feet.

'This can't be happening,' said Lawrence. 'You're wasting your time. I can't tell you something I know nothing about.'

'Yes, you're very good at that,' said Southall. 'You still haven't told us where and when you hurt your arm. Just saying, "I caught it on some barbed wire," isn't good enough. You might want to think about that while you're waiting down at the station.'

* * *

Within half an hour there were two patrol cars and a SOCO van parked outside Greg Lawrence's house. Such was the commotion that several neighbours came out to see what was going on.

While Southall supervised the search inside the house, Norman and Thomas were going from house to house around the dozen properties in the vicinity to see if anyone could recall seeing Greg Lawrence on the night Kim died.

It proved to be a fruitless quest. It seemed it was so quiet around here that no one ever saw or heard anything, and Norman wondered if anyone would notice if a bomb went off nearby.

The only exciting moment occurred when one elderly gent opened his door and allowed his dog to escape. The dog had snapped at Thomas when he extended a hand to stroke it, but the young detective had impressed Norman with the speed of his reflexes, and the dog missed its intended target by some distance. The old man had quickly forced his dog back inside the house and slammed the door without answering any of their questions.

Then, after Thomas had knocked again, the man seemed to freeze upon reopening the door. Norman had briefly thought the man was having some kind of seizure, but after a short coughing fit, he seemed to recover sufficiently to deny everything and then hastily close the door again.

'I didn't think, "did you see anything?" qualified as an accusation that needed such a vehement denial,' said Thomas, as they walked away from the house.

'It did seem a little unnecessary,' said Norman. 'Maybe he was feeling guilty about the dog trying to eat one of your fingers.'

'Yeah, he was a snappy bugger, that dog,' agreed Thomas. 'It's a good job I had my wits about me.'

CHAPTER 41

'Are you sure you don't want a solicitor, Greg?' asked Southall.

'I don't need a solicitor.'

'Okay, if you insist. I just want to make sure you understand your rights.'

'Yes, I understand, but I haven't done anything wrong, so I don't need one.'

'How do you explain the red shoe we found in your house, Greg?'

'I can't explain it.'

'That's not good enough, I'm afraid. As I said before, it's one of the shoes Kim was wearing the night she died. We found the other shoe two miles away, so it's not looking good, is it?'

'I honestly have no idea how it got there.'

Southall stared at Lawrence but, to her surprise, he didn't flinch and stared right back at her.

'Okay,' she said after a few seconds. 'We'll come back to the shoe. Let's start with the night Kim disappeared.'

Lawrence sighed.

'What, again?'

'Yes, again. And we'll keep going over it until I think you're telling the truth. Now, you said you were at Nick Rose's house playing snooker. Is that right?'

'Yes, that's right.'

'Are you sure? The thing is Alan Evans told us Nick wouldn't let you play because you were so drunk he thought you might damage his table.'

'Okay. If you want to be pedantic, I didn't actually play snooker that night. But I was there.'

'I have to be pedantic, Greg, because it's the little details that can be so important.'

'Whatever,' said Lawrence, sullenly.

'So, you admit you were already drunk by the time you got to Nick Rose's house?'

'Yes, I suppose I must have been.'

'You suppose. Either you were, or you weren't?'

'All right, I admit it. I was drunk. Okay?'

'Can you remember what time you went home?'

'I'm not sure. I think Alan left at about half past ten. Nick wouldn't let me play snooker, so I went home.'

'And how did you get home?'

'Nick says he took me home in his car.'

'I'm not interested in what Nick says. I want to hear it from you. Tell me how you got home.'

'I don't know. If Nick says he took me, I would think he took me, wouldn't you?'

'Hmm. The thing is, Nick also says Alan Evans helped to take you home, and we know that's not true. Why d'you think he would lie about that?'

'I have no idea.'

'Okay, we can come back to that,' said Southall, calmly. 'Now, what about that arm of yours? You told us you caught it on some barbed wire on a job. Which job was that?'

'I can't recall. I do a lot of jobs.'

Southall smiled.

'Now, we both know that's not true,' she said. 'In fact, we're pretty sure you haven't done a job in weeks that would involve fencing. Are you suggesting that wound on your arm is weeks old?'

Lawrence looked pleased with himself.

'I'm not averse to working for cash, you know. I don't have to record that.'

'So, who did you do cash work for?'

'I can't tell you that!'

'You can't tell me, because it's not true, is it, Greg?'

Lawrence licked his lips but said nothing.

'You're a terrible liar, Greg. You haven't done any cash work recently, have you? Come on, Greg. Why don't you tell us the truth? How did you hurt your arm?'

'I don't know how it happened, honestly. When I woke up the next morning, it was like this, all bandaged up.'

'Are you telling me you've not even changed the bandage?' asked Southall. 'You're kidding, right?'

'I don't know what you mean.'

'Well, let's put it this way. If that hasn't healed by now, it'll be seriously infected.'

Lawrence played the silent card again. He had his arms folded on the table before him.

'I think that must be healed by now. Why don't you take that bandage off and show us?'

'You can't make me do that.'

'Why don't I call a doctor, and have that dressing changed? Just to show how caring we are.'

'Nick said you'd be like this, and not believe anything I say.'

'Did he tell you that if you stop telling lies, I might be more inclined to believe you?'

'I'm not telling lies.'

'Oh, really? So, what did Nick tell you to say about that arm of yours?'

'He said if I told you it happened the night Kim died you'd say it proved I killed her.'

'Does Nick run your life for you?'

'Don't be bloody stupid, of course he doesn't.'

'He seems to be telling you what to do all the time.'

'He's a mate. He looks out for me, that's all.'

'And you think his suggestion that you lie to us is a good idea, do you?'

'I didn't kill Kim.'

'Okay, in that case, you've got nothing to lose by telling us the truth, have you?'

Southall sat back and waited for Greg Lawrence to speak, but he didn't seem to be able to decide what to say.

'Look at it from our point of view,' said Norman. 'We know whoever did it isn't going to put their hand up and confess, so anyone telling lies is going to be of interest. We also know from statistics that killers often know their victims well. So, from where I'm sitting, right now, you tick both those boxes.'

It was clear this was something Lawrence hadn't considered.

'It's not rocket science,' said Norman. 'You keep on lying, what else are we supposed to think?'

'If you tell us what happened to your arm, and we can confirm it, we might be able to prove you didn't kill Kim,' added Southall.

'But I honestly don't know how it happened. I told you, I was drunk.'

'You can remember a detail like leaving Nick Rose's house just after ten thirty, but you can't remember injuring your arm? I find that hard to believe,' said Southall.

'I don't remember leaving Nick's at ten thirty. I know I left then because he told me.'

'And he told you he took you home in his car?'

'Yes.'

'But he didn't tell you how you injured your arm?'

'No, he didn't.'

'Don't you find that strange, Greg? You say you woke up the next morning and your arm was bandaged. Now, I would assume Nick was the person who bandaged the arm so in that case he would have witnessed the accident, and yet he's never mentioned it.'

Lawrence was confused.

'And you're sure it's a good idea to follow Nick's advice, are you?' said Southall. 'I think you need a little time to yourself so you can decide if this bullshit strategy is the right one for you.'

'You mean, I can go?'

'No, I mean you can spend some time in a cell. We'll resume this interview later.'

CHAPTER 42

'I'm beginning to think Nick Rose is up to his neck in this,' said Southall, when Norman got back to the incident room.

'He does seem to be pulling a lot of strings in the background, doesn't he?' said Norman.

'His alibi is non-existent now,' said Southall. 'Alan Evans wasn't there, and now we know Greg Lawrence wasn't either. That means Rose was on his own from about half ten, so he had plenty of time to find Kim and murder her.'

'D'you think he's been advising Greg to lie to draw our attention to him?'

'It's worked so far. He created a little confusion by telling his lies, supposedly to protect Greg, but subtly pointing us towards him. Then he let slip about the time Greg said he'd happily murder Kim. In the meantime, he's persuaded Greg to lie to us, which makes him look even more suspicious.'

'What about the shoe?'

'If he had planned to murder Kim, perhaps it was always part of the plan to plant some incriminating evidence at Greg's house. He was quick to rush to Greg's side when we told him Kim was dead. And he's been at the house every time we've been there. He could easily have planted the shoe for us to find.'

'Do you want to bring him in?'

'Not yet. Once he knows we've let Lawrence go, I'm sure he'll expect us to turn up again, and I'm just as sure he's got plenty of answers lined up. This time I want to know the answers before we ask the questions.'

'It sounds like you have a plan.'

'Remember that fancy car outside Rose's house?'

'The Maserati?'

'That's the one. A fancy car like that has telematics, just like Mike Gordon's Jaguar. I've put in a request, and Superintendent Bain has promised to lean even harder than he did last time. With any luck, we'll have some results later today.'

Norman's phone began to ring.

'Is that DS Norman?'

'Yeah, that's me. Who wants to know?'

'There's a Mr Watkins down here at the front desk. He wants to speak to you.'

'What does he want?'

'He won't tell me. He says it's important, but he'll only speak to you.'

'Really? Okay, tell him to take a seat. I'll be down there in a couple of minutes.'

* * *

As soon as Norman saw the man, he recognised him and was relieved to see he didn't have his snappy dog with him.

'Mr Watkins? I'm DS Norman.'

'You came to my house this afternoon with a young colleague. I'm afraid my dog snapped at him. Would you pass on my apologies?'

'Ah, yes, I remember,' said Norman. 'But you needn't have come down here to apologise. There was no harm done. He probably shouldn't have stuck his hand out like that. I expect the dog wasn't expecting it.'

'That's only part of the reason I'm here,' said Watkins.

'Okay. So, what can I do for you?'

'Is there somewhere we can talk?'

'Sure,' said Norman. 'Follow me. We can use one of the interview rooms.'

Watkins followed Norman down a corridor and into an empty interview room. Norman invited him to sit down, and then sat opposite him.

'Now, Mr Watkins. What can I do for you?'

'You won't take my dog away, will you? He's all the company I have since my wife passed away. I'd be lost without him.'

'Take him away? Why would we do that? Has he attacked someone?'

'It wasn't the dog's fault. If he hadn't been drunk, it would never have happened.'

Norman was confused.

'Your dog was drunk?'

'No, not the dog. That man you arrested, Greg Lawrence. He's the drunk one. I was walking the dog, and it was dark. Lawrence appeared from nowhere, stumbling all over the place. He startled the dog and then, when he fell over, I think the dog thought he was attacking me, and it bit him. If he's made a complaint, he's wrong. It was all his fault.'

Now Norman thought it was all beginning to make sense.

'So, you were walking your dog, Greg Lawrence was drunk, he fell over, and your dog bit him, is that right?'

Watkins nodded vigorously.

'Yes, that's what happened,' said Watkins.

'Can you tell me where the dog bit him?'

'There's a footpath that runs along the back of the houses—'

'I meant where on his body.'

'Oh. I see. On his arm, just about here.' He pointed to his forearm just above his wrist. 'I took him inside and cleaned it up for him. I even put a bandage on to stop the bleeding.'

'And you say it happened on the footpath behind the houses. Can you remember when this was?'

'A couple of weeks ago. I know it was a Monday because I have a routine, you see. Monday, I watch the news at ten, then walk the dog before I go to bed.'

'What time would this have been?'

'The news finishes at ten thirty, and we only walk for ten or fifteen minutes, so it would have been around ten forty, ten forty-five when the dog bit him.'

'And you said you took him home to clean up his wound?'

'Well, yes, I couldn't just leave him. I cleaned up the wound and bandaged it for him, and made him a cup of tea. I offered to take him to the hospital for a tetanus injection, but he insisted he would go the next day. I don't know if he did.'

'Can you remember how long he was at your house?'

'To be honest, I thought it would be nice to have some company, but a sentimental, incoherent, drunk isn't the best company. It took me ages to persuade him to leave. It must have been at least forty-five minutes or more. I know it was nearly midnight by the time I had walked him home and got back here.'

'You walked him home?'

'I know it's barely a hundred yards, but I was feeling so bad about the dog bite, and incoherent or not, he was still quite shaky, so I thought it best to make sure he got home safely.'

'Would you mind writing this down in a statement?' asked Norman.

'Lawrence isn't making a complaint, is he?'

'Honestly, Mr Watkins, I think the last thing Greg Lawrence will want to do is make a complaint against you. I think he's going to be much too grateful to complain.'

'D'you really think so?'

'I'm sure of it.'

CHAPTER 43

'We have a complication,' Norman told Southall. 'I've just been talking to one of Greg Lawrence's neighbours. The wound on his arm is a dog bite.'

'A dog bite?'

'Apparently, Greg Lawrence fell over as this guy was walking his dog that night, and the dog bit him.'

'So, we won't find his DNA under Kim's fingernails.'

'This guy can also account for Greg's whereabouts up until midnight.'

'Bugger! I'm sure Kim was picked up before then.'

'Yeah, exactly. Greg can't have been in two places at once.'

'This neighbour isn't another one of Kim's boyfriends, is he?'

'You're thinking conspiracy, right? Greg and the neighbour? The problem is Mr Watkins is in his eighties. He's not Kim's type.'

'Why didn't he come forward sooner?'

'It seems he was worried Greg would make a complaint and we'd take his dog away. I told him I didn't think Greg Lawrence would be making a complaint and was more likely to offer to buy his dog a steak dinner.'

'But if Greg has an alibi, why does he keep lying? Do you think he paid someone to kill Kim?'

'He's broke. How could he pay someone to bump her off?'

'I don't know. Maybe I'm wrong, but something doesn't quite seem to add up. D'you think he's protecting someone?'

'Who, Greg? I dunno,' said Norman. 'How about I go and speak to him in his cell? Maybe I can get him to loosen up a bit.'

Southall considered the idea.

'We're going to have to let him go now he has an alibi.'

'We still have the shoe.'

'Yes, but we're only assuming it's hers. We don't know for sure.'

'I'm sure the mud will prove it's a match.'

Even so, she could have had two pairs the same.'

'Women and their shoes, huh?' said Norman, tongue in cheek. 'Do you want me to speak to him before I release him?'

Southall looked at the clock.

'I'd like him to stew for a couple of hours first, and then you can go for it. It's worth a try.'

CHAPTER 44

Lawrence was sitting on the bed in the tiny cell when Norman squeezed in and sat down next to him a couple of hours later.

'I'm having trouble getting my head around this game you're playing, Greg.'

'What game?'

'All the lies. I'm beginning to wonder if you're protecting someone.'

'Protecting someone? I don't understand.'

'Why didn't you tell us your neighbour's dog bit you?'

'A dog bit me?'

'The wound on your arm; your neighbour, Mr Watkins, says he was walking his dog when you came past. You were so drunk you fell over and the dog bit you. Don't you remember?'

'I honestly don't remember anything.'

'Jeez, he says you were around his house for almost an hour while he cleaned you up, and made you a cup of tea. He says he even took you home.'

'Is this true? He really said that?'

Norman nodded.

'You won't believe how relieved I am to hear that.'

'How d'you mean?'

'Can I be honest with you?'

'I wish you would,' said Norman.

'The not remembering thing. I've heard it can happen. Sometimes your brain can deal with traumatic stuff by just blanking it out. I was beginning to wonder, you know?'

'I'm not quite sure what you're suggesting, Greg. Are you saying you think you could have killed Kim?'

'Good God, no. Of course not! When I told you I loved her, I meant it, no matter how difficult it may be for you to understand.'

Norman stared at Lawrence, not quite sure what he was getting at, but if he hoped Lawrence would fill the silence with an explanation he soon realised it wasn't going to happen.

'We're going to release you now,' said Norman, eventually. 'But don't think that means you're out of the woods. There's still the issue of the shoe we found.'

'I honestly have no idea how that got there.'

'My boss isn't going to accept that. She'll probably want to ask you about it again, so I suggest you go home and try to work out how it could have got there.'

'Oh, don't worry, I intend to,' said Lawrence.

'Go home, and stay there,' said Norman. 'And don't do anything stupid like trying to make a run for it, okay?'

'Why would I run away? I keep telling you; I didn't kill my wife!'

'Yeah, right. I'll get someone to run you home.'

CHAPTER 45

Wednesday 30 October 2019

After a sleepless night Greg Lawrence had taken the unusual step of going for an early run. It was just after eight thirty, when he got back home.

'Are you all right?' asked Nick Rose the moment Lawrence opened his front door. 'I saw them take you away yesterday. What did they want?'

Lawrence was annoyed to find Rose waiting inside the house for him. He had been thinking hard while he was running, and now he felt he was beginning to make sense of everything. What he wanted now was some peace, so he could think it through and get things straight in his head.

He barged past Rose and strode into the kitchen, busying himself making a cup of tea.

'They took me in for questioning,' he said, turning to face Rose, 'because they wanted to know why I had one of the shoes Kim was wearing the night she died.'

Rose scratched his head.

'I'm sorry. I don't understand,' he said.

Greg Lawrence returned to making his cup of tea, his back to Rose.

'When they searched the house, they found one of Kim's shoes.'

'What?'

'They found one of the shoes she was wearing the night she died; it even still had mud on it. So, of course, they took me away for questioning. What else would they do? They wanted to know how the shoe got here.'

'But how did it get here?' asked Rose. 'My God, Greg, they don't think you—'

Now Lawrence swung round to face Rose, his eyes blazing. When he spoke, there was a menace in his voice Rose had never heard before.

'Of course, they don't think I killed her! You should know that better than anyone.'

'What the hell is that supposed to mean?'

'What do you think it means, Nick?'

The two men stared at each other, silent for a moment, until Rose spoke.

'But if they found the shoe here, they must have thought you killed her. So, how come you were released?'

'It turns out I have an alibi until midnight, and they're sure Kim was abducted before then.'

Lawrence watched as disbelief became etched on Rose's face.

'You have an alibi?'

Lawrence smiled.

'You sound surprised.'

'But I lied for you. I agreed to tell the police you were so drunk I brought you home and put you to bed.'

'Ah, yes, but I don't need your alibi now. I've got a much better one.'

'But they'll think I'm involved now. I did what you asked without question, and they already suggested they might charge me with obstruction. Now they're going to think, well, I don't know what. Jesus, at the very least, I've committed perjury.'

'Oh, I see,' said Lawrence. 'You're my friend and you were looking out for me, is that it?'

'Exactly. It's what any guy would do for his best mate.'

Lawrence pointed his finger at Rose.

'I know how these things work. They always assume it's the husband, that's what you told me, Nick,' said Lawrence. 'But did you seriously think I could murder my own wife?'

'If you must know I didn't give it much thought,' protested Rose. 'You asked me for help, so I assumed you must have done it, but it never for one minute occurred to me that I should refuse to help you.'

'Is that right?' said Lawrence. 'The thing is, Nick, I'm not sure I believe you.'

Rose licked his lips. There was an unnerving confidence about Lawrence he'd never seen before.

'Look, it's all worked out, in the end, hasn't it?' he said, apologetically. 'I'll just have to deal with the fallout. I have friends in high places. Maybe I can sweet talk one or two of them, so they don't charge me with anything.'

'Oh, well, that's all right, then,' said Lawrence. 'We'll just forget it ever happened, shall we?'

Rose smiled uncertainly.

'Yes, let's do that, shall we? I mean we've known each other for years. We shouldn't let a little white lie come between us.'

'All right,' said Lawrence. 'I'll forgive your "little white lie" as you call it.'

Rose exhaled the breath he had been holding, but then he froze at the next words.

'But I'm not going to forgive you for planting the shoe where the police could find it.'

'What? Don't be ridiculous, Greg. You can't believe I did that. I mean, where would I have got the shoe from, for God's sake? It's more likely to have been the police who planted it. I mean, were you following them when they found it? They were probably hoping you would crack and confess once they showed you the shoe.'

For the briefest moment, Lawrence regarded Rose with something like disbelief but quickly broke into a smile.

'I'm not going to confess to something I haven't done, am I? Someone else did it, not me.'

'Look, I understand you need to say this stuff in front of the police, but you don't need to keep up the pretence with me, Greg.'

'What bloody pretence? What are you talking about?'

'No one would blame you, you know,' said Rose, his usual calm assurance reasserting itself. 'Let's face it, Kim could be a total bitch when she felt like it, couldn't she? And, even if we agree it was "someone else", as you put it, it's probably the best thing that could happen. If you ask me, "someone else" did you a real favour.'

Lawrence swung around, his face a picture of fury.

'What did you say?'

'Well admit it, Greg. Kim made your life a misery. She was always on your back. Everyone else thought the same. I could never work out how you two stayed together, or how you came to be married in the first place.'

'Really? Well, I'll tell you. We stayed together because I loved her.'

'That's all very well, but it needs two people to make a marriage. You might have loved her, but she despised you. Why d'you think she was always screwing other guys?'

'Rubbish.'

'It's not rubbish.'

'So how come you never said this to me before.'

'What would be the point? You wouldn't listen. You're not listening now, but, deep down, you know I'm right.'

'That's bullshit. Kim didn't despise me.'

'Yes, she did. She told me so herself.'

'When? When did she tell you?'

'It doesn't matter when. You don't want to know.'

'Yes, I do want to know. Come on, Nick, you've said this much, now tell me when she told you she despised me.'

'Forget I said it. It doesn't—'

'Was it when you were screwing her, Nick?'

Rose felt his calm reassurance draining away.

'What? You knew?'

'Of course I knew. I thought you were the one guy I could trust, but it turns out you're no different to the others, are you?'

'You knew, and you never said anything?'

'I know about all of them. She kept a bloody diary and left it where I could read it. Oh, she thought if she used silly little code names, I wouldn't know who was who, but it wasn't that hard to work them out. I'm afraid Kim wasn't as clever as she liked to think she was, and I'm afraid you're not either.'

'Look, it wasn't like that, Greg.'

'Oh, piss off, Nick. Of course, it was like that. Did you really think you were something special to her?'

Rose was struggling for the right words to say, but now Lawrence's face broke into an evil grin.

'Oh, I get it now,' he said. 'There was a piece in the diary that I couldn't quite figure out at the time, but now it makes sense. You wanted Kim all to yourself, didn't you? You're so bloody sure of yourself you actually thought she was going to leave me for you, but then she dumped you, didn't she? Ha! That must have been hard to take for an ego like yours. You always like to think you're better than everyone, but Kim didn't think you were anything special, did she?'

Rose's face reddened, and his eyes blazed angrily, but Lawrence didn't give him time to speak.

'She dumped you just like she dumped everyone else, didn't she?' he insisted, angrily. 'You see, there was only ever one person she stayed with, Nick, and that was me! I was the only one good enough!'

'In your dreams,' sneered Rose. 'She despised you, more than you'll ever know.'

'You didn't like being dumped, though, did you? You were so angry about it that Kim was scared of you. Did you know that, Nick? You managed to scare a woman. How does that make you feel? Proud?'

Rose could see Lawrence was as angry as he was, but he was confident he didn't need to worry. After all, he looked after himself, and this was Greg Lawrence before him, and everyone knew he was a gutless, soft touch of a man.

'I lied for you, Greg. She was destroying you. I couldn't stand by and watch any longer, and I was happy that you had finally found the guts to do something about it.'

'Me?' said Lawrence incredulously. 'I didn't kill her. You did.'

'Don't be so bloody stupid. You know it wasn't me. Why would I kill her?'

'Because she discarded you like a piece of trash, and then you planted the shoe to pin the blame on me. It must have been like a gift from heaven, finding I needed an alibi for that night. No wonder you were so quick to agree.'

'I agreed because I wanted to help you. Anyway, you can't prove I killed Kim, or that I planted the shoe because I didn't do it.'

CHAPTER 46

'Next day delivery,' said Southall, waving an envelope at Norman. 'How fast is that for telematics?'

'How come these guys are so keen to help us?' asked Norman. 'Normally with stuff like this they quote data protection, and anything else they can think of that might slow things down?'

'Did you know Nathan Bain has a brother? It just so happens he owns the company that has the data.'

'Ha! Now, that explains a lot,' said Norman.

Southall spread the map out on an empty desk and stared at it.

'Bollocks!' she said, turning away in dismay, and staring up at the heavens.

'Jesus!' said Norman. 'I was hoping we were going to find he had been in town, and at the crime scene, that night.'

'Not a bloody sausage,' said Southall, bitterly, returning her gaze to the map.

'It looks like the car was in his garage all night,' said Norman.

'This doesn't make sense,' said Southall. 'He told us he drove Lawrence home. He must know we can use this data to track his car and prove he didn't.'

'Maybe he doesn't realise,' suggested Norman.

'Does he look that stupid to you?' asked Southall.

'Yeah, good point,' agreed Norman. 'But we can still bring him in for questioning. This information is irrefutable proof his story about his whereabouts the night Kim died was bullshit. And we know he's had plenty of opportunities to plant the shoe.'

'You're right,' said Southall. 'Let's get Nick Rose in here, now. I want some answers.'

Morgan and Thomas were at their desks, aware of the growing excitement across the room, and desperately hoping to be involved.

'Catren,' called Southall. 'With me, please. Dylan, I want you to go with Norm.'

'Come on, then, let's go,' said Southall. 'This arsehole has been playing with us all along. I don't want him to get away.'

* * *

Fifteen minutes later their two cars were parked outside Rose's house, and Norman was hammering on the front door.

'Either he's not in, or he's stone deaf,' he said to Southall, 'and he wasn't deaf last time we spoke to him.'

Morgan and Thomas appeared from the back of the house.

'There's no sign of life around the back,' said Morgan.

'Bugger,' said Southall. 'Dylan, can you check the garage, please.'

Thomas ran over to the enormous garage and peered through the window. He looked across to them, shaking his head.

'No sign of the Maserati in the garage,' he called. 'There is another vehicle in there, but it's dark inside, and I can't make out what it is through the frosted glass.'

Norman led them across to join Thomas. He walked around to the back of the garage where there was a door.

Reaching for the handle, he was surprised to find it opened easily. He peered inside.

'Round the back here,' he called. 'This door's open.'

Without waiting, Norman pushed the door wide open and stepped inside. The garage was wide enough to fit two cars alongside each other and deep enough to allow the back half to be divided off from the rest. This room, where Norman was standing now, was where Rose had installed his snooker table.

'Jesus,' he muttered as he walked around the table towards a door on the other side. 'There's enough room here to make a family home without that damned great house!'

He reached the other door, swung it open and walked into the garage space proper. To one side, there was a space for the Maserati. On the other, a small, black, jeep-like pick-up truck was parked. He turned as Southall entered, followed by the others.

'I guess if you wanted to go out at night and not be tracked in your Maserati, this would do the trick,' he said, pointing to the vehicle.

'Well, fancy that,' said Southall. 'An open-back truck. That would be perfect for carrying a body.'

'Yeah,' agreed Norman. 'A quick whack across the head, bundle her in the back of the truck, and off you go.'

Southall turned to Morgan and Thomas.

'I'd like you two to stay here, call forensics and get a team down here. I want this car given a thorough going over. Tell them to take it apart if necessary.'

Now she turned to Norman.

'I'm guessing Rose will be at Lawrence's house.'

'Yeah,' said Norman. 'That seems to be where he spends most of his time since Kim's death. But I think it might be a good idea to get some back-up.'

'Come on,' said Southall. 'Let's go. You can call them on the way.'

CHAPTER 47

It was only a ten-minute drive to Greg Lawrence's house. As they climbed from the car, they could hear the familiar hee-haw, hee-haw, of an approaching patrol car's siren.

They jumped from the car and headed towards the house. The front door was open, and now they could see Greg Lawrence sitting on the front step. He seemed to be staring into the distance but looked surprisingly serene. As Norman followed Southall, he felt his guts run cold. Instinct told him something wasn't right about this.

Southall stopped to speak to Lawrence, and as he looked up at them, they could see blood splashed all over the front of his shirt.

'Greg? Are you okay?' asked Southall.

At first, he stared as if he didn't know her, and it seemed to take an age for him to recognise her.

'Yes,' he said, finally. 'Yes, I'm fine.'

'Is Nick Rose here?'

Lawrence nodded.

'He's in the kitchen.'

'What happened?' asked Norman.

'I had no choice. It was self-defence.'

Norman stepped around him and headed into the house. The kitchen door was open, and he could see the usually tidy kitchen was in disarray, a sure sign there had been a struggle. He stepped through the door and stopped in his tracks.

'Oh, crap!' he muttered, as he stepped his way through the debris to where Nick Rose lay on the floor, in a large pool of blood. What Norman guessed was a kitchen carving knife protruded from his chest.

A minute later, he was back outside. The backup had arrived in the shape of two patrol cars, and Greg Lawrence was being guided into the back of one of the cars by two uniformed officers.

'Did he say what happened?' asked Norman.

'He says Rose confessed to killing Kim, and then attacked him with a kitchen knife. He fought back, and in the struggle for the knife, he accidentally stabbed Rose. Is he—' said Southall.

'Dead? Oh, yeah, for sure,' said Norman. 'It looks like there's enough blood to fill a swimming pool on the floor in there.'

'Shit!' said Southall. 'This is all my fault. I should have brought Rose in before we let Lawrence go.'

'And Lawrence said he "accidentally" stabbed Rose?' asked Norman.

'Yes, why?'

'Can you accidentally push a six-inch carving knife up to the hilt into someone's chest? I mean, an inch or two, maybe, but six inches? The knife's nearly gone right through and out the back of the guy.'

'We would have a hard job proving it wasn't an accident,' said Southall.

'Yeah, I know,' said Norman, 'but I suspect maybe Lawrence knows that, too.'

CHAPTER 48

'So, tell us what happened, Greg.'

Southall sat back in her seat alongside Norman and studied Greg Lawrence across the table. He had refused a solicitor, despite Southall making sure he knew his rights. Now he showed confidence they had not seen before. It was bordering on arrogance which, according to everything they knew about him, was totally out of character.

'I already told you.'

'Yes, you did,' agreed Norman, 'but now we need you to tell us again,' he pointed to the nearby recording machine, 'for the record.'

Lawrence sighed.

'When I got home, that arrogant twat was inside the house, waiting for me.'

'By, "that arrogant twat," I take it you mean Nick Rose?' asked Southall.

'Yes, that's right.'

'But didn't you tell us he was your best mate who always looks out for you?'

'If he was my best mate, why was he shagging my wife?'

'He was having an affair with Kim?'

'That's right.'

'And you knew?'

'I'm not completely stupid. Of course I knew. I know about that bloody Mike Gordon, she works with, too.'

'So, you didn't just know Kim liked to play games; you knew who she was playing the games with?'

'Not the one-night stands, but I knew who the steady boyfriends were. It was all in the diary. That's how I first found out about Nick Rose. You know Kim was scared of him, don't you? Of course, you do; you've read the diary. So, he should have been the first person you arrested, but you didn't. Why not?'

'If you remember,' said Norman, 'you gave him an alibi when you insisted he had been the one to take you home and put you to bed.'

It was evident from Lawrence's face that he hadn't remembered.

'You say Nick Rose told you he killed Kim,' said Southall. 'Did he tell you why?'

'I can tell you why,' said Lawrence. 'He was so arrogant he thought he had swept her off her feet, and that she'd leave me for him, but she didn't. She dumped him and stayed with me.'

Norman was tempted to argue the point that Kim was actually 'with' him, but he decided against it. They could argue semantics later.

'Did he tell you this?'

'He didn't have to. You see, for all his arrogance, Nick has a fragile ego. He couldn't handle the fact she rejected him. It was because of the way he reacted that she became scared of him.'

'Did he tell you how he killed her?'

'He said he enticed her into his car, hit her over the head, and then drove to a spot by the river where he tied her up with fishing line, and then pushed her into the water.'

'And what car did he use?'

'He didn't say.'

There was a knock on the door.

'I'm sorry, Greg, can you hold on a moment,' said Southall. She couldn't hide her irritation as she turned to Norman. 'I told them—'

'I know,' he said, soothingly, 'I'll see what it is.'

He went over to the door and opened it just enough to see who was outside.

'This had better be important, Catren,' he hissed.

'Trust me it is, Sarge,' whispered Morgan, 'and I think you're both going to want to hear it.'

'Okay, we'll be there in a minute.'

'I think we're going to have to call a temporary halt to this interview,' said Norman as he closed the door and turned to Southall.

'Why?' she demanded.

'There's a bit of an emergency, and they need your input,' said Norman.

'Can't it wait?'

'I'm afraid not.'

Greg Lawrence had been looking on with ill-concealed amusement, but now he spoke.

'You carry on, Inspector,' he said. 'I can wait.'

The uniformed PC who had been on standby outside was called in to sit with Lawrence, and Southall stormed from the room, scarcely giving Norman time to keep up. He had to move quickly so they could enter the incident room together.

'I hope this was important enough to warrant interrupting a crucial interview,' she said.

It was Judy Lane who replied.

'I think you'll find it is, boss.'

'I'll be the judge of that,' said Southall, before adding, impatiently. 'Well, come on then, let's hear it.'

Lane shuffled through the papers on her desk.

'The first point of interest; it seems Nick Rose has removed the tracker from his car.'

'Aren't they supposed to trigger an alarm if they get tampered with?' asked Norman.

'I don't know about that, Sarge, but they found a tracker in Rose's garage, and it's identical to the one that should be in the car. As we speak, they're trying to find out if it's the actual one that should be in the car.'

'So he could have used his car the night Kim died, and we'd be none the wiser,' said Southall.

'Not necessarily,' said Lane. 'Forensics have been in touch about the pick-up truck. The mud underneath, and on the floor of the cab is a match for the site by the river.'

'Well, since we can't prove the Maserati moved from the garage that night, we'll take that as confirmation the pick-up was the vehicle used to carry the body, but it's hardly a surprise,' said Southall. 'Is that it?'

'Oh, no,' said Lane, a smile tugging at the corners of her mouth. 'There's more, and it gets better. They've also dusted the pick-up for fingerprints, and the only prints they can find—'

'Are Nick Rose's,' said Southall.

Now Lane's smile widened.

'Apparently not. It seems there is only one set of prints, and they belong to Greg Lawrence.'

'Lawrence?' said Southall. 'Are you sure? There were none belonging to Nick Rose?'

'That's what they say,' said Lane, before adding, 'I don't know how much it helps, but they also found a set of keys for the pick-up at Greg Lawrence's house.'

Southall looked quizzically at Norman.

'How does that work?'

Norman scratched his head.

'Well, we know Rose had an ego, and he liked to pose in the Maserati, right? We also know Greg Lawrence hasn't used his van in weeks, but someone lets him borrow a vehicle. So, what if Rose doesn't use the pick-up much but let's Lawrence use it for work?'

'So, you're saying you think Lawrence killed Kim?' asked Southall.

Norman shrugged.

'He's got motive.'

'He's also got an alibi, remember, the dog bite?'

'Oh, crap! Yeah, I forgot that.'

'It's a good job he has got an alibi,' said Lane. 'When they were searching his house and garden, a sharp-eyed technician decided to poke around in the garden shed. She found a box on a shelf that didn't look as dusty as everything else. When she opened it up, she found a wedding ring and a pair of used ladies knickers. They also found traces of dried mud. They think it's possible the shoe found in the garage could have been stored in the box after the murder.'

'This doesn't make sense, does it?' asked Southall. 'If Rose planted the shoe to frame Lawrence, why would he risk keeping all this stuff at Lawrence's house where we might find it?'

'This is going to sound far-fetched,' said Norman, 'but what if Greg Lawrence has played us?'

'In what way?'

'What if he planted the shoe himself? It's pretty clever when you think about it. I mean, who would do that, right? We certainly didn't consider it, did we? We all assumed Nick Rose must have planted the shoe to frame Lawrence, which meant Rose was the killer, but what if Lawrence is the killer and he's framing Rose?'

'Why would he do that?' asked Lane.

'Because Nick Rose had been having an affair with his wife,' said Norman. 'This way, he gets rid of the cheating wife, and makes the lover pay by framing him for murder.'

'There's just one problem,' said Southall. 'We may have a story that works, but he's got an alibi that says we're wrong.'

Catren Morgan had just come into the room.

'Are you talking about the Greg Lawrence alibi?' she asked.

'Yes, why?' asked Southall.

'It's bollocks,' said Morgan. 'I've just been talking to the younger Mr Watkins. He tells me his father's showing signs of dementia, and he gets easily confused.'

'So his dog didn't bite Lawrence?'

'Oh, the dog bit him all right, but the old man was confused. It happened a week earlier than he said.'

'Are they sure?' asked Southall.

'Would you forget the night your elderly father phoned after midnight because he was worried he would have his dog taken away for attacking someone?'

'I can believe the old guy did that,' said Norman. 'When I spoke to him, he kept asking me if we were going to take his dog away. That dog is his world. He said it's all he's got left now his wife is dead. I felt sorry for him.'

'Right. Let's get this straight,' said Southall. 'We're now saying we believe Lawrence killed Kim, that he used Rose's pick-up truck to move the body, and that he was trying to frame Rose for the murder. Are we all agreed on that?'

There were no dissenting voices.

'But I can see a problem, you're all missing,' continued Southall. 'If we're right about this, why didn't we see that pick-up truck on any of the CCTV footage from the town?'

'What if he never actually came into town?' suggested Norman. 'Remember Gordon said he drove around town looking for Kim but he never found her. Up until now we've assumed that was because someone had abducted her before he got there.'

He paused for a few seconds.

'Don't stop, Norm,' urged Southall.

As Norman explained his alternative theory, Southall added questions to test it and make sure it held water. Ten minutes later they had a plan.

'I'm sure his defence will argue the evidence is all circumstantial,' said Southall, finally, 'but I think we have enough.'

'I'm still not convinced he killed Nick Rose in self-defence,' said Norman. 'It takes a lot of force to plunge a knife six inches into someone's chest. I don't believe you could do it accidentally.'

Lane's computer pinged to announce a message, and she leaned forward to read it. Then she clicked her mouse, and a few seconds later, the printer started making the wheezy noises that meant it was about to kick into life.

'Right, Norm,' said Southall. 'Let's get back to Mr Lawrence and see what he's got to say now.'

'Hang on, boss,' said Lane, as she retrieved a single sheet of paper from the printer. 'You might want this.'

CHAPTER 49

They were back in the interview room, opposite Lawrence. Norman had set the recorder in motion and made the introductions. Now Southall smiled at Lawrence.

'Now then, Greg, I'd like you to explain how the shoe we found came to be in your garage.'

'I told you. Rose planted it. He was trying to cover his own arse and frame me for the murder.'

'Now, I'm a little confused as to why he would think he could frame you for murder when he had previously provided you with an alibi. How would that work?'

Lawrence frowned.

'I'm not sure I understand what you're getting at.'

'Come on now, Greg, it's not rocket science,' said Southall. 'Nick Rose had already told us you were with him the night Kim died. Now he expected us to believe you had killed her? At the very least that would have meant admitting he had lied to us about your alibi, and at the same time destroying his own alibi. He seemed like an intelligent man to us. What you're suggesting doesn't make sense.'

Lawrence narrowed his eyes.

'You mean you think I'm lying? Why would I do that?'

Southall smiled sweetly.

'I don't know, Greg, you tell me?'

'I've got nothing to lie about, and anyway, what does it matter if I can't explain why he framed me. You know I couldn't have killed Kim because I was with that old guy whose dog bit me.'

'Ah, yeah, Mr Watkins,' said Norman. 'I was the one who interviewed him. It was very public-spirited of him to come forward like that.'

'Yes,' agreed Lawrence. 'It's a pity there aren't more people like him around.'

'Yeah,' said Norman. 'He's a nice old guy. He thinks the world of that dog, you know; says it's all he has left now his wife is dead. D'you know how old he is, Greg?'

'I have no idea,' said Lawrence. 'We never got around to discussing stuff like that.'

'Mr Watkins is eighty-one years old. He has a son older than you. Can you imagine that?'

Lawrence sighed. He was beginning to tire of Norman's condescending attitude. Did he think he was talking to a ten-year-old?

'What difference does it make how old his son is?'

'You're right; it doesn't matter how old he is,' said Norman. 'He's a nice guy, though. It just so happens he came in to speak with one of our team earlier today.'

'Why are you telling me this?'

'I just thought you might be interested in what he had to say,' said Norman.

'Why should I care what he said?'

Norman beamed a smile at Lawrence.

'Patience, Greg. I'm just going to explain why you should care. You see, as I said, Mr Watkins is eighty-one, and you must be aware that sometimes people that age can get a little confused. Mr Watkins is no different. He's probably worse than most as he's suffering from the early stages of dementia. His son tells me it's getting to the stage where he probably shouldn't be living on his own. To get ready for when this time arrives, the son is converting his garage into a self-contained flat so the old man can go and live there.'

'I don't see why this is my concern.'

'It's not his condition I expect to concern you,' said Norman. 'But what will concern you is the fact that Mr Watkins's son told us the dog bit you a week earlier than the old man told me.'

Lawrence suddenly sat bolt upright. He wasn't bored with Norman's attitude now.

'No, that's not right, there's been some mistake,' he said.

'I don't think so,' said Norman. 'You see, his son remembers vividly.'

'How can he be so sure?' asked Lawrence.

'He's so sure because his dad called him the night it happened. You don't forget when an elderly relative calls you a few minutes after midnight because, when it happens, you automatically fear the worst, and it stays with you for quite a while.'

'Why would he call that late?'

'Because he thought you were going to make a complaint about the dog, and someone would come and take it away. He loves that dog; the idea of losing it terrifies him.'

'He's making it up.'

'Why would he do that, Greg?'

'I don't know, but I'm sure there must be some reason.'

'Well, we thought you'd probably say something like that, so we've got someone checking the call log for Mr Watkins's phone. We'll know soon enough.'

'This is bollocks,' snapped Lawrence.

'No, it's not,' said Norman, breaking into a smile, 'but your alibi is.'

Lawrence was so angry he couldn't speak.

'My, my, that's quite a temper you have, Greg,' said Norman. 'Maybe you're not exactly the quiet downtrodden guy everyone seems to think you are.'

Lawrence scowled at Norman.

'No comment,' he said.

'My sergeant is right,' said Southall. 'You're not down-trodden at all, are you, Greg? We're sure you killed Kim, and you planted the red shoe in your garage to make us believe Rose was trying to frame you.'

'I've never heard such bullshit,' said Lawrence. 'I told you before: I knew about the affairs, and I didn't care. I put up with it because I loved Kim, so why would I kill her?'

'Maybe you did put up with the affairs at first. But it must have eaten away at your self-esteem, and then when you found out Nick Rose, your best mate, someone you thought you could trust, was taking his turn with Kim, that was one affair too many. You killed her, used Nick's pick-up truck to dump her body, and then tried to convince us he was to blame.'

'That's very imaginative, but where's your proof?'

'We found the keys to Nick's pick-up at your house,' said Southall.

'I told you he let me use it for work.'

'Oh, yes, that's right. Did he use it himself?'

'Only when he didn't want to get his precious Maserati dirty.'

'Doing what?'

'Like taking stuff to the council tip. Nick was into recycling in a big way. He took all his garden waste down there.'

'How often was that?'

'Once or twice a week.'

'So you were both using the vehicle?'

'Yes.'

'Can you explain why only your fingerprints are all over the inside?'

'Only mine? That can't be right; Nick must have wiped his prints off.'

Norman laughed.

'Yeah, right,' he said. 'So he knew exactly where your prints were and managed to remove only his own? Dream on, buster.'

Lawrence looked pleadingly at Southall, but she ignored him and carried on with her questions.

'Or perhaps you can explain why we found Kim's wedding ring and underwear in a box in your garden shed?' she asked. 'There's mud residue in the box, too. We're pretty confident that will be the same mud that was on the shoe found in your garage. Are we right?'

Lawrence banged a fist on the table.

'Nick Rose planted that stuff,' he yelled. 'It has nothing to do with me!'

'We think it's all to do with you, Greg, because we think you killed Kim.'

'I keep telling you she didn't come home that night. You should be looking for whoever she hooked up with that night.'

'I'm glad you mentioned that,' said Norman. 'Because we found someone she called that night who thought he had hooked up with her. He was so sure his luck was in he drove twenty miles to meet her, but she didn't wait for him. We think she just wanted to make him angry.'

'Maybe you should be speaking to him, then?'

'Oh, we have,' said Southall. 'And we know he didn't set eyes on her. We think she called him to set him up on a fool's errand, and then came home. And when she got home, we think the argument you had been having earlier kicked off again, only this time you lost it, and you killed her.'

'This is bullshit,' said Lawrence. 'You can't prove any of it.'

There was a knock on the door, but this time Southall showed no irritation. This would be Thomas, as arranged.

'Excuse me a minute,' said Norman.

He walked to the door, opened it enough to collect a sheet of paper from Thomas and exchange a few short, whispered words, then he came back to the table and sat down. He placed the sheet of paper on the table and slid it across to Southall who studied it for a minute.

'Let me continue,' said Southall, staring at Lawrence. 'After you killed Kim, you trussed her up with fishing line, put her into the back of the pick-up truck and took her out to a site next to the river.'

'This is twaddle,' said Lawrence.

'The mud on the underside of the pick-up proves it was there,' said Norman.

'Yes, and I keep telling you that's because Nick Rose killed her, not me.'

Now Southall showed Lawrence the sheet of paper Thomas had delivered.

'D'you know what this is, Greg?'

Lawrence looked at the paper with disinterest, then looked up at Southall.

'Some sort of map?' he said.

'A lot of people don't know their smartphones record their location all the time,' said Southall. 'But we think you do know. We think that because when we looked at your phone, we could see you've switched tracking off. But did you know that particular model of mobile phone is notorious for continuing to track even after tracking is switched off?'

Lawrence licked his lips, his face suddenly pale.

'Now look at the map, again,' said Southall. 'You see those little crosses? They show the location of your mobile phone between the hours of two and three a.m. on the night Kim died. You don't need me to identify the location, do you?'

Lawrence stared silently down at the map.

'While you were in that location, we believe you were putting Kim into the water. I suppose you were hoping she would drown and then wash out to sea and never be found.'

'This doesn't prove I killed her,' said Lawrence. 'And anyway, I thought you said I'd killed her back at the house. How could she drown if she was already dead?'

'Ah, that's the thing, Greg. You see, Kim didn't die at the house.'

'She didn't?'

'No. Kim was unconscious, but the post-mortem showed her lungs were full of fresh water. That means she was still breathing when she went into the water. What we can't decide is whether you thought she was dead, or whether you trussed her up so she couldn't save herself from drowning.'

'If it was the first one, you could maybe argue it was an accident, and you could plead manslaughter,' said Norman, 'even though she wasn't dead until you drowned her.'

'But, if you trussed her up to make sure she drowned,' said Southall, 'that's a particularly cruel way to kill someone, and there's no doubt its murder.'

Lawrence was pulling the weirdest of faces. Norman couldn't tell if he was horrified at what he'd done, or terrified that they'd worked it out.

'You've got it all wrong. I didn't kill Kim,' he insisted. 'I loved her.'

'Yeah, you can tell that to the jury,' said Norman.

'Nick Rose killed her. He confessed, just before he attacked me,' said Lawrence.

'Did you get him to write it down?' asked Norman. 'Or record it?'

'Well, of course, I bloody didn't.'

'Then it's not going to help you much, is it?' said Southall.

'But he attacked me with one of my kitchen knives.'

'I'm glad you mentioned that,' said Norman. 'I'd nearly forgotten.'

He opened the folder before him, picked up a sheet of paper and slammed it down on the table before Lawrence.

'This proves that's yet another lie. If Nick Rose used this knife to attack you, why aren't there any of his fingerprints on it? Are you suggesting he cleaned them off before he bled out?'

'It was self-defence.'

'No, Greg, it was murder.'

EPILOGUE

It was midday. It had been a hectic thirty-six hours since Greg Lawrence had been charged with the two murders, but they were confident they had enough evidence to prove their case. Now they just had to make sure it was all presented correctly, which was a tedious but necessary part of the job.

Southall and Norman had taken an early lunch break. At Norman's suggestion, after collecting a coffee and panini from the coffee stall by the harbour, they were now perched on a bench high up on the hill above the cemetery, looking out to sea and enjoying some welcome sunshine on their faces.

'It's hard to believe how peaceful it is up here,' said Southall.

'Yeah, I found it the first full day I was in town,' said Norman. 'It was sunny that day, too. I intended to have lunch here every day that first week, but then Catren found the body on the beach and that sort of changed my plans.'

Southall turned to him.

'Is she all right?' she asked.

'Who, Catren? Yeah, as far as I know. Why?'

'She's been very quiet around me the last few days. I'm worried she might have got tangled up with that dickhead from Region again.'

Norman was puzzled for a moment, and then he grinned at her as he realised who she meant.

'You mean Hickstead? You don't need to worry about him. He tried his luck, but was never in with a chance. She has better taste than that.'

'So, what's up with her, then? Why is she suddenly avoiding me, and looking embarrassed to be around me?'

Norman turned back to stare at the sea. On the outside, he looked calm and collected, but inside he was squirming. He had known this was probably going to happen sooner or later, but now it was here he realised he had no idea how best to deal with it.

He had told Catren to forget it, and act like she knew nothing, but of course, it's easier said than done. He sighed as he realised there was only one way to do this. He had to be honest.

'Okay, you're going to find out sooner or later, and it's probably better you hear it from me.'

'Hear what?'

'I told you how the guys had checked out your past career, and you agreed that yes, we'd all done it, right?'

'I would have preferred it if they hadn't but, as you say, we've all done it. Anyway, I thought you said you had put them straight about that?'

'Well, yeah, I did, and they're all cool with what happened. They agree the guy who got shot was an idiot.'

'So, what's the problem with Catren?'

Norman sighed. He was finding this even more challenging than he had thought it would be.

'The thing is Catren was impressed that you had achieved so much so young. I think maybe she's looking for a role model, so she wanted to learn a bit more about you.'

'I don't think I'm a good role model for anyone,' said Southall. 'I certainly wouldn't recommend . . . oh, I see . . .'

Her voice trailed away into silence, and now she, too, stared out to sea. There was an awkward silence, but Norman felt they couldn't just leave it at that. They had to get past this.

'I'm sorry,' he said. 'It was the other, private stuff Catren found. That's what's wrong with her.'

'It was years ago, but nothing's ever private with newspapers, and the bloody internet, is it?' said Southall, bitterly. 'Do they all know?'

'I told her to keep it to herself.'

'And has she?'

'As far as I can tell, yes she has.'

'I suppose this means you know all about it, then?'

'Actually, I told her I didn't want to know.'

They had both kept their eyes out to sea, but now Southall turned to stare at him.

'Really?'

Norman returned her gaze.

'Yeah, really. All I'm interested in is, can you do your job, and can I get on with you? That's all I need to know. I figure if you want me to know anything about yourself, you'll tell me. If not, then that's okay by me.'

They both looked out to sea again and sat in silence for a couple of minutes before she spoke.

'So, can I do my job?'

'It's early days, but I reckon so.'

She turned to look at him again.

'I'm not sure if that's good, or not.'

'Trust me, it's good,' he said, offering her a wry smile. 'I have to temper my praise. I don't want you getting big-headed.'

A smile teased at the corners of her mouth.

'And can you get on with me?' she asked.

'It's early days, but I reckon so. What about me? Do I make the grade?'

Now it was her turn to smile.

'It's early days, but I reckon so,' she said.

They sat in silence for another minute or two.

'Are you going to stay?' she asked.

'I'm sorry?'

'Superintendent Bain told me you had come on a month's trial. I know the month's not up yet, but do you think you're going to stay?'

Norman sighed.

'If I went back, I'd be bored to tears with nothing to do. To be honest, I wasn't sure I'd like being so far from home, but something must have happened to me when I crossed that bridge. Now I'm here, I realise the place I thought of as home isn't home at all.'

'I couldn't tell if that was a, "yes, I'm staying" or a, "no, I'm going back".'

'Despite my reservations, I feel as if I belong here,' said Norman. 'I like this place, and I like the people around me. So, it's a, yes, I'm staying.'

'I had reservations too,' admitted Southall, 'but now I'm here I quite like it, especially the slower pace of life.'

'Yeah, it's kinda like another world,' agreed Norman. 'I'll have to find somewhere to live, though. I don't fancy spending winter in a holiday chalet.'

'Yes, me too. A hotel is all very well for a few weeks, but I need to find myself a house. You get a lot more for your money here, so I'm quite looking forward to house hunting.'

Norman looked at his watch.

'I guess we ought to be heading back.'

'Let's go back through the cemetery,' said Southall. 'I'm always intrigued by the headstones.'

* * *

Ten minutes later, she called out to Norman who strolled over to join her. She pointed to a small headstone, and read the inscription out loud.

'To the unknown lady found in the woods. We don't know who you are, or where you came from, but we will remember you. RIP.' Then she turned to him, 'That sounds intriguing, don't you think?'

'It was twenty years ago,' said Norman. 'I wonder what happened?'

'I was hoping you'd be interested,' she said. 'You see, I have this idea for training the team, but it will only work if you're on board with it, too.'

'We're going to need something to investigate if it's as quiet around here as they tell me it is. So, what's the plan?'

'Cold cases. I've spoken to Superintendent Bain, and he thinks it's a great idea, but he says it will only work if you're staying and you agree it's a good idea.'

'I think it's a great idea,' said Norman. 'Maybe this grave will be a starting point for our first case.'

THE END

Thank you for reading this book.

If you enjoyed it please leave feedback on Amazon or Goodreads, and if there is anything we missed or you have a question about, then please get in touch. We appreciate you choosing our book.

Founded in 2014 in Shoreditch, London, we at Joffe Books pride ourselves on our history of innovative publishing. We were thrilled to be shortlisted for Independent Publisher of the Year at the British Book Awards.

www.joffebooks.com

We're very grateful to eagle-eyed readers who take the time to contact us. Please send any errors you find to corrections@joffebooks.com. We'll get them fixed ASAP.

Milton Keynes UK
Ingram Content Group UK Ltd.
UKHW031259220824
1353UKWH00052B/540

9 781804 056370